ORHAN'S INHERITANCE

ORHAN'S
INHERITANCE

a novel

ALINE OHANESIAN

ALGONQUIN BOOKS OF CHAPEL HILL   2015

Published by
ALGONQUIN BOOKS OF CHAPEL HILL
Post Office Box 2225
Chapel Hill, North Carolina 27515-2225

a division of
WORKMAN PUBLISHING
225 Varick Street
New York, New York 10014

This is a work of fiction. While, as in all fiction, the literary perceptions and insights are based on experience, all names, characters, places, and incidents either are products of the author's imagination or are used fictitiously.

LIBRARY OF CONGRESS CATALOGING-IN-PUBLICATION DATA
Ohanesian, Aline.
Orhan's inheritance : a novel / by Aline Ohanesian.—First edition.
pages cm
ISBN 978-1-61620-374-0
1. Inheritance and succession—Fiction. 2. Family secrets—Fiction.
3. Domestic fiction. I. Title.
PS3615.H345O74 2015
813'.6—dc23   2014031970

10 9 8 7 6 5 4 3 2 1
First Edition

For Vram,
who made it possible
and for Alec and Vaughn,
who made it necessary

The past is not dead; it's not even past.
——WILLIAM FAULKNER

Language is the house of being.
In its home man dwells.
——MARTIN HEIDEGGER

ORHAN'S INHERITANCE

The
Ottoman
Empire
1915

BLACK SEA

TRABZON

Location of The Melkonian House

SIVAS

ERZINCAN

YOZGAT

KANGAL

Deportation Route

KAYSERI

Location of Fatima's Inn

MALATYA

Euphrates

ANATOLIA

ADANA

ALEPPO

MEDITERRANEAN SEA

Euphrates

Deportation Route

DER ZOR

SYRIA

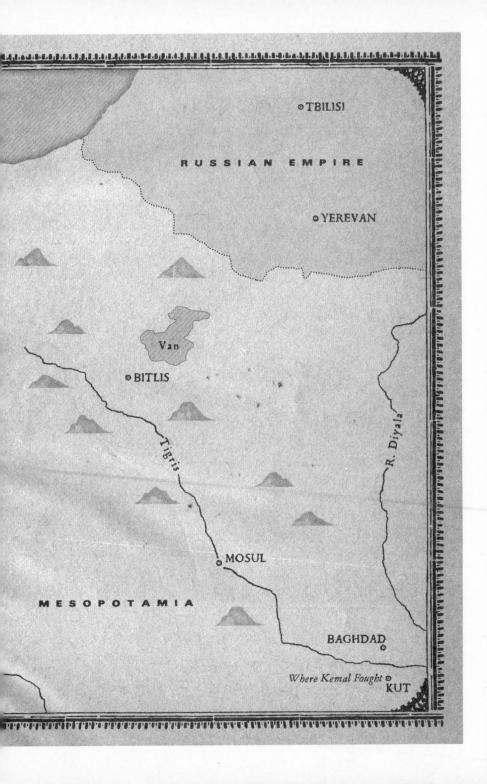

PART I

1990

CHAPTER 1

An Axe in the Forest

THEY FOUND HIM inside one of seventeen cauldrons in the court-yard, steeping in an indigo dye two shades darker than the summer sky. His arms and chin were propped over the copper edge, but the rest of Kemal Türkoğlu, age ninety-three, had turned a pretty pale blue. Orhan was told the old men of the village stood in front of the soaking corpse, fingering their worry beads, while their sons waited, holding dice from abandoned backgammon games. Modesty forbade any female spectators, but within hours the news spread from one kitchen and vendor's stall to the next. Orhan's grandfather, his *dede,* had immersed his body, naked except for his britches, into a vat of fabric dye outside their family home.

Orhan sinks into the backseat of the private car, a luxury he talked himself into when the dread of a seven-hour bus ride back to the village started to overwhelm his grief. He wanted to mourn in private, away from the chickens, the elderly, the traveling merchants, or worse yet, the odd acquaintance that could normally be found on a bus ride to Anatolia, the interior of Turkey. He told

himself he could afford a little luxury now, but the car showed
up an hour late, sporting a broken air conditioner and a driver
reeking of cheap cologne and sweat. Orhan lights a cigarette and
shuts his eyes against the sting of the man's body odor.

"Going to visit your family?" the driver asks.

"Yes," answers Orhan.

"That's nice. So many young people leave their villages and
never come back," he says.

The truth is it's been three years since his last visit. Had Dede
had the good sense to move out of that godforsaken place, there
would be no reason to go back. The car veers off the highway,
making its way along a recently paved road toward the city of
Sivas, on whose outskirts Karod village is located. The driver
slows down and opens a window, letting the *terroir*-laden scent of
soil waft into the car's cavity. Unlike Istanbul, whose majesty is
reflected in the Bosporus, Central Anatolia is the quintessential
other Turkey, in which allusions of majesty or progress are much
harder to come by. Here shepherds follow the bleating of long-
haired goats, and squat village women carry bundles of kindling
on their backs. Time and progress are two long-lost relatives who
send an occasional letter. The ancient roads of Sivas Province,
once a part of the famed Silk Road, have seen the stomping of
Assyrian, Persian, Greek, and Roman feet. Dry-rotted timber,
blocks of concrete, and sheets of corrugated tin stand feebly upon
ancient Byzantine stone structures whose architectural complex-
ity suggests a more glorious past. Layer upon layer of earth and
civilization washed downstream by the muddy waters of the Kizil
Irmak, the Red River, produces a kind of sedimentary aesthetic.

Orhan thinks of the unbearable heat of Anatolian summers acting as an adhesive for all these different layers.

"You have siblings?" the driver asks.

"No," answers Orhan.

"Just your parents then?" he asks, glancing at Orhan through the rearview mirror.

"Father, grandfather, and an aunt," he says, looking out at the barren landscape. How is it that even without a single structure weighing down on it, the land is heavy, the atmosphere so pressed it makes it hard to breathe? It was these very fields, burdened with a history he could not name that first inspired him to pick up Dede's Leica. Somewhere around age fifteen, Orhan discovered that if he blurred the image in the lens enough, Karod would no longer threaten to crush him. Through the lens, the slopes and valleys of his childhood started to resemble abstract paintings, broad strokes of yellow and green, hidden patches of lavender, set against an ever-changing sky of blue and orange. It was only later that he realized he was imposing meaning upon the world, by the way he chose to capture it. Those first photographs were like butterflies suspended in glass panes.

"I grew up near Sivas," the driver continues. "What's your family name? Maybe I know it."

There is no escaping this constant need for placing one another in Turkey. It's one of the few things Orhan loved about living in Germany: the anonymity. "Türkoğlu," he says finally.

The driver's expression, framed in the rearview mirror, changes. "I'm sorry for your loss," he says. "Kemal Bey was an extraordinary man. Is it true he fought at Ctesiphon?"

Orhan nods, taking another drag from his cigarette.

"They don't make them like that anymore. That generation was full of real men. They fought against all of Europe and Russia, established a republic, and founded entire industries. It's something, huh?"

"Yes," agrees Orhan. "It's something."

"The paper says he immersed himself in dye for medicinal purposes," the driver says.

It's not the first time Orhan has heard this preposterous theory. It's a story crafted, no doubt, by his cunning little aunt. Though Dede had been a well-respected World War I hero-turned-businessman, he was also an eccentric man, living in a place where eccentricities needed to be explained away or covered up.

In villages like Karod, every person, object, and stone has to have some sort of covering, a layer of protection made from cloth, brick, or dust. Men and women cover their heads with skullcaps and head scarves. These standards of modesty also apply to their animals, their speech, their ideas. Why should Dede's death be an exception?

The car veers left onto a loosely graveled road that leads into the village. Orhan searches for the wooden post that used to announce the village's name in unassuming hand-painted white letters, but it's nowhere to be found. A young boy in a bright orange shirt and green shorts walks behind a herd of cows. He sweeps a long stick at their backs, ushering them into one of many narrow corridors sandwiched between mud-caked houses.

"Is this it?" asks the driver.

"Yes," says Orhan. "Just follow this road until you see the house with the large columns."

The sound of crunching gravel comes to a halt as the car stops. Orhan extinguishes his cigarette and steps out. He can hear the singular sound of hired wailers, their practiced percussion luring him out of the car: two, maybe three female voices filled with a kind of sorrow and vulnerability that comes only with practice. The two-story family home is a dilapidated old ruin by any standards, but here in the forgotten back pocket of Central Anatolia, it is considered a sturdy and grand affair. A thin film of mustard-colored stucco advances and retreats over hand-cut stones of putty and gray, reminding Orhan of a half-peeled piece of dried-out fruit. The Victorian-looking house, complete with parlor and basement, is the birthplace of Tarik Inc., which began as a small collection of workshops and which, over the past six decades, grew into an automated firm, exporting textiles as far away as Italy and Germany. Here, inside these ruinous walls, according to family legend, Orhan's great-grandfather had woven a *kilim* for the sultan himself. That was before the empire became a republic, before democracy and westernization revolutionized what it meant to be a Turk. In the courtyard to the left of the house, the massive copper cauldrons stand guarding the wilting structure. Through the decades they've gone from holding fabric dye to sheltering children playing hide-and-seek, to storing the discarded ashes of hookah pipes and cigarettes. These vessels have contained the many bits and pieces of Dede's life. Perhaps it is only fitting that they also housed his last breath.

Orhan weaves a familiar path around the cauldrons. All empty, except one holding a murky sledge like dye that looks more black than blue, the color of a good-bye.

Above the wooden frame of the front door, a stone arch inscribed with indecipherable script and the date 1905 welcomes guests into the time warp inside. No one really knows what these letters above the door announce or in what language they're written. Orhan hunches his six-foot frame in order to step inside the home and into a sea of curious townspeople and villagers come to pay their respects and graze on food and gossip. The head wailer, a rich woman by the looks of her gold teeth, orchestrates a powerful atmosphere of lamentation with a chant from the Koran.

"He drowned himself," someone whispers.

"If he drowned himself, why is his head not blue?" another asks.

"Consider how neatly he folded his clothes," someone else says, as if that alone could prove something.

"Apparently, medicinal dye is all the rage in Istanbul."

"He was always a forward-thinking man."

Orhan recognizes only a handful of people in the room. Anyone with any sense or prospects left Karod a long time ago, peeling it off like an ill-fitting coat. A few old men and women, the aging parents of his childhood friends, people he politely calls auntie and uncle, pat his face and shake his hand. Village girls, none older than twenty, roam around the room offering tea and cookies on plastic trays, their black head scarves framing eyelids lowered in modesty. They wear traditional baggy *şalvar* pants beneath their brightly colored cotton dresses. Orhan thinks he recognizes one or two of them. Suddenly conscious of his Italian suit and loafers, he grabs a cup of tea and makes his way to the living room, where every flat surface—tables, bookshelves, mantels, even the television—is covered with handcrafted doilies. Their intricate geometric and floral designs in various shades of beige provide every exposed horizontal surface with a measure of modesty.

A young girl, flanked on both sides by older women, one of whom he remembers as the village marriage broker, silently offers Orhan a tray of baklava.

"*Maşallah*," says the marriage broker, scanning her eyes along the length of his body. "We heard you came by private car." She nods in solemn approval. The girl standing to her left keeps her eyes glued to the plastic tray of sweets, and the broker gives him a conspiratorial smile. Orhan lifts his hand in protest, sure that the gesture is universal enough to decline both the baklava and the girl.

Six years ago, when Orhan first returned from Germany, these same "aunties" shunned him like a leper. The word *communist* was thrown at his back and sometimes to his face. Now they parade their single daughters in front of him, fantasizing about becoming the mother-in-law of the prodigal grandson and successful businessman. It was the combination of their scorn and his father's that made him settle in Istanbul, where no one knew a thing about his past. To his city friends, Orhan's stay in Germany was not a forced and shameful exile but an acceptable part of a rich man's education.

The girl still stands before him, awkwardly holding the tray of baklava in her calloused hands. They look so much older than the rest of her. These girls are a completely different species from the gazelles that make up the social elite of Istanbul, a modern crowd of which Orhan's ex-girlfriend, Hülya, is a member. Perhaps, with his inheritance only moments away, Orhan could pursue Hülya, with her excellent lineage and perfect tan, in the manner she was accustomed to and win her back. Though by the standards of Turkish inheritance law, the majority of Dede's wealth will no doubt go to his useless father, Orhan is sure to receive something. Hülya could move into his apartment, its ancient walls covered in what her posh friends perceived as high art. He would have to buy a large china cabinet for all her cherished relics of the West, a collector's plate with Lady Diana's face lodged at its center, her collection of Duran Duran albums displayed prominently on the shelf. All the symptoms of Western capitalism without the pesky virtues like freedom of expression and minority rights.

Orhan gulps down the remainder of his tea, sets the tiny cup on the girl's baklava tray, and moves to the sitting room, where it is less crowded. The room has only three occupants, his aunt, father, and a man in a modern suit whom he recognizes as Dede's lawyer. They sit in an uncomfortable silence that goes undisturbed by his arrival at the door. Auntie Fatma sits at the back wall, in her usual garb—a long-sleeved peasant dress of dark rayon challis fabric over baggy *şalvar* trousers—doing her best to remain invisible. Orhan is surprised by the black cotton head scarf that covers her head and frames her prunelike face. Though it is customary

for village women of a certain age to cover their heads, his aunt
has never been one to follow convention.

She balances a large aluminum tray on her knees, as she guts
the insides of a dozen tiny squash. Her hands work at a frenzied
pace, but Orhan suspects she will be listening carefully to every
word spoken. He bends down and gives her a quick peck on the
cheek. Seeing him, her face cracks into a smile, revealing a mouth
full of gold teeth. Orhan takes the seat closest to her in silence.
Light bounces from Auntie Fatma's tray to her golden mouth and
back again. The smell of garlic and red pepper paste lingers in the
air. She scoops handfuls of ground beef and rice into the hollows
of each vegetable, her legs spread apart to steady the tray. The
yellow and green squash glow like tiny gems in a jewelry box.
Orhan's hand instinctively reaches toward the middle of his chest
where his camera used to hang, before remembering he hasn't
got one. It's a reflex that almost never happens in Istanbul, where
he now lives. His body still remembers that long-lost object like
the severed limb of an amputee.

His Leica is probably still somewhere in the house. Orhan
hasn't seen it since his arrest a half-dozen years ago, and he doesn't
want to. She is a skilled lover. If he got close to her again, pressed
a firm finger on her shutter release button, she would open her
aperture just enough to let the light penetrate and then shut it
again. She would release that familiar and intoxicating sound,
somewhere between a clap and a moan, and wait for him to wind
her up again. The act would be blissful no doubt, but it would end
badly. It always did. The last time he took a photograph in Karod,

the country was coping with the military coup of 1980. Orhan was only nineteen when he took that final photograph. It was the sharp contrast of colors and textures that interested him. So focused on the abstractions that he failed to see the world around them. The Leica did that. It stole all his perspective.

Yes, much better to stay away from it.

Orhan tries hard not to look at his father who sits in the opposite corner, in Dede's favorite chair. He balances a cane on his knees, fingering a set of worry beads hanging from his left hand. It is the middle of August and Mustafa Türkoğlu is, as always, dressed to rural standards, beige skullcap, oxford shirt, sweater vest, and a dark gray wool sports jacket paired with baggy *şalvar* pants. Orhan can't remember a time when his father wasn't dressed this way. The sweltering heat of the Anatolian sun seeps through the window, threatening to suck the oxygen from Orhan's lungs, but his father sits unfazed. Nothing, not even the death of his father, much less a little heat, can produce the slightest change in the man.

Mustafa does not acknowledge Orhan's presence. His eyes, hard little marbles of contempt, stare straight ahead. It is probably the position he's assumed all day, throughout the long funeral service and the endless cries of hired wailers, the procession of handshakes and sorrowful faces. As the funeral guests leave, he regresses to his belligerent old self. All those years in exile it was his Dede, who had sustained him, who'd written long letters and accepted phone calls. How ironic to be left with this one, this angry little man whose perpetually sunburned skin had hardened like his heart.

Dede's attorney clears his throat. He must have a fine mahogany desk back in Istanbul, but today Mr. Yilmaz has been relegated to a straight-backed wooden chair so small that the man's knees practically touch his chest. It is a testament to his father's remarkable powers of subjugation.

"Shall I begin?" the attorney asks.

Orhan's father gives the man a nod.

"Upon my death," the attorney reads, "I give and bequeath the apartment building in Nishantashi to my son Mustafa, with the provision that he provide for our beloved Fatma Cinoglu throughout her life."

Auntie Fatma does not respond to the mentioning of her name. Head bent, she continues her merciless impaling of squash.

"The total of my estate, including the textile factories in Ankara and Izmir, as well as any and all properties and assets belonging to Tarik Inc., shall be entrusted to my grandson, Orhan Türkoğlu."

The words wash over Orhan like a bucket of warm water. Orhan feels himself floating in their warmth, the tension in his muscles relaxing. Except for the sound of Auntie Fatma's scraping, the world and all its noises drown in the syllables pouring from the attorney's lips. So this is what approval feels like. The company is now entirely his. It is not what he expected. Since Turkey's inheritance laws are still heavily influenced by Sharia Islamic law, it may not even hold up in court, but it is what his grandfather wanted.

Mustafa leans forward in Dede's chair. Embracing the cane with both arms, he looks like a man drowning. His lips are pressed together, as if holding his breath. Dede's words carry a lifetime of a father's disapproval for his son, and for a split second Orhan feels sorry for his father.

"Lastly, I bequeath the family home located in the village of Karod to . . ." The attorney pauses, looking around the room at each person before he proceeds. "To one Ms. Seda Melkonian."

Who?

"The bastard," Orhan's father says. "Son of a whore!"

Orhan isn't sure whose mother is being cursed here—his own, the attorney's, or Dede's. Maybe all mothers everywhere.

"Who?" Orhan hears himself say.

"You listen to me, you piece of shit." Mustafa turns to the lawyer, spit flying out of his mustache. "I'm going to ram that will so far up your ass, you'll be able to gargle with it!"

Orhan feels he may be sick. He needs to take control of this situation, to compose himself and concentrate. How could Dede turn his aunt and father out of the only home they've ever known? Orhan stands and looks around the room dumbfounded.

"This doesn't make any sense," he says.

"Who is this Seda Melkomam?" Mustafa asks.

"Seda Melkonian," the attorney corrects him.

"Do you know her, Mr. Big City Attorney? Huh? Did some she-devil seduce that simpleton in his old age? Trick him into giving her my house?" his father shouts.

"No, Mr. Türkoğlu," the attorney says, "I do not know her, but I do have an address. Your father's will clearly states that this house now belongs to Ms. Melkonian."

"No one is kicking me out of my home," Mustafa says.

"This can't be," Orhan says, pushing past a horrific mental image of his father and aunt moving into his flat in Istanbul. "This house has been in my family for a hundred years. My father was born in this house," he says. "My aunt has lived here for over seventy years. Where would they go?"

"This should help you locate Ms. Melkonian," the attorney says, pulling a large manila envelope from his briefcase and handing it to Orhan.

"No one is locating anybody," Mustafa says, lighting another cigarette. "Any lawyer in Turkey will tell you this will is garbage."

Orhan rips the envelope open and pulls out one of Dede's tiny black sketchbooks.

"It is part of the will. It belongs to you now," the attorney says. "There is an address on the last page where you can find her."

Orhan stares down at the tattered tome. The black cloth cover and white string keeping its pages tight are familiar to everyone in the family. Although he never called himself an artist, Dede was always drawing. He carried a sketchbook the way most men carry their worry beads. When he was young, Orhan would find them in every corner of the house, in his toy bin, a kitchen cupboard, or behind the chicken coop. There were entire volumes dedicated to things as mundane as Auntie Fatma's dishes, but there were also books filled with wondrous animals, real and imagined. Once, at fourteen, Orhan had the pleasure of seeing the body of a woman, her breasts and legs and buttocks drawn in meticulous detail. He spent a great deal of time with that particular collection, until Auntie Fatma discovered it under his mattress and gave him a proper beating. One never knew what lay between the two soft black covers of these volumes. The thrill in opening one of Dede's sketchbooks lay in this not knowing.

"Typical," barks his father. "He plunges us into ruin and leaves a handful of drawings as consolation."

"There is also a letter, addressed to you," the attorney says. Turning to Mustafa, he extends a small sealed envelope to him. The letter stays suspended in the air for what seems like a long time until finally, Mustafa, his eyes never leaving the attorney's face, snatches it from his hand.

Orhan turns the sketchbook around and around in his hands. The weight and feel of it does what the wailers and well-wishers could not. He bites his lower lip until the pain overwhelms his grief.

"I'm sorry if this confuses you," the attorney says as he rises to leave.

"No one is confused," Mustafa utters the last word like a curse.

Turning to Orhan, the attorney says, "Perhaps you could walk me to my car."

Orhan jumps at the chance to leave the dark room and his father's presence. Outside the pomegranate trees prevail against the dry wind, but their leaves are less reserved. They shimmy and sway, reflecting light and creating the kind of fleeting negative space of which Orhan often dreams. Their playful existence stands in direct contrast to the dilapidated buildings lining the streets of Karod.

Orhan walks alongside the attorney whose steps are quick despite his old age.

"I'm sorry about what happened in there. My father isn't himself," Orhan says.

"He's nothing like your grandfather," the attorney says.

Orhan realizes for the first time that this man is roughly the same age as his late grandfather.

"Were you and Dede friends, Mr. Yilmaz?"

"You could say that, yes," says Yilmaz. "He was very proud of you. You know that?"

"God knows I tried to please him," says Orhan. "Do you think he was in his right mind toward the end?"

"If you're asking me if he knew what he was doing, my answer is yes. He wanted to give you control over Tarik Inc. But that doesn't mean it's legal, not when your father is still alive. I tried to dissuade him from this business about the house, knowing it would only exacerbate things, but he insisted."

Orhan nods.

"Your grandfather was a good man," the attorney says, placing a hand on Orhan's shoulder. "He wouldn't do this if he didn't have a good reason. You understand?"

"Yes," he hears himself say, though he understands nothing.

"Look, the will is highly unconventional. The part about the house can be easily contested as it goes against our inheritance laws to forgo immediate family and favor a stranger. But if one part of the will is contested, then the rest of it is suddenly open to questioning. We don't want that."

"No," agrees Orhan.

"Go see her. Find out what this is all about. It's what he wanted. But take these papers along," he says, removing a new envelope from his briefcase. "It's an offer for compensation in place of the house. Try to get her to sign the house back to you. It will calm your father down. Whoever she is, a dilapidated house in the middle of nowhere can't be of much interest to her."

"I hope you're right," says Orhan.

When the attorney's car can no longer be seen, Orhan returns to the house. His father, still seated in Dede's green chair, glares at him through a cloud of cigarette smoke.

"He never loved me, you know." They are the first words his father has spoken to him on this day of mourning and they come out in a low ominous whisper.

"He would have put his eyes out to avoid looking at me as a child. Avoided me like the plague until you came along. Now he's put it in writing. Skipped me like I never existed. Made it official."

"Every father loves his son," says Orhan, "even if he doesn't know the best way to show it." He should know.

"A perfect stranger," his father says in disbelief.

Orhan reminds himself that this is not his fault. And though it isn't, he feels guilty just the same.

"You know that attorney is no friend of ours. What will you do next, shine his shoes?"

"Dede trusted him," Orhan says.

"Your *dede* was an old fool." His father's voice grows louder, making Orhan wonder how soon the family's plight will spread from the balconies and stalls of Karod to the streets of Istanbul, where Tarik Inc. is located. "Everything we have has just slipped through our fingers. And what do you do?"

"Not everything," says Orhan. And not *our* fingers, he thinks. Just yours.

"You have been charmed, you know. Bewitched by the West, its shiny coins and godless women," Mustafa says, rubbing his index finger against his thumb.

"I live in Istanbul. How is that the West?" Orhan says, thinking he hasn't had anything shiny or naked in such a long time.

"Be quiet!" Mustafa says, propping himself up with the help of his cane. Despite himself, Orhan reflexively recoils from the menacing rod.

"You are not to contact that woman," his father says.

"Don't you want to know who she is? Why he's done this?"

"No, I don't want to know. And I forbid you to go stirring up shit that no one cares about."

"I have to go and see her to get the house back," says Orhan.

"Always, I am living among heathens," Mustafa says, raising his voice again. "I ask nothing of you. Only to be a good Turk, a good Muslim. And what do you do? You shame me. You turn communist. You spread leftist propaganda and get kicked out of the country."

"I was a photographer, not a communist." Orhan is shouting now. When will his father understand this? Every conversation turns to this perceived betrayal.

"You've given me nothing to be proud of," Mustafa says. "I hang my head in shame while you go around without remorse."

"I have nothing to be remorseful about. I've been pardoned, remember?" he says, thinking that it must be easier to dwell on a son's perceived betrayal than a father's disapproval. Orhan stands to his full height and begins pacing, towering half a meter above his father. He knows all about a father's disapproval. If it were up to his Mustafa, the country would be run by mullahs, every woman in a head scarf, bureaucrats so busy praying five times a day, they can't see straight.

"You godless louse," Mustafa says. "You think you are so much better with your art and your pictures."

"I haven't taken a picture in years," Orhan says.

"Yes, yes, Mr. Big Businessman," Mustafa says, making wide circles with his arms. "You think you would have that job if it weren't for your *dede*? Hmm, Mr. Exile?"

"Well, he didn't give it to you, did he?" Orhan says. "He gave the company to me." Even as the words leave him, Orhan wishes he could take them back.

Mustafa's face turns as gray as his mustache. "You are nothing but a traitor," he says finally. "To your faith, to your country, and most of all, to this family. I want you out of this house by morning. And take his fucking letter with you," he says, throwing Dede's letter at Orhan and limping toward his room.

Orhan watches his father walk out of the room with the help of his cane. Unable to face the funeral guests that litter the house, he steps out into the family courtyard, where Auntie Fatma is waiting for him on one of two plastic chairs. Free of her dark head scarf, she carries her grief, raw and exposed to the dry wind, in the creases of her face.

"I've brought tea," she says. "Sit. Let him fester."

Orhan accepts, though he isn't thirsty, and settles into the other chair.

"I see you've found God," he says, lighting a cigarette and pointing to the discarded head scarf draped on a low table between them.

"Nonsense," she replies. "Those idiots in Ankara have outlawed it, so naturally I decided to take a new fancy to it." A new law banning head scarves in universities had just passed. It was the Kemalist state's way of curbing fundamentalist Islam and embracing modernism. But the rule was meant for young university students, not village women in their nineties.

"Always the rebel," Orhan says.

She reaches over and takes the letter in Orhan's hand. She rips it open. "Here, read it to me," she says.

Orhan hesitates for only a moment, before his curiosity and the need to hear Dede one last time overcome him.

Dede's narrow slanted script dominates the page. There are no drawings here. Only words.

My dearest Mustafa (and you are dear, though I never let you feel it),

I trust that by now you will be seeking the comfort of religion through our good imam. And I am glad of that, though I cannot believe as you do. I lost that ability a long time ago. To tell the truth, I'm not sure I ever had it. My words here are meant to be another salve, for you and also for Orhan and Fatma.

I have spent the last year chasing my past. Or rather, it chased me. At first, I hid from it, looked the other way, busied myself, but then I grew tired and turned to face it. I met with it in secret places. On the highest branches of our now barren mulberry tree, at the lap of the red river where I first caressed your mother. I even climbed inside the cauldrons. Each time my past did not disappoint me. It came, explaining everything and nothing. Rest assured that whether you find me in my bed, at the base of a tree, or inside the river: I did not jump, or drown, or in any way harm myself. I simply went looking for my past and was mercifully relieved of its burden.

I'm sorry I did not love you better as a child. You were, for me, a daily reminder of her. I hope that my love for Orhan has made up, in part, for my failures as a father. I ask only for your forgiveness and that you oblige me this one last time, as I try to meld my past to your present. Forgive me. For your sake and for Orhan's too.

Your loving father,

Kemal

"Well, that explains all the tree climbing," says Auntie Fatma.

Orhan remains speechless. Part of him had hoped there would be an explanation of the will. His heart aches for his father, and his mind is racing with questions.

"Give it here. I'll see to it that your father reads it."

Orhan hands her the letter and opens Dede's sketchbook, hoping there might be a clue to his reasoning. Almost every page is filled with sketches of the old mulberry tree that still stands in the center of their courtyard. The row of cauldrons looms sometimes in the background and sometimes in the foreground. How many times did Dede sketch these cauldrons before stripping his clothes and immersing himself for his very last breath?

"Tell me, who is this Seda?" asks Orhan.

"No 'How are you, Auntie? How have you been, Auntie?' Are you like this with your girlfriend too? What was her name?"

"Hülya," Orhan replies. Auntie Fatma and Hülya were like the two parts of Turkey itself, one grasping for modernity, the other with both feet planted in the fertile soil of a rural village. The last time Auntie Fatma paid a visit to his apartment in Istanbul, she fastened a garden hose to the bathtub and proceeded to "do a proper washing." Hülya and Orhan came home to find half his furniture piled high on the balcony and the other half dripping with soapy water. It was an amusing story he told at dinner parties.

"How is Hülya?" Auntie Fatma asks.

"Don't know. We broke up," he says, thinking about the curse of the Türkoğlu men, always being left by their women.

His grandmother passed when his father was only a toddler and
Orhan's own mother died in childbirth. Auntie Fatma, never having been a Türkoğlu wife or mother, is the only female constant
in the family.

"Her loss," Fatma says. "You're a handsome devil, like your
grandfather, may Allah's blessings be upon him. I'm supposed to
say that now," she says, laughing, "every time I mention your *dede*.
As if Allah would take commands from me."

"Are you going to tell me what this is all about, Auntie?"

"Why should I? Besides, why do you suppose I know?"

"Because you knew Dede best. And because you're old," he
adds, winking at her. "As old as this house, maybe older."

"Why, you son of a goat. For your information, the house is at
least a decade or two older than I am. Don't let the date on that
stone arch fool you. And I'm as strong as an ox," she says crossing
her arms. "Besides, you're no schoolboy yourself. What are you
now, thirty-five?"

"I'm only twenty-nine and you know it," he says.

"Got any pictures to show me?"

"No. I don't even own a camera. Since when do you want to
see my photos, anyway? You're just trying to change the subject,"
he says.

"Clever little boy."

"Man," Orhan corrects her.

"Boy, man—what's the difference? And I have always liked
your pictures. Look, I even kept this here for you." Auntie Fatma

lifts her head scarf that is draped on the table to reveal the Leica, familiar yet titillating, its silver and black fascia hinting at all kinds of possibilities. Underneath it is a portfolio of his photography.

Orhan hasn't seen either object for years. Like the stone arch above the main door of the house, his camera and portfolio are remnants from a forgotten life.

"Take them," she says. "It's not good to keep a grudge, especially against one so dear."

Orhan reaches for the camera, running his hand across the silver knobs and leather creases. His breath slows down, quelling his anxiety. There's no harm in touching the thing. It's only a camera, an inanimate object.

"What am I supposed to do about all this?" he asks, trying to concentrate on the problem at hand.

"You'll do what you've always done," she says. "Follow your Dede's wishes. Just promise me you'll get the house back."

"Just like that. Like I'm picking up some *simit* on the way home from work."

"Yes, like that," Auntie Fatma says. She sighs, letting her shoulders drop. Never one for serious conversation, his aunt has a special talent for trivializing all of life's little unhappinesses. But this time, for once, she seems worried.

"You don't have to worry," says Orhan. "I'm not going to let some stranger turn you out of your home," says Orhan.

"*Benim paşam.* My prince," she says, patting his knee. "You've got her information. Go and find her. Only be careful."

"Careful?"

"Yes, careful," she says. "You know what the trees said when the axe came to the forest?"

"No, what?" asks Orhan.

"The handle is one of us," she says, smiling her devious smile.

Orhan knits his brows together in confusion.

"I don't get it. Am I the tree or the axe?" he asks.

"Who knows?" she says.

⸙CHAPTER 2⸙

Pilgrimage to Ararat

WHEN THE BOEING 747 finally pulls its wheels up during take off, Orhan literally feels lighter. The more space between himself and his father, and that damned house and Karod, the better. He shuts his eyes and tries to push the terrifying thought of Mustafa moving to Istanbul and taking ownership of Tarik Inc. out of his mind. He tries instead to imagine California, where Seda Melkonian lives. Sunny beaches and German-dubbed reruns of *Knight Rider* come to mind. He thinks of the tall American in that show, David somebody, singing "Looking for Freedom" on top of the Berlin Wall minutes before it was torn down.

Orhan's own freedom is in the hands of a total stranger. The thought lands him right back where he's been since Dede's funeral: wallowing in a pool of dread. Maybe the old man really had lost his mind. Maybe Orhan was too busy with the company to notice. Reports of Dede's growing eccentricities did sometimes reach him, but indulging the old man's whims was a time-honored tradition in the Türkoğlu house. Auntie Fatma and his father didn't agree on much, but neither of them balked when

Dede started making strange requests. As a boy, Orhan watched as his father washed all the coin money before placing it in a wooden box Dede had labeled TEMIZ, clean. His grandfather was always going on and on about the evil stench of money. One afternoon, Orhan found Auntie Fatma ironing the paper money. She placed the bills flat onto the board, then covered them with a linen pillowcase. The iron hissed as hot steam rose up from the bills, through the white linen and into the hallway. When he asked her what she was doing, she said, "I'm purging the money of all its evil." Not questioning it, Orhan helped her hang each bill to dry on the clothing line.

Last month, the old man wrote a letter to the supervisor at the factory demanding that all the red fabric dye in the plant be the exact shade of a red mulberry he'd included in an envelope. The discreet manager had placed the letter with smudged fruit on Orhan's desk and ignored its directives.

Orhan knew Dede's requests were growing stranger and stranger, but he could never have predicted this. A battle begins in the pit of his stomach between the forces of anxiety and grief. Just when grief takes hold of his insides, a wave of anxiety sweeps in and coats everything with its venom.

Orhan orders a whiskey on the rocks and stares into the amber liquid, trying to make sense of what Dede has done. Is this Seda woman a relative? Even so, what would possess Dede to leave the house to her? Even if the family home is the least valuable of Dede's assets, it encompasses four generations of Türkoğlu life.

Dede started Tarik Inc. inside those walls sometime after the

First World War. The company specialized in handwoven rugs and grew significantly in the mid-seventies. By the time Orhan came along, the business had moved to the city. To Orhan, the house was always a place of confinement and conflict, a place where Mustafa's menacing rod and booming voice faced off against Auntie Fatma's iron will. As a boy, he'd escaped to the outdoors. But as a teenager, Dede's Leica had saved his sanity. The truth is, when he first picked up the camera, he wasn't trying to change the world or make it better; he was trying to escape it. The Leica gave him a legitimate reason to capture the world, without having to join it.

ALL THAT WAS before he was exiled to Germany, before he stopped taking photographs. But Orhan doesn't want to think about that. What matters is not what the world does to you but how you respond.

Upon his return to Turkey, six years ago, Orhan had imagined himself a prodigal son, returning to claim his rightful place in his country, his home, his family business, maybe even his father's heart—that most impenetrable of caves. He flew straight into Istanbul, took a cab to his grandfather's factory, and never looked back. He worked tirelessly and without looking up. He collected patterns from all the most remote corners of the country and mined ottoman archives for designs that would have otherwise been extinct. Recently, Orhan designed his own line of kilims. He merged ancient patterns with the clean lines and a monochromatic color palette more suitable for younger buyers. He stopped

thinking about photography altogether. The business, Dede's fail-
ing health, and his father's incompetence left little room for anything of his old life. He chased stability like a blind dog on a scent.

And now he was sniffing his way to Los Angeles.

Orhan downs the rest of his whiskey in one big gulp and eyes
his travel bag. His Leica lies on its side, on top of Dede's sketchbook and his old portfolio. Black on black on black, a triumvirate
of dark casings that contain his past. Auntie Fatma insisted that he
take the camera and his portfolio with him. He hasn't cracked the
portfolio open and doesn't plan to. Looking at the images would
be like rummaging through the things of an old lover and he's got
no need for that kind of pain.

Before leaving Karod, Orhan found an old roll of unused black-
and-white film. He chose a 50 mm lens and stood staring at the
house of his childhood. The once mighty mulberry tree prevailed
over the aging structure, its black barren branches hanging like so
many veins in God's arm. The dark downward lines crisscrossed
against the bright sunlit mustard of the house's stucco. He took
the photo, thinking of all the drawings of the mulberry tree and
cauldrons in Dede's final sketchbook. He pressed the shutter release and the camera snapped and moaned, but it brought no
new knowledge about the tree, the house, or the man who loved
them.

Chapter 3

Home

SEDA FINGERS THE letter tucked inside her sleeve, where its crumpled surface has molded into the shape of her left wrist. Pulling it out, she smoothes its creases against her knee. Her eyes roam around the page, like they've done again and again in the past few weeks, resting on the spots where the black ink stops and begins again, then to the white spaces in between. Thinking, sometimes, there is more in between words than within them.

I am the grandson of Kemal Türkoğlu . . . he's written. Kemal's name, warm and sweet, swims through her blood and down into her belly before it somersaults into her throat and threatens to escape. She presses her lips together, refusing to let him out.

It is a strange thing, receiving a letter from a dead man's grandson. A letter from a place so far away and long ago that opening it was itself an act of heroism. Even in death, Kemal would not let go of her. He has reached through time and space to grab hold of her once again.

She feels the sheet of paper releasing an ancient djinn, a demon that threatens to uncover the past she's painstakingly buried. She stares at the letter's folds and creases, the frayed edge where it's been torn out of a legal pad, reading the awkward English translation of Turkish thoughts.

From her room, she can see the other residents shuffling to and fro, searching for God knows what. Morning medications, breakfast, companionship, a reason to live. The first time she saw the words *Ararat Home for the Aging,* they were printed on a white folder sitting on the kitchen counter. Beneath a large photo of Mount Ararat was captioned: "Named after the holy mountain in Armenia where Noah's ark is believed to have landed, the home is a refuge for an aging Diaspora." It was the word *refuge* that bothered Seda the most, so similar to *refugee,* a word she was all too familiar with. She thought about flinging the brochure into the yard, burying it deep in that cactus soil that her niece liked so much. Ani was her only living relative, the daughter of her long-deceased younger brother. Seda knew Ani loved her. Still, a month later she found herself living in the Ararat Home. It is a museum for the living, breathing relics of an unburied past, built by a community for whom everything, from the church picnic to the baker's son passing the bar exam, is a testament to survival.

"You coming?" Old Kalustian pokes his bald head into her doorway. The old goat thinks he's got pull with the ladies just because he uses a fancy cane instead of a walker.

Seda clicks her tongue and waves him and his silver-headed cane away. Can't hold his stool but still thinks he can command his pecker.

"Come on. The kids from St. Nishan are reenacting the great battle of Sardarabad," he says, eyes shining.

Seda lifts both her eyebrows and clicks her tongue, before turning her wheelchair around in refusal.

"Suit yourself," he says.

There's no dignity in this place, thinks Seda. No privacy either. Some fool is always poking his or her head into your doorway. And as if the residents and nurses aren't bad enough, lately all kinds of people keep showing up, waving their tape recorders in her face, asking her questions about the past. Everyone is an amateur historian. They use words like *witness* and *genocide,* trying to bridge the gap between her past and their own present with words.

She wants nothing to do with it. But the other residents have fallen under a confessional spell. They're like ancient tea bags steeping in the murky waters of the past, repeating their stories over and over again to anyone who will listen. Who can blame them? Driven from their homes not by soldiers this time, but by their own loved ones, to this place so cleverly labeled "home," a second exile. In some ways, Seda thinks it's worse than the first: to the lexicon of horrific memories is added the immense shame of surviving, of living when so many others did not. Yet they all bask in their rediscovered relevance. But all the words in every human language on earth would not be enough to describe what happened.

When the past wells up inside her, Seda knows not to let it out. "I can't remember," she tells those who ask. When the river of words comes billowing out, it poisons everything. It taints the present with the blood and tears of the past. She wouldn't mind the forgetting that comes with age, but whatever is eating at her brain is only wiping out the freshest of memories. It leaves the undigested past alone, lets it fester, decomposing in her mind. Despite her best efforts, the scents and visions of her girlhood come bubbling up to the surface. Yesterday, she thought she smelled pistachios and almost threw up her lunch.

Seda rolls her chair to the window and opens the blinds. She places a palm above her brow to block the sun. She can see three rows of plastic chairs facing the great fountain. A splattering of costumed boys and girls in varying heights are scattered between the fountain and the audience. One fat boy wears an Armenian priest's robe complete with pointy black hat. She spots Kalustian limping toward the back row and leans forward to hear a few phrases.

"Let the bells of every Armenian church ring," bellows the boy priest.

"To battle!" A girl dressed as a soldier waves a plastic rifle.

A stout woman kneels in front of the children, mouthing every word. She waves her arms, encouraging the remaining soldiers to take center stage. The audience is eating it up, Seda can tell. There may even be a few veterans of that battle in the audience. There'll be claims of that sort by Kalustian for sure. All this incessant probing and recording of the past has made celebrities of them all. Outside these walls, these old people may be overlooked, their past a narrative the world insists upon forgetting. But here among the residents of the Ararat Home, they are esteemed as survivors of the genocide, bearers of unspeakable horrors, guardians of their people's past.

"Morning Ms. Seda." Betty Shields, Seda's favorite orderly, enters the room, her shoes squeaking against the linoleum floor. "Not gonna leave the building today, are we? Well, it's a damn shame, that's for sure. It's a mighty fine day out."

Seda likes it when Betty speaks this way, adapting a comfortable vernacular that exaggerates her southern black roots. Being the only non-Armenian in all of Ararat Home, let alone the only black person, can't be easy. It's always amusing when in the presence of others, especially doctors, Betty Shields alters her speech, stripping it of all its color. Is it conscious? Seda wonders.

"You hear about the genocide exhibit? It's next week, you know," Betty says.

"I heard," Seda says. She folds the letter in half then twice more and tucks it back inside her sleeve.

"They say the governor may come. Imagine that. The governor coming here."

Seda shrugs her shoulders. It's not all that hard to imagine. California's governor, George Deukmejian, is Armenian American. The art exhibit is the brainchild of Seda's niece, Ani.

Betty kneels before Seda's wheelchair. She reaches over to stroke Seda's silver bob.

"I'm not an invalid you know," Seda says, waving her hand away.

"I know," says Betty, "but you've been awfully quiet lately. You all right?"

"I'm ninety," Seda answers. "How all right can I be?"

"You got a visitor. Not Ms. Ani. No ma'am. This one's a gentle-man. Checked in at the front desk a few minutes ago. Tall and handsome too. Like a Mediterranean Clark Kent."

"Lucky me." Seda rubs her fingers against the letter in her sleeve. Let him wait. She's got nothing to say to him. The past is dead and now so is Kemal. Uttering even a single syllable might bring it all back and she isn't going to let that happen. *I will breathe. I will sign whatever he wants and make him leave.* She repeats this mantra to herself whenever the panic sets in.

"Well, all righty then. Show's over," Betty says, jutting her chin at the window. "You ready for lunch?" Without waiting for a reply, Betty takes the handles of Seda's wheelchair.

"Did I say I was ready?" says Seda. "I don't remember saying I was ready."

"All the same, it's time for lunch," says Betty.

Seda takes a deep breath and picks up the embroidery in her lap. She hunches over her hands, letting her fingers work the deli-cate piece of stitching. Three rows of red and yellow diamonds mark the pattern as Anatolian in origin. Despite her resolve, the past is bleeding out of her fingers, staining everything she touches.

CHAPTER 4

White Days

ORHAN STANDS IN the parking lot of the Ararat Home for the Aging, sucking on a cigarette and feeling more than a little intimidated. Inside the sprawling grounds and behind the palm-lined walkways are hundreds of elderly Armenian men and women, some of whom may have been alive during World War I. Singed and scattered by history, they are united in their hatred of all things Turkish. When Auntie Fatma told him to use the Armenian alias "Ohan," Orhan had laughed at the suggestion. He's done nothing wrong, and as far as he knows, neither have his ancestors. But he's heard that they are an angry people, angry enough to inflict violence upon themselves and others over something that may or may not have happened seventy-five years ago. He extinguishes his cigarette on the side of a trash can and walks inside.

The reception area is a large rectangular room decorated in muted sea foam and mauve. Three loveseats surround a tiny coffee table much too small for the room. The sofas are upholstered in a floral print made of a vinyl most resistant to human waste.

Silk flower arrangements grace the dusty piano. The place reminds Orhan of the prized living rooms of Turkey's growing middle class: rooms stocked with every Western comfort but still uncomfortable. Rooms to be viewed but not used.

A bronze bust stands on a large pedestal, placed in the center of the room so that one must walk around it to get to the front desk. Below the bronze man's creased forehead and comic mustache is a plaque identifying him as the writer, William Saroyan. A paragraph below the bust reads:

> I should like to see any power of the world destroy this race, this small tribe of unimportant people, whose wars have all been fought and lost, whose structures have crumbled, literature is unread, music is unheard, and prayers are no more answered. Go ahead, destroy Armenia. See if you can do it. Send them into the desert without bread or water. Burn their homes and churches. Then see if they will not laugh, sing and pray again. For when two of them meet anywhere in the world, see if they will not create a New Armenia.

Orhan stands dumbfounded by this strange collection of words. In this homage to survival, the author actually invites an imagined enemy to try and destroy his race. At least the writer acknowledges that they are an unimportant people. The only thing that's left to give them importance is this claim to a tragic past, in which Orhan's people, the Turks, play the villain intent

upon destroying them. Orhan knows all about the difficulties mi-
norities face in Turkey, but that doesn't make all Turks murderous
thugs.

"Can I help you?" the receptionist asks.

"I'm here to visit a . . ." He considers the word *relative* or *friend,*
but neither word fits comfortably in his mouth.

"Name?"

"Orhan."

"The name of the resident, sir?"

"Oh, yes. Her name is Seda Melkonian," Orhan says, suddenly
aware of his thick Turkish accent.

"Room 1203," she says. "But it's lunchtime, so they're all in
the dining hall now. Go down this main hall and turn right. You'll
see the sign."

Orhan walks a maze of corridors and hallways before finding
the dining room. He pauses just before the glass-paneled French
doors. The room is filled almost entirely with old women. A handful of men sit at a rectangular table, huddled together for cama-
raderie or protection. They roll dice into wooden backgammon
trays, the way men in his village have done for centuries. Women
in mint green scrubs roam the room, adjusting wheelchairs and
spoon-feeding hesitant mouths. He steps over the threshold and
is immediately confronted by a din of noise coming from a television in one corner of the room. On the screen, a man with
perfectly coifed white hair and matching teeth is presiding over a
game show of sorts. The contestants stand before an enthusiastic
crowd shouting out prices of things ranging from a blender to a

new car. Orhan stares at the screen, marveling at the spectacle of garish colors, a celebration of consumerism and wealth accompanied by shiny smiling people and loud music. Distracted, he does not at first notice the robed and slippered woman approaching him. She cradles a plastic blue-eyed doll and calls out to him in what he assumes is Armenian.

Oh God, please don't be Seda. He never considered the Melkonian woman might be senile or suffering from some kind of dementia. He gives the woman with the doll a cautious smile. She points an accusing finger at him, and holds the matty-headed doll tight in her other arm. It stares at him too, its rosy lips and cheeks in direct contrast to its shorn locks and tattered dress. Orhan tries to ignore the woman, but she points her crooked finger straight at him.

"Don't mind her. This is Mrs. Vartanian," says a hefty black woman, wearing a uniform. Her name tag is decorated with stickers of puppies and reads "Betty." She takes the woman with the doll gently by the arm.

"She thinks you're a soldier," says Betty. The woman presses her plastic doll to her chest before spitting at Orhan's feet. He looks down in disbelief, his ears burning with disdain.

"She don't mean nothing by it," says Betty. "Do you, Mrs. Vartanian?"

"It's okay. I understand. She's . . ." He fishes for the appropriate English word and finally settles for "old."

"We like to call it mature," Betty says.

Orhan nods, making a mental note to look up the word *mature* later in his English-language dictionary. "I am here to see Seda Melkonian," he says.

She scans his face for a moment.

"She is expecting me," he adds.

"Right over there," Betty says, pointing to a woman with short hair the color of unpolished steel. She is bent over a piece of needlework. Orhan can see her gnarled fingers, hooked like a great eagle's talons, working diligently at a delicate piece of fabric. He takes a few steps toward her, then stops. Unlike the woman with the doll, Seda Melkonian is impeccably dressed. She wears a navy blue cardigan with a violet silk scarf around her neck. Orhan takes a deep breath and continues toward her, stopping only when his feet are planted right in front of her chair. She smells strongly of jasmine.

"Mrs. Melkonian?" His voice is smaller than it's been in years.

The old woman raises her head. She has a lovely face, despite its creases. Her eyes have a haughtiness to them. Greenish gray with flecks of gold, they take him in, starting at his shoes and pausing at his shoulders before finally coming to rest on his face.

"Orhan Türkoğlu," Orhan announces, extending his hand. When she doesn't take it, he clears his throat and fixes his eyes upon her, looking for a clue about her identity. She looks nothing like his father but a bit like himself with his own hazel eyes and tawny skin. Could this woman hiding in a nursing home in Los Angeles be flesh of his flesh? Orhan's grandmother had died of tuberculosis within a year or two of his father's birth. Her sister, Auntie Fatma, arrived shortly after to take care of Orhan's father, the young Mustafa. No photographs survive of his paternal grandmother. But then, few in Anatolia could have afforded such things back then.

When Orhan's own mother died in childbirth, Mustafa watered the repressed seeds of his anger with large amounts of raki. And later, when he found God, he replaced the raki with a stronger cocktail of theology and nationalism. Mothers birthed, then died, in the Türkoğlu family. Not even their ghosts stayed behind. Perhaps this is why Orhan is almost thirty and unmarried.

Suddenly, Orhan is eager to get beyond the awkward introductions. He considers how best to explain his presence. A flock of generalities swirl in his head about the importance of his mission, but all he can manage is "I sent you a letter."

She does not respond.

"I speak perfect English," he says.

The old woman raises an eyebrow at this.

Embarrassed by the exaggeration, Orhan adds, "I mean, I am fine speaking English."

After an uncomfortable silence, he grabs an empty chair. "May I sit?" he asks, then before she can respond, he sits down. He waits for her to say something, about the letter or its contents, but the old woman picks up the embroidery in her lap, arranging it just so.

"As you know, my grandfather, Kemal Türkoğlu, has passed." The words cut through him, forming fresh wounds. Orhan looks for a hint of sadness in her eyes at the news and, finding none, continues, "And he's left our family home in Karod to you."

The old woman lowers her head so that her silver hair falls forward, masking the sides of her eyes.

"Do you have any idea why he did that?" he asks suddenly.

She does not answer.

"Are you a distant relative? A friend maybe?" The question seems idiotic as soon as it leaves him.

Orhan looks around for someone with authority, only to find Betty staring at him suspiciously. He has every right to be here. So why are his hands sweaty?

"Excuse me," he says to Betty, lifting a finger in the air.

Betty continues looking at him, but does not move. "Yes?" she says.

"Does she speak?"

"Pardon?" says the orderly, her southern twang lingering on the first syllable in a way that makes Orhan feel even more foreign.

"Mrs. Melkonian—does she speak?"

"When she wants to," says Betty, arching one penciled eyebrow at him.

Orhan sighs. Will that be soon? he wants to ask.

He turns his attention back to Seda, who's making small loops with her needles. Her gnarled fingers move slow and steady in circular motions. Orhan wills himself to be patient, trying to remember that all this may be too much for her. But as a hexagon emerges in the needlework, he feels himself growing more and more angry. Say something, he wants to shout at her. He stretches a hand out and places it on top of the needlework, stalling her hands.

"Do you know who I am?" he asks her.

The old woman looks into his face for a long defiant moment. "*Evet,* yes."

Orhan is silenced by her answer, spoken in the familiar language of his mother tongue. There is no mistaking the disdain in her voice. Her eyes bore into him, offering up a challenge he can't quite comprehend.

"You want the house," she says in English, looking away from him again.

"That's right," he says, recovering. "It's been in my family for almost a century."

The old woman does not respond to this.

"Can you imagine how we must feel? No, of course you can't," he says, answering his own question. He presses his lips together in an effort to contain the emotions. This is when he remembers the photo.

"I wanted to show you this," he says, pulling out the last photo he took of the house before leaving Karod. He looks at it again before handing it to her. He had hoped that the barren tree and the crumbling facade of the house would discourage this Seda woman from seizing the property, but the intense chiaroscuro makes it a powerful image. The tree and the house have never looked more exotic. He hands it to her anyway.

"You see, the house he's left you is not in very good condition. Barely standing, really. It's in the middle of nowhere, but it's got a lot of sentimental value for my family. My father and aunt live there now."

The old woman exhales audibly when she's confronted with the photograph. She recoils back from it when Orhan holds it out toward her.

"I am prepared to offer you more than what the property is worth," he says. "All you have to do is sign this agreement stating you will take payment in exchange for the property. It's incredibly generous, given that the house rightfully belongs to my family."

"I don't want your money," she says, her eyebrows knitted together with scorn. "If I sign, you'll leave and never come back?" she asks.

Orhan nods. "You have my word," he says.

"Give me your pen," she says, without looking at him.

Orhan exhales, letting all the air trapped in his chest out. He extends the legal papers and a plastic pen in her direction and waits for her to sign.

ᴄᴈᴑCHAPTER 5ᴑᴈᴇ

The Staff of Moses

IT IS A nothing pen, the kind of pen people discard without thinking, but he holds it out to Seda like the staff of Moses. If a wooden staff could part the Red Sea, then surely a plastic one could do the same. And the sea of her past is red indeed. She's managed to stay away from its shores all her life, to ignore its gurgling sounds, its demand for more sacrifice.

Mrs. Vartanian points a finger at the young man's back, yelling, "Turk eh." A few residents look him up and down, then turn away. Betty was right. He is handsome in a rugged sort of way, with insistent eyes set deep in his square skull. He smells of cinnamon and cigarettes.

"What's going on here?" Betty is standing above their hunched figures.

Seda immediately spreads her hands over the documents. "None of your business," she says.

"Those look like legal papers," says Betty. "Does Ms. Ani know you're signing those?"

"Don't be a busybody," Seda snaps.

"It's not really right to ask little old ladies to be signing things without legal counsel, is it?" Betty says to Orhan, ignoring Seda.

"She doesn't need legal counsel," says Orhan.

"Last I checked, I'm an adult," says Seda. "I can sign whatever I damn well please."

"It's only a small matter," Orhan says.

"Then you won't mind if she sleeps on it," says Betty.

"I don't need to sleep on it," says Seda.

"I think you should leave now," Betty says, grabbing the documents from Seda's lap. "Visiting hours are over."

Orhan rises to his full height, still staring into the orderly's dark eyes. "You don't understand," he says.

"All the same, visiting hours are over," she says, handing him his documents. "You're gonna have to come back tomorrow."

Seda, still holding the pen, stares at the documents in the young man's hands. Without removing his eyes from the orderly, Orhan bends his lanky frame down to Seda's ear.

"*Ak gün ağartır, kara gün karartır.*" It is a Turkish proverb spoken in the tongue of her forgotten past. A white day sheds light; a dark day sheds darkness.

"The days are white now, Mrs. Melkonian," he says in English. "I'll see you tomorrow." And she swears she can see the thin white sheet that hangs between her past and his future go flapping in the wind.

Before Seda can say another word, he is gone and Betty is pushing her chair again.

"How dare you?"

"How dare I what?" says Betty, casually.

"You know what!"

"I'm only looking out for you, Ms. Seda."

"I don't need you to look out for me. I'm perfectly capable of looking out for myself."

"Is that right?" asks Betty.

"Yes, that's right."

"I seen this TV show last week, where some con man romanced this widow and swindled her out of her savings."

"Did I look like I was being romanced to you?"

"You know what I mean."

"No, I don't know what you mean."

"All the same, you should tell Ms. Ani about whatever this is."

"This has nothing to do with Ani." Seda can feel her face burning and her voice rising. "What I tell and don't tell my niece is none of your business."

"Whatever," says Betty, stopping in front of Seda's doorway.

"No, not whatever. You are an orderly," Seda says, pointing her finger. "Your job is to bring me my food and pills. Bathe me. Not to give me legal advice."

"Is that so?"

"That's so. When I need help, I'll ask for it. Otherwise, leave me alone."

"Fine," says Betty, closing the door behind her.

Good, let her leave, Seda thinks. A closed door is a rare blessing around here. Tomorrow. All this will be over tomorrow. The young man will come back and get what he needs, then go back to Turkey before Ani or anyone else notices him.

It's as if Kemal put every painful memory in the shape of that ancient house, wrapped it like a Christmas present, and forced his grandson to deliver the gift. Well, she would return that thing right back to where it came from.

PART II

1915

CHAPTER 6

Normal

LUCINE WAKES UP as she always does, to the slow rhythmic sounds of Anush's ivory comb. The gentle scrape and pull is her own private rooster call. She opens her eyes to the thousands of tiny particles that dance in the light from their only window. They dodge and duck and swirl around to the music of her older sister's comb.

Anush is seated in her usual place, before the oval mirror. She wears an emerald silk dress with gold filament at the neck and wrists, an Easter present from their parents. Her black hair cascades across her shoulders, a dark, wide cloak of vanity.

"Will you help me with the braid?" Anush asks.

Ordinarily Lucine would groan and refuse, but now that the world is changed, she cannot bring herself to decline. She slips into her own dress, which is cinched at the waist and mercifully nothing like the emerald silk of her sister's.

"Sit down. It's easier that way," Lucine says.

She parts and weaves the three ropes of Anush's hair, over, under, and in between, until a long tight snake winds its way beyond her sister's shoulders and down to the back of her chair. In the village, where most women cover their heads, Anush's exaggerated locks are considered indecent or Western, depending on whom you ask. Today, together with the rich green fabric of her dress, Anush's illustrious mane seems even more out of place, like an unsuppressed laugh during the liturgy.

When the braiding is done, Lucine remains standing behind her sister. The blue haze of the morning has burned off. In this new light, Anush's rosy complexion stands in stark contrast to Lucine's own tawny skin. They are an unlikely pair. Anush, the elder, pressed and tamed and trusting, sweet like her name professes. Anush of the many ribbons and even more suitors.

"Now you sit. Let me do your hair," says Anush.

"What for?" asks Lucine, pulling her unruly locks into a tight bun.

"To look pretty, silly," she says, rising from the chair.

"I don't want to look pretty," Lucine says.

"Why not?"

Because it's stupid to worry about one's hair when the world is turning inside out. "I just don't," she says.

"You're fifteen. You need to start taking an interest in your appearance," Anush says. "Besides, it's Wednesday."

Lucine starts at the news. *Wednesday already? Has it really been one week since Uncle Nazareth was taken away?*

"Wednesday," Anush repeats by way of explanation. "Our bath day." She places a hand on Lucine's shoulder and ushers her into the chair before the mirror.

Lucine's heart sinks at the thought of the hushed whispers of the community bathhouse, the thought of village women arching their eyebrows as they relay Nazareth's plight to one another.

"Don't worry, Mairig says we aren't going today," Anush reassures her. "But I thought we should make an effort anyway. Cheer things up a bit." Then, changing the subject, "You're really very pretty, you know. I will never forgive you for inheriting Grandmother's green eyes."

"Are you sure we are not going to the *hamam*?" Lucine asks.

"Yes, of course I'm sure. Now sit down. We will just pull the sides back," Anush continues, pulling Lucine's unruly curls away from her face and fixing a small pin at the base of her skull. "There, a compromise. This way you look properly reserved from the front and free from the back."

"How stupid. Who's going to look at me from the back?"

"Oh, I know someone who is always looking at your back." Anush smiles at Lucine's reflection.

"Who?" Lucine can feel her face reddening.

"Oh come now, Lucine. Don't tell me you haven't noticed Kemal lurking behind you on our walks to school."

There was a time, long ago when Lucine had not yet given up sucking her thumb, that Kemal, the Turkish boy whose father works for Hairig, was her closest friend. Though he was a few years older, Lucine used to tease him profusely, getting a keen sort of pleasure from beating him in a race and pulling at his ears. But she must have offended him somehow, because he hardly ever spoke to her anymore, preferring the company of her charismatic uncle. Whenever she tried to engage him in conversation, Kemal would either look away or turn bright red.

"We all walk together. If he's looking at anyone, it's probably you," she says.

"Nonsense. Every time you cross the courtyard, he drops the wool or spills the dye."

"That's ridiculous. Besides, he doesn't count," Lucine says. "He's like an extension of Uncle Nazareth." She regrets the words as soon as she speaks them. The mention of their uncle's name hangs in the now stagnant air like a sorrowful melody. He is gone, and there are no more practical jokes and no more laughter. There is no one to spread the balm of frivolity over their all-too-serious lives.

"He'll be back before the end of the summer," Anush says. "You'll see."

Lucine fights the urge to take Anush's braid in her hand and whip her with it.

Instead she says, "Maybe you're right."

"Of course I'm right. As Ottoman subjects, our men must serve in the Ottoman army. It's normal."

Lucine winces at the word *normal*. She wonders how her sister has managed to forget the way the gendarmes woke them in the middle of the night, how they dragged Nazareth by the collar of his nightshirt and kicked him out the door. She wants to explain the difference between real soldiers and unarmed labor battalions. Uncle Nazareth says there is nothing normal about a government licking its wounds from the Balkan wars by making a scapegoat of its Christian Armenians. Every defeat the empire suffered meant more nationalism, more ethnic conflict, and more violence. Her people would never be Turkish enough or Muslim enough to be blameless.

"We better get the boys ready for breakfast," Anush says. It is understood. Anush will take care of six-month-old Aram, while Lucine will attend to Bedros, their ten-year-old brother. In the seven days since their uncle's disappearance, Lucine and Anush have taken over their mother's role while she hides in her room, mourning her brother's loss.

She hasn't left her bedroom since that night. *A headache* is how their father describes it. Tending to her is an unpleasant but necessary task—emptying her bedpan, bringing her food—but the thought of her mother sitting in the stench of her own filth is unthinkable.

Lucine places her hand on the doorknob and prays that her mother is still sleeping. When Mairig sleeps, her eyes don't stare vacantly into the distance, her mouth does not betray the dark roads where her mind roams. When Mairig is sleeping, Lucine can pretend that she will soon get up from under her embroidered coverlet and resume mothering.

The door squeaks open despite all of Lucine's precaution. The air, trapped by the red velvet curtains, is thick and sticky. Mairig's head is propped up at the center of her pillow, like a rare jewel. She blinks at the wall when Lucine stands before her four-poster bed. Lucine waits for Mairig's gaze to land on her. When it doesn't, she breathes a sigh of gratitude, thinking today Mairig will not put her despair into words.

"He was all I had left here. The only thing I brought with me. That and my dowry. Silk dresses, tablecloths, gold and him, body and mind."

Lucine ignores her words. She bends down and retrieves the bedpan with both hands, careful not to spill anything on Mairig's Persian rug, the one she brought with her from the city.

"I've got nothing left here that is my own," Mairig continues. "Nothing from that life before." She is referring to her other lives again. The life she lived in Istanbul and the one she was meant to live in Paris. The lives in which her hands worked at a piano instead of the rearing of children, where she was not limited to hobnobbing with missionaries but instead conversed with composers and actresses.

Lucine can't understand why Uncle Nazareth's presence made it all bearable, but it did. She can't understand why she and her siblings are not enough for Mairig. Why she needs her brother, the missionaries, and all kinds of news from the capital. What Lucine does understand is that her mother's unhappiness began long before Nazareth disappeared. She can trace it back even further than her own birth, back to the moment her parents met and fell in love. Falling in love had derailed Mairig's life; Lucine has heard the story many times. Uncle Nazareth's disappearance is only the last episode in that derailment.

"Hairig will find him," Lucine whispers.

"Yes, yes he will," Mairig says, turning her face away.

Lucine drags her feet to Bedros's room, wondering why Anush is so eager to marry and spend the rest of her life taking care of a brood of children, an as-yet-undetermined but no doubt foul-smelling husband, and a host of new family members that may or may not include a domineering mother-in-law.

Bedros sits up in bed, his eyes still shut. As she pulls the night-shirt off her brother's back, Lucine notices that he is still clutching the slingshot their uncle gave him for Easter.

The morning of Uncle Nazareth's disappearance, Lucine tip-toed past her sister's bed, careful not to touch the door, which creaked at the most inopportune times. In the darkness of the hallway, she stepped over the seventh floorboard, knowing it too would betray her if given the chance. Downstairs Mairig was al-ready busy preparing for their trip to the public baths. Lucine could hear her slippered feet brushing against the stone floor of their kitchen, filling the damp air with the smell of stuffed cab-bage and soap. Lucine's plan was to slip out the front door, take her uncle's horse for a ride, and disappear into the nearby fields, thus avoiding all the ogling and nakedness of the community bath. She managed to get to the door and unlock it before the smell of Turkish coffee wafted up the stairs to awaken her father. But before she could open it, a violent banging came from the other side.

The door swung open and Muammer Bey, the governor, en-tered the house. She didn't dare look up, fixing her eyes instead on the yellow-and-brown marble of the worry beads hanging from his hand; they looked like the gouged eyes of a dozen slain tigers. He clicked one round orb against the next. One, two, three . . . stopping at twelve, though there were twenty-one more to go. Lucine knew there were thirty-three beads in all because she counted them on one of his last two visits, when he had tried and failed to persuade Hairig to give him Anush's hand in marriage. Everywhere in the province young Armenian men were being taken from their homes, but only the Melkonians had the honor of a visit from the governor himself. There was a time long ago when the governor was considered a friend in their house. He would spend Friday evenings playing backgammon with Hairig, but Lucine liked him best for his magic tricks. If you caught him in the right mood, Muammer Bey would pull a pebble out of your ear.

But there were no magic tricks and pleasantries that day. Muammer Bey ascended the stairs, two by two, with two young soldiers at his heels. One minute her uncle was upstairs sleeping soundly, and the next, he was gone. Her parents clamored to the front door, and Lucine was relegated to the back of the house with her siblings. She didn't get a chance to say good-bye or to take one last look at his face. There was no more talk of going to the *hamam* that day. And today would be no different.

Downstairs, Hairig is already seated at the dining table, waiting for his morning coffee. He is dressed in his three-piece suit, an affectation he assumed many years ago when he was courting Mairig, who was and still is enthralled with the West. His red fez and stained leather apron sit on the table, in bold contradiction to his European clothes—a reminder that he never quite managed to meld who he is with who she wanted him to be.

Anush hums softly to herself, as she enters the room carrying plates of black olives and white cheese in one hand and the baby in the other. She places a half-eaten loaf of bread at the center of the table, before serving the tea and coffee. Her cheerful sounds and everyday movements are an affront to Lucine. Aram presses his cheeks into her chest, sucking in air in place of mother's milk.

"Where is the fresh bread?" Bedros asks, eyeing yesterday's loaf.

Anush looks at Hairig before turning to Bedros. "There is no bread anywhere. There's a queue outside the baker's shop, but his door is closed and the windows are boarded up."

Her words send shivers down Lucine's spine. Months ago, the government charged several Armenian bakers with poisoning the bread of Turkish troops stationed in Sivas. Groups of Armenian men, regardless of their profession, were imprisoned, until a medical inquiry proved the charges baseless. The bakers returned safely to their homes. But where were they now? Why were they not at their ovens?

"Never mind that," Hairig says.

Steam rises from his tiny coffee cup, a delicate thing made of white porcelain with tiny blue flowers dancing their way toward a gold-leafed rim. *From Paris,* Mairig likes to say. Forgoing the delicate handle, Hairig places his dye-stained fingers around the rim, a habit Mairig detests. With her hiding in her room, there is no one to chide him about the proper way to lift a cup.

"I want to explain some things to you." There is a long silence, during which Hairig stares into the rising steam of his coffee cup. "Turkey has entered the war," he says finally. "I know what you witnessed the other night must have been upsetting. But you mustn't be frightened. Many things change when a country is at war. We have to prepare for what may be some difficult days."

Upsetting? Losing a favorite trinket is upsetting. Spilling one's soup is upsetting. Having your uncle dragged out of the house by soldiers is another thing entirely.

"Who are we fighting, Hairig?" Bedros asks. Her little brother, his eyes wide with excitement, has brought his slingshot to the table. The perfect symmetry of his face is interrupted only by a scar that goes from the center of his left eye to the top of his left cheek.

"We are not fighting anyone, my lion. We are trying to sell carpets, but our government has sided with Germany against the French, British, and the Russians," Hairig says.

"What about the Americans?" Lucine asks, thinking of her beloved teacher, Miss Graffam, who hails from someplace called Maine.

"They have not entered the war as of yet," Hairig says.

"You told us about all this in the winter," Anush says, bouncing Aram on one knee.

"Yes, but things have gotten worse, particularly for Christians. We are viewed as an internal threat, an enemy living within the state. The Armenian intellectuals in the capital were rounded up and arrested a month ago. The politicians, poets, priests, and composers have all disappeared." His voice trails off. All four children follow Hairig's eyes to the spot at the center of the table where his words have landed.

"Under the circumstances, I cannot export my carpets anymore. I have made some difficult decisions," Hairig continues, his voice hollow.

"Yesterday I dismissed most of my men. For now, I will do what's left of the dyeing myself. Anush, you and Lucine will help Mairig with her responsibilities."

"I can help, Hairig," says Bedros, raising his hand like an eager schoolboy.

"Good," says Hairig. "You will all stay home from school for now, until things are clearer."

Clearer? How much more clear could things be?

"We will have to wait and see which way the tide is turning. The best thing to do now is to cooperate and show our government that we are not a threat."

Lucine bites her lower lip to keep from speaking. With Mairig in bed and Uncle Nazareth gone, there is no one to reason with Hairig. "Uncle Nazareth would tell us to leave," she says finally.

"Your uncle is not here and we have seen where his ideas got him," says Hairig. "I'm afraid your lessons at the American school will have to be postponed. I will send a note to Miss Graffam."

"No." It's out before she can retract it, but the idea of giving up her lessons and waiting indoors for the gendarmes to come back is too much. "Miss Graffam will help us. We can go to France or England. Mairig speaks French and my English is improving,"

Lucine begs, but Hairig's eyes are still focused on the thick mud of his coffee cup.

"Men and women of God do not represent their governments, Lucine," he says.

"I'm not staying in this house and hiding," Lucine says. "For what? What exactly are we waiting for anyway? We should try to find Uncle Nazareth. We could leave now, before it's too late."

"Lucine, be quiet." It is Anush, the keeper of all things pretty and fair and *normal*.

"No, I will not be quiet. And what do you know? You've got your nose so far into your dowry chest, you can't see what is happening right in front of you."

"That's not true!"

"It is true, Anush. Why do you think Father Sahag was killed like a dog in the street? Or Professor Fenjian was running in the streets stark naked a few nights ago? Huh?"

On New Year's Day, Father Sahag, the thirty-eight-year-old vicar, was driving toward his home town, in Sivas Province, when he was murdered by Halil Bey and his cete forces, men who only weeks ago were incarcerated criminals. There was no time to dwell on this or any other event because within days the authorities began their "interrogations." Professor Fenjian, the mathematician from Roger's College, returned from the questioning naked, except for a black sock strategically placed on his genitals, blowing in the breeze. Soon families all over Sivas were grieving the loss of their young men, conscripted into the army, arrested under suspicion, or simply gone missing.

"Stop it!" Anush screams.

"Enough!" Hairig pounds his fist on the table, tipping the delicate Parisian cup and startling the baby who's still waiting for milk.

Lucine propels herself away from the table. She hurries in the direction of the stable where Uncle Nazareth's horse awaits.

CHAPTER 7

Red River

KEMAL MOVES SLOWLY, careful not to wake anyone. At eighteen,
he is tall and lanky for an Anatolian and therefore moves cau-
tiously, almost apologetically through the world. He does not fold
his bedding and store it in the low compartments of the *sedir,* as
he usually does. Instead he looks around the solitary room and
tries to absorb this rare moment of peace in the house. His grandmother lies sleeping on her straw mat in the left corner of the
room, her broad back turned to the rest of the house. Wrapped
in a shawl woven by her own hand, she lies at the foot of a mighty
wooden loom. Bundles of yarn form a rainbow at the very top
and strands of turquoise and saffron-colored wool weave in and
out of one another, cascading at her chapped feet. She placed
her bedding in this spot a few weeks ago, soon after the arrival
of Emineh, his father's new wife. Emineh lies in the opposite
corner, on the right side of the house, where the family stores its
foodstuffs. She huddles behind a small collection of flour sacks
and bulgur barrels, carefully arranged to protect herself from his
grandmother's wrath.

His father sleeps in the center of the room where a seven-foot post holds the ceiling up. His wooden leg is propped nearby, at a safe distance from the *tonir,* the sunken circular oven around which they eat all their meals. In more peaceful days, when his mother had been alive, they would crowd around its glowing embers, cracking seeds and telling stories before falling asleep.

It will be hours before the voices of the *muezzin* chant the first of the five calls to prayer. Kemal heads toward the stable, where hidden among the chickens, sheep, and his father's donkey is an old sack where he keeps his sketchbook. Kemal was only ten when he first saw it in the hands of Gevork, the Armenian apothecary, who scribbled something inside it every time someone made a purchase. Soon Kemal was making daily visits to the shop, leaning over Gevork's shoulder, until the sly Armenian agreed to trade the half empty tome for two kilims of fine woven wool. It took Kemal a year to weave two kilims without his father's knowledge. Nazareth had slipped him the extra wool, and his grandmother, ever the one to entertain his whims, helped him weave. At first, he did not know what he would do with the journal, since he had not been taught his letters. He ripped away the pages of indecipherable scrawls by the apothecary and began making his own markings, delighting in the way the graphite sounded against the smooth page.

He holds it now and thumbs through the many drawings that fill its pages. It all started innocently enough, with drawings of bottles, flutes, and flora. Soon he moved onto the goldfinch, the bulbul, and finally to his grandmother's face, always sitting before

the loom. She posed for him unknowingly, like all the other crea-
tures in Sivas.

Drawing, and the way of looking it necessitated, became second nature to him. One day, seated at the foot of the imam, who
was pontificating about the many authenticated miracles of the
great prophet, Kemal picked up a stick and drew a portrait in the
dust. It was a mindless act, like throwing stones into the river, and
the likeness was not very good, but it was enough to make the
imam stop midsentence. The old man spent a full minute stroking
his wiry beard before taking Kemal's left earlobe into his plierlike
knuckles and dragging him all the way home. On the road, the
imam made Kemal repeat the following words, pinching harder
when the boy was not loud enough:

> It is not permitted to draw anything that depicts animate
> beings, because the Prophet (peace and blessings of Allah be
> upon him) said, according to the sahih hadith: "Every image
> maker will be in the Fire." And he (peace and blessings of
> Allah be upon him) said: "The most severely punished of
> people on the Day of Resurrection will be the image mak-
> ers, those who tried to imitate the creation of Allah." And he
> (peace and blessings of Allah be upon him) said: "The makers
> of these images will be punished on the Day of Resurrec-
> tion, and they will be told, 'Give life to that which you have
> created.'"

When the imam knocked at the door, it was Kemal's grandmother who answered. She assuring the imam that the boy

would be properly whipped. But when the bearded cleric left, Kemal's grandmother simply swatted his head and returned to her loom. Despite her indifference, Kemal thought hard about what the imam had said. Not about the sin and its punishment but about the very last bit. What if he could give life to that which he created?

It wasn't the last time his sketching would cause him trouble. Just last week, in a fitful rage over the warring women of the house, his father spotted Kemal sketching listlessly by the *tonir*. Before Kemal realized what was happening, his sketchbook landed in the embers next to the roasted chestnuts. "This is not Constantinople," his father said. "There is no poetry here. Only survival." He then made Kemal promise to pay less attention to sketching and more attention to the weaving. It was a difficult promise for the young man, but he intends to keep it, at least between the hours of sunup and sundown. The rest of his time, Kemal reasons, is his own.

He sits on the floor of the stable, drawing by the light of an oil lamp. A magnificent peacock struts across the page, peculiar only in that it has the lovely breasts of a young woman. Before Kemal can ponder why breasts have become so prominent in his recent drawings, he hears the shouting.

"She's taken it! She's taken my silver thread off the loom!" his grandmother screams.

"I did no such thing," Emineh says.

There is a low murmuring from his grandmother, followed by the booming sound of his father's voice shouting, "Enough! Kemal! Where in Allah's name is he?"

"I'm here, Baba, preparing the donkey," Kemal calls out.

"Hurry it up. We are due at Hagop Effendi's this morning."

The news immediately brightens Kemal's mood. The Melkonian family is an enchanted lot. Hagop Melkonian is one of the few men who's called effendi, a man of authority and education. His great big house stands on top of a hill, overlooking the entire valley. It has two stories, as opposed to one, and no animals are allowed anywhere near it. The whole place is crowded with furniture the likes of which he has never seen before. They eat their meals on a long wooden table, as opposed to a rug. Mrs. Melkonian plays the piano and entertains missionaries, switching from French to Turkish and back again with the same ease as someone who goes from milking a goat to a cow.

And then there are the two girls. They eat with the men and exchange ideas and opinions freely. Now the thought of seeing his friend Nazareth or catching a glimpse of the lovely sisters makes him feel lighter on his feet. Ignoring the morning call to prayer, the father and son make their way out of the valley.

"These women are driving me mad, Kemal," his father says.

"I know, Baba."

"Your grandmother doesn't understand a thing. But you do, don't you, boy?"

Kemal nods.

"You know why I've brought Emineh. She is a good weaver and young . . . young enough to bear more children. Soon you'll have brothers and sisters. Won't that be nice?"

When they're not arguing, Emineh and his grandmother

are in charge of weaving the kilims, the small prayer rugs Mr. Melkonian exports throughout Turkey, England, and Persia. His grandmother is the sole master of the massive loom, where large rugs worth far more than a kilim are woven. She sits before her altar of wool from sunup until sundown, her hands moving feverishly, tying up to three knots per second. Sometimes her hands are so fast that even Kemal's keen eyes cannot make out their movements.

"Is that why we're going to Hagop Effendi's? To get more wool?" Kemal asks.

"We were supposed to get more wool days ago. He's probably noticed an increase in our productivity since Emineh arrived. Maybe he will be forced to offer us more for each piece. That kilim your grandmother wove last month was easily worth forty *paras*."

Kemal remembers the piece, a geometric pattern, lush with six different shades of green. "It *was* lovely," he says.

His father stops his mule and looks down at his only child. "Get your mind out of the clouds, boy. Pay less attention to the colors and more to the coins. Do you want to work for an Armenian dog for the rest of your life?"

"No," Kemal whispers, although he would like nothing more than to spend his life working alongside the Melkonians. He spends the rest of the journey imagining himself in the bosom of that boisterous clan. Racing on horseback against Nazareth, the lace and ribbons of the lovely Anush, the refined elegance of Mrs. Melkonian, and finally the sharp wit of the clever Lucine, in

whose company he grows quiet and light-headed. God knows he
has been very careful, trying hard not to stare at her or be alone
in her presence.

A web of narrow streets, worn by centuries of use, leads to
the ancient Armenian churches and monasteries, some of which
date back to the Crusades. Beyond them is the town's center,
encompassing the market square, city hall, and other government
buildings. There is an invisible border that separates the Muslims
from the Christians, the Turks and Kurds from the Armenians and
Greeks. Kemal and his father cross this border, leaving behind the
orchards and vineyards of the lower valley and climbing toward
the fertile wheat and barley fields of the upper plateau.

The remainder of the journey is a silent one, except for the
sound of the Kizil Irmak, the Red River, whose water is stained
crimson by the clay hills it passes on its way to the Black Sea.
Kemal fixes his eyes on the horizon, toward the village of Karod,
where the Melkonians live.

Despite the morning fog, Kemal can see the house clearly. Cut
stones, each a different shade of gray, are stacked one upon the
other. The upper two stories are timber frame filled with sun-
dried bricks and plastered with lime, and the roof is capped with
tile. His father describes it as "offensive," and most of the Turkish
villagers agree with him. It isn't the size of the house that they
find so distasteful, nor its location, perched high above the hill,
overlooking all of Sivas, but its occupants that they cannot toler-
ate. Prudence demands that Christians in Anatolia show a certain

amount of modesty, and the villagers agree that Hagop Melkonian has trouble keeping his head down.

Inside, the massive courtyard has lost its usual ordered rhythm. Seventeen copper cauldrons stand in their circular formation, but the customary bustle is missing. Only Demitrius, the Greek half-wit and son of the village midwife, is loitering around the cauldrons, waiting for instruction. The six men, including Hagop and Nazareth Melkonian, who soak, stir and dry the wool, are nowhere to be found. Kemal's father eyes the bushels of wool lying around the yard.

"Our sheep are sheared once a year. Where in God's name do they get all this wool every month?" his father whispers.

"Magic sheep," Kemal says, suppressing a smile.

Before his father can respond to his son's indolence, Hagop Effendi bounds toward them, spectacles in hand, vest uncharacteristically unbuttoned, a furrowed brow in place of the placid tranquillity that usually graces his face.

"Kemal, where have you been?" he says, breathless.

"Good morning, sir."

"Nazareth's gone. He was taken in the night," Hagop Effendi says.

"Taken where?" Kemal asks.

"He's been assigned to the labor battalions."

"Perhaps we should come back later, at a better time," his father says, already inching his way out of this family drama. Whispered rumors of impending doom have been circulating for weeks. The fate of these infidels is no concern of his. Kemal, on the other hand, feels as if he's been struck.

"And Lucine," Hagop continues. "She is upset. She left the house hours ago. I've looked everywhere. Go and find her."

Kemal mounts the rough back of his father's mule and races to the river, where he knows she likes to take Nazareth's horse. The landscape, like his grandmother's shawl, melts into multiple shades of green wool. In his mind's eye, he can see Nazareth being dragged out of the house. Did they press the tip of a bayonet firmly to his back? Was there time for him to pack a few things: his dagger, his lucky riding coat, the one with the missing button?

His thoughts are interrupted by the sound of the Red River, whose chatter grows louder by the minute. Kemal sees Nazareth's horse and dismounts. He ties his animal to an apricot tree about a hundred yards away from the riverbank and makes his way toward the water. His heart thumps with excitement when he realizes he will finally be alone with Lucine.

She is seated on a sunburned slope of honey-colored grass. Her hair is loose and wild from the morning ride, her swollen eyes fixed upon the river, the stillness of her gaze confronting the river's restlessness. Kemal doesn't see the steady stream of tears or her small chest heaving silently until he is standing just above her.

He says nothing and lowers himself onto the grass beside her. She takes a deep breath but does not look at him.

"He's gone," she whispers between sobs.

"I know," Kemal says. They are the first words he's uttered to her in a long time, ever since the sight and scent of her became too much to manage.

"You mustn't worry," he says. "He is brave and clever. He will persevere." Kemal puts a timid arm around her shoulder. It is the first time he's touched her in so intimate a manner. When they were little, he would hoist her up by the waist as she climbed a tree, and console her when she inevitably fell, but all that was a very long time ago. Kemal lets his palm cup her shoulder. The gesture releases a flock of tears as Lucine folds into him. He knows he should say something, but the feel of her soft hair brushing against his face, the scent of her, a hint of honey and jasmine, the curve of her neck make him dizzy. She's just a child, he tells himself. A rich Armenian child.

"If he isn't safe, then nothing, no one is . . ." she says, removing herself from under his arm and turning her eyes back to the river.

"Shh, that's enough. How long have you been crying?" he asks, trying to coax her back to the present.

Lucine shakes her head. "You don't get to tell me what to do," she says. "You're not him. Since when did you start talking to me again anyway?"

"Since right now," says Kemal.

"You don't just stop talking to people for no good reason and then change your mind. You're either a friend or you're not."

"You're right, I'm sorry," he says. "Now no more crying. What's this business about quarreling with your father and running away?" he says, trying to look stern. This time her head snaps to attention, and she is looking straight at him. He braces himself for the fury she will pour into him. It's happened before. Twice. Twice he's been the lucky recipient of that hot fiery liquid of emotion and intellect, only they hadn't been alone.

"What would you have me do? He won't go looking for Nazareth. And he forbids me to go to school. If you think I'm going to sit around and wait to be taken like Nazareth or, worse yet, cower in a corner of my room, then you're as foolish as he is."

"No one is asking you to cower," he says.

"No? They've taken my uncle, your friend, and no one seems to want to do anything about it."

"What does that have to do with your schooling?" Kemal says.

"The only chance I have of happiness is hidden somewhere in my books. I'm going to be a teacher, like Miss Graffam, not some woman slaving over a *tonir*."

"But you're only a child," Kemal says.

"I am not a child! There are fifteen-year-olds all over Sivas getting married, having children, and who knows what else. I am no child, Kemal. Besides, you're only a few years older."

Kemal lingers on the sound of his name in her mouth, between her lips.

"Well, if you're not a child, I suppose you're a woman then," Kemal says. There is a pause, and he wonders if he's gone too far.

"You think you're so clever don't you?" she says, straightening her spine.

"What? Something wrong with being a woman?" he asks.

"I know your definition of a woman, and it does not interest me," she says.

"Really? What is my definition of a woman?" Kemal has never had a conversation so sweet.

"Someone who bows her head and mends your socks and bears a half-dozen children."

He laughs as she mockingly bows her head and makes to mend an imaginary sock.

Lucine stops quite suddenly and looks up at him, adding, "Someone who suffers silently." She grows quiet and serious now, her eyes filling with a knowing melancholy.

I will never make you suffer, he thinks. His hand is at her cheek, but only for a moment. The contact wakes her from her moral slumber and she jumps to her feet.

"I better go home now," she says.

CHAPTER 8

The Crier

KEMAL: THE TURKISH boy. Kemal: the weaver's son. Kemal, her uncle's keeper, who always stood quietly at his right. He had not only talked to her but let her cry on his shoulder, making her angry and energized all at once. Lucine blushes when she remembers burying her face in his chest. She did not know how much she missed him until he started talking to her again. *Ach pazoog,* my right hand, Uncle Nazareth called him. Kemal hadn't extended a fist to the enemy but an open palm to her face.

She whips the horse into a frenzied speed, racing away from the river and her confusion. Inside the courtyard, she hurries past bubbling cauldrons, past Hairig's expectant eyes. She knows she should apologize for storming off—a dutiful daughter would. But looking at Hairig would mean confronting the fear in his eyes with the shame in her own.

Once inside, she heads to the library, which is not a library at all but a set of bookshelves, carefully arranged perpendicularly against one wall of the parlor. She sinks into Hairig's red velvet floor cushion and places her trembling hands under her thighs.

Her eyes dart from one title to the next, looking for answers to questions not yet formed in her mind. But the titles offer no answers, only reprimands.

"Daughter," Hairig whispers from behind her. Lucine, wishing to avoid his eyes, fixes her gaze on the volumes above her. He too searches the shelves and finally selects a thin leaflet she recognizes as the collected poems of Daniel Varoujan, the poet of Sivas. Hairig lowers himself to the divan and opens to "The Longing Letter." He points a finger to the seventh stanza, and waits for her to read it.

> *Oh, come, my son, your ancient home restore!*
> *They burst the door, they swept the larders bare.*
> *Now all the swallows of the spring come in*
> *Through shattered windows, open to the air.*

"It's about a mother waiting for her son's return," he explains. Lucine nods, eyes lowered to the words. "Isn't it lovely?" Hairig asks.

Lucine shrugs. "All our songs and poems are so sad," she says.

"Poets write about what they know to be true," Hairig says. "And we Armenians, we know about loss. When I was young," he continues, "I only read poetry. Your grandfather was mortified. He wanted me to be fierce like my brothers, but I didn't have it in me." Lucine's ears perk up at the mention of Hairig's family. He lost all but one brother in the Red Sultan's massacres, so named for all the blood he managed to shed before the Young

Turk Revolution instilled constitutional law. Hairig rarely ever spoke of his lost brothers.

"What your grandfather didn't understand is that strength comes in different disguises. It does not always ride a mighty horse or wield a shiny sword. Sometimes we have to be like a riverbank, twisting and turning along with the earth, withstanding swells and currents. Enduring.

"You," Hairig says, pointing his finger at her, "are like my brothers. Strong and fierce. But sometimes it's better to be like the river. *Gu hasganas?* Do you understand, Lucine?"

"That is how I survived," he says, closing the leaflet. "I may have shamed my father by refusing to fight along with my brothers, but what matters is I survived and my mother lived to see it. And the same will happen with your uncle Nazareth," he says, smiling at Lucine and stroking her hair. She gives him a weak smile and wills herself to believe him.

"I wooed your mother with the help of these books," he says, waving the volume in his hand. "There was a time I could recite whole poems to her. She didn't expect that from a merchant. Did I ever tell you how we met?"

Lucine nods. It is a favorite story among the family, retold so many times that she is almost sure she witnessed it herself. He begins it anyway. "She came into your uncle Varouj's store in Constantinople with her mother. She was planning to leave for that music school in Paris within weeks and needed fabric for her fancy new dresses. I was there delivering wool and taking inventory. I'd been in that store a thousand times, surrounded by rare silks and deep wools. I had been swimming in a sea of color for so long, nothing really stood out anymore. But the moment she stepped inside, every color and cloth in the room was crisp again and focused. Like someone had finally cleared my vision by giving me a pair of spectacles. Oh, I am not ashamed to say that I was love-struck immediately. Of course, it took a lot of hard work, especially with your grandmother, to take me seriously as a suitor," he says. "I didn't speak French and I had never been to a proper school."

"Kemal touched my cheek." The words spurt out of her mouth like discarded watermelon seeds. They drop into his story, inter-rupting it, staining its familiar beauty with their unwanted pres-ence. Her words make Hairig's mouth fall open and the kindness in his eyes disappears.

"What?" he says, his breathing shallow.

"He was only trying to . . ."

"What? He was only trying to what?" Hairig demands to know.

"Comfort me," Lucine says, eyes lowered.

"Stop." His voice is steady and firm. "Stop before I get any angrier."

"But you've always liked him," she offers, still not daring to look up.

"I like succulents as much as I like tulips, but you don't see me planting both in the same patch of land." Hairig's body shoots up from the divan. "You stay away from him. This is no time to disgrace the family. There is an ocean of spilled blood between us, the blood of my brothers included." His hand, still holding the leaflet, shakes violently.

"He is an employee, a common villager, and a Turk." Hairig spits the last word out like a piece of phlegm. He takes Lucine's chin between his thumb and forefinger, lifting her head until her eyes meet his. "Just because we live side by side, does not make us the same," he says.

Lucine wants to object, but he holds her in his stare until she winces from the shame.

"It is a sin against God. We are Christians first, Armenians second, and only after, Ottomans. He doesn't even have a last name, for God's sake.

"Don't disappoint me Lucine," he says finally. "My heart could not take it."

When he's gone, Lucine thinks about his words and wonders where the longing in her own heart fits into the order of things.

The next four days are spent in a familiar fog of house chores, away from the courtyard and the river, away from her father's averted eyes and far away from Kemal. A tray of green beans for de-stringing, a carafe of coffee for Mairig's headache, a game of marbles with Bedros, and sometimes, when Anush allows it, a sweet cuddle with the baby. Lucine likes to press her nose into the soft fold of Aram's neck, to breathe in his sweet tangy smell. She is *enduring* the way Hairig prescribed. But it is not enough to quell the foreboding and excitement of her nights, when she lies awake alternately reliving the moment when Kemal's palm pressed her cheek and the dreaded night of Uncle Nazareth's abduction.

On the fifth day, Lucine is busy soaking lentils, delighting in the way the smooth little pebbles slip through her fingers, when Bedros walks into the kitchen. His dark mass of hair, jutting in every direction, hangs well past his earlobes, covering the left side of his face where his scar hides. Even his eyes, so black they lack irises, wear an expression of neglect. In his hand, he holds the wooden slingshot.

"Kemal said to tell you thanks," he says.

"What?" She can hardly believe what has just come out of the child's mouth.

"For the book," he says. She suddenly notices a small volume in his left hand. "I didn't know he could read English," says Bedros. "Anyway, he says thanks for lending it to him."

"Yes. Yes, he can read English," she lies, struggling to think of something else to say, but Bedros has moved on, the way children do. She runs her fingers across the volume, knowing that the same palm that caressed her cheek has fingered its pages. She knows, without opening it, that the book does not belong to Kemal. Most of the Muslim villagers cannot read, and Kemal is no exception. She knows, without opening it, that the book belongs to her teacher, Miss Graffam, the missionary. It's not just the leather binding that is exquisite and foreign but also the title, *The Missionary Herald*, written in English, which gives the owner away. The thought of Kemal sneaking into the American girl's school and taking a book for her makes Lucine's chest swell with gratitude, and she smiles at his daring. She is about to tuck the volume in her apron, when a single leaf of paper floats to the ground.

Long graphite pencil marks, dark and light, weave seductively across the page, creating an image of her hair, wild like it was that morning. Hidden in the mass of hair is an image of her face, her deep-set eyes, mouth slightly open, an image at once familiar and disturbing. Lucine marvels at the skillful drawing she knows to be his and blushes when she tries to think about how carefully he's looked at her. She folds the sheet of paper twice before tucking it in her sleeve.

"What's wrong with you?" Anush is standing at the doorway. Aram sits on her right hip, sucking at the dimpled fingers of his right hand.

"What?" Lucine says, startled.

"I said, what's wrong with you?" Anush repeats.

"I'm being helpful. Soaking lentils."

"Since when are you helpful?"

"Since always."

"I'm surprised you haven't got your nose in a book."

"I'm not allowed to go to school, remember?" Lucine holds the tiny volume low so it remains hidden under the table.

"It never stopped you before."

"There are people disappearing out there, Anush. The priest has lost his mind, and Mairig refuses to leave her room." And Kemal has stroked my cheek, she almost adds. "How would you have me react?"

"Well, you can stop sulking, for one thing. There's no need to be walking around like you've got a noose around your neck. You're scaring Bedros."

"She is not." Bedros materializes from behind a bulgur barrel. The sight of him, disheveled and dirty, makes the sisters forget their differences. It is clear that despite their best efforts, the child suffers.

"Your pants are falling off your hips," Anush tells him.

Bedros shrugs.

"Come on." Lucine places the volume in the pocket of her apron and puts an arm around his shoulders. "Let's go take your pants in."

She arranges four Easter cookies in front of him, two plain and two with walnuts, while she works on his trousers. "You need to eat more, Bedros," she chides gently. "It will make you big and strong."

The boy nods, his mouth full of sweet dough. "When is Mairig coming out of her room?" he asks.

"Soon. Maybe today. Tomorrow the latest," Lucine says, dragging the needle back toward her. The truth is she has no idea when her mother will resurface.

Just then the sound of the town crier comes floating through the window, stopping her hand.

"All Armenian men between the ages of twenty and sixty must report to a town meeting. Town meeting at the square. Seven thirty tonight! The rest of you start preparing for relocation. Each family will be given one oxcart for their possessions. Take only what you need."

He shouts at the top of his lungs, repeating the phrases over and over again, until finally he goes hoarse. Bedros, who is only ten and shouldn't quite understand the meaning of any of this, lowers his chin to his chest. Lucine stands up without a word, dropping his trousers at her feet, and goes looking for Hairig. Surely now he will take action. She finds him standing outside their chicken coop, huddled with several other Armenian men from the village.

"We were better off under the sultan," says Gevork the apothecary.

"Nonsense," says Hairig. "The Young Turks have established a constitutional monarchy."

"Don't be naive, Hagop," says Arzrouni the blacksmith. "They are more like a dictatorship, always preaching about expansion, about Turkey being a great land united by language and religion. Where does that leave us?"

"There is nothing we can do but show up," says Gevork the apothecary. He is still wearing the silly white coat he ordered from England, the one meant to give him the authority of a Western doctor.

"No," says Arzrouni. "We need to flee at once. There are men in the mountains who will help us."

"What men?" her father interrupts.

"Murad the Brave and his men," someone answers.

"Murad and his like are revolutionaries," says Hairig. "Fighting the Ottoman army with a handful of guns is tantamount to mass suicide. That's exactly why they don't trust us. Violence only invites more violence. We need to show them we are loyal subjects of the empire."

"Loyal subjects are not removed from their homes and deported," says Arzrouni.

"It is only a temporary relocation," says Hairig. "I say we go peacefully so that we can return to our homes when the war is over."

Their hushed tones and gesturing hands remind Lucine of the few remaining chickens trapped in the coop. But it is their eyes that scare her the most. In them, she sees a paralyzing and all-consuming fear. This is what Hairig means about being like a river.

Lucine turns on her heels and walks toward the house. She takes the stairs two at a time, gaining momentum, until she swings Mairig's bedroom door open.

"You have to get up now," she says to the ghost of her mother, pulling the covers up and back. "They want to take Hairig."

"Take him? Where?" asks Mairig.

"They've called a meeting. He will go. You know he will go. It's time for you to get up."

"He can't go. What will we do without him?"

"Get up. Please, Mairig."

An hour later, Mairig emerges from her cocoon, trembling fingers picking at the cross at her neck. "Don't go," she tells him, but Hairig is already kissing each child on the forehead. He is dressed in his finest three-piece suit, his brushed fez sitting at an angle on his head. He whispers something into Bedros's ear but says nothing else. Nothing about the dyeing of the wool in his absence, nothing about provisions, nothing about future plans, nothing to his daughters or his dumbstruck wife.

At daybreak, Mairig is still sitting at the oak table with a bowl of lamb stew warmed up thrice over. When she finally notices her daughters standing at the doorway, she rises. Walking past them, she says, "Don't cut Bedros's hair. Promise me."

CHAPTER 9

Under the Mulberry Tree

THE NEXT MORNING, Mairig's headache disappears, along with her evening robe. The cream-colored Easter frock she dons makes her look like a china doll meant for preening. But Mairig wears it to prepare the oxcart.

"I want everything ready for when your father gets back," she says, her voice cheery.

The Armenian families of Karod are all preparing their oxcarts for what the authorities call relocation. They push the rumors of mass graves along the routes out of their heads and prepare for survival. The Melkonian wagon is nicer than all the others, with a proper door that swings outward, tiny mustard-colored tassels hanging from the window openings, and a brown velvet cushion in the front for Firat, the Turkish coachman Mairig manages to hire. She pulls a wire frame along the back, over which Anush places a blue comforter for privacy and to keep out the wind. They lay two wool mattresses in the bed of the wagon for warmth. Over these, they place a steamer rug with soapstone, a hot-water bottle, and enough food for a few days. Everything else must fit in the foot-and-a-half space between Firat and the wagon. The suitcases and provisions are piled one on top of the other until they form a wall between the coachman and his wares. Lucine places a sack of dried figs in the back, wondering how long the makeshift cushions in this springless wagon will serve as a source of comfort.

The memory of Kemal's hand on Lucine's cheek presses itself upon her again and again. Each time she pushes it away, it surfaces back up pounding at her chest.

"That's enough," Mairig says finally. "The rest we can do when your father gets back." Lucine does not ask her when exactly that will be.

"Now get your things ready for the bath," Mairig adds.

"Do I have to go?" asks Lucine. "I don't want to walk all the way across town just to sit in the bathhouse with all those giggling naked girls and women."

"No one will be giggling," says Mairig.

"Is it safe to be walking about freely across town?" Lucine asks, appealing to Mairig's fears.

"Don't be ridiculous," says Mairig. "It is Wednesday, our bath day. There is no law against bathing. We may be on the road for days."

Mairig and the girls make their way down a wide, unpaved road that winds through the Armenian quarter past the two-story houses, the great domed church, narrowing at every turn, so that by the time Mairig and the girls approach the market, it is only as wide as a single cart.

Lucine tries not to dwell on the gawking villagers. Mairig lifts the hem of her cream-colored dress and walks before her daughters with her back straight. No one dares to approach her, although the cobbler's apprentice sneers as they pass by. Lucine pretends not to hear the word *gâvur,* infidel, slip past his lips. She tries to keep her head down as she follows Mairig. She adjusts the linen bundle carrying the necessities of their bath on her shoulder. For the first time ever, Lucine longs for a head scarf. The bonnets that shield them from the blazing midday sun do nothing for the suspicious glares of their Muslim neighbors. They scream "Christian" to anyone who looks their way.

"Why are we walking toward the market?" says Anush.

"I have to see the midwife before we go," Mairig answers.

"What for?" asks Lucine.

"I need her to keep something safe for me," says Mairig.

"Why not give it to the reverend's wife?" asks Anush.

"Because Iola is Greek and not Armenian," Mairig explains, exasperated. "What's more, she is a midwife. No one will dare touch a hair on her head if they know what's good for their wives and daughters."

"Why not give it to Miss Graffam?" asks Lucine.

"Because the school is too far. We cannot risk it," says Mairig.

The market is a porous borderland between the Christians and the rest of Sivas. Here all kinds of different people trade goods and words. They forge acquaintances, rivalries, and sometimes friendships. Yet it is not the kind of place for the likes of Mairig, who has always relied on a servant to do her shopping.

Now the vendors who usually shout above one another slouch behind their sparse stalls. There's only a handful of haggling women, and the vendors seem nostalgic for more formidable opponents. An old widow in a black head scarf answers their prayers by complaining about the price of garlic. Since the war began, food is scarce and whatever is left is triple in price. But the Melkonian women do not want for money, nor are they here to purchase food. They need only to pass this place safely.

A lemon vendor near the entrance sits in front of the bright yellow pyramid of fruit. He squeezes one golden lemon in his left hand, turning it around and around in his palm, his eyes never leaving the three women making their way toward him. Mairig looks directly in front of her, leading her daughters past him when the lemon comes flying from behind her, hitting her squarely on the back of the head. Lucine rushes to her mother's side, but Mairig only stumbles for a moment. She presses a palm to the back of her head. Saying nothing, she turns her back on the jeering of the vendors and resumes her straight-backed walk through the market. Lucine stands frozen, her closed fists pulsing with rage. She makes a sharp turn to face the vendor, when Anush steps before her. "Don't," she whispers, resting her hand on Lucine's chest.

They see Iola's son, Demi the half-wit, first. He stands at the front door of the apothecary's house, something he does whenever he accompanies his mother to work. Lucine blushes, remembering an old joke of Uncle Nazareth's. He liked to say that

Demi had seen more bare-breasted women than any eunuch in the sultan's palace.

Gevork the apothecary is with all the other men of the village, but a few feet away his elderly father, one of the few Armenian men not called in for the "meeting," paces back and forth. Normally there would be a half-dozen women bustling about, carrying news of the birth out of the house, to the expectant father and his male relations. But today, the old man waits alone. In his arms, he holds the apothecary's precious white coat, the Western symbol to announce his status to the world.

The apothecary's father lifts the coat up like a sacred shroud. "He left his coat. Pray for a son so I may pass it down."

Mairig seems confused by his words. "He will be back shortly. You can give him his coat then," she answers him. Then, "We've come to see Iola."

"Yes, yes. She's been in there all morning. My wife is inside helping. Any minute now they will come out with the child."

A guttural scream comes from inside the apothecary's house.

"We better go in and see if she needs any help," says Mairig.

Inside the dark inner room, Iola squats before the wailing woman. Gevork's mother scatters bread crumbs and sprinkles water around the room, warding off the evil eye. Iola's seven birthing brooms hang from the walls, along with ropes of garlic. At the foot of the bed lies the Koran and the Bible, over which is the largest string of blue beads in Sivas. No one, Christian or Muslim, dares protest over one item or another.

A moaning from the mother escalates until an infant's wail cuts through the air. Iola pulls the baby out and places it right on its mother's chest. Pausing briefly in front of Gevork's father, Iola makes the sign of the cross. "A son," she says simply. "May God bless him."

The old man hurries back into the house, and Iola turns her attention to Mairig.

"Wise at birth," she says in Turkish. "Didn't want to enter this black little world. Had to pry him out. His first memories will be on that dusty road, poor thing."

"Yes, we are to leave tomorrow," Mairig says. "I have a favor to ask," she adds, pulling a scroll of paper from her bosom. Lucine reads the words *New York Life Insurance Company* typed in block English letters.

"Will you keep this safe?"

Iola looks at the scroll with great suspicion. Everyone knows that few things mystify the midwife like the written word. "I don't bear other people's talismans," she says finally.

"It's not a talisman," says Mairig, though from what Lucine understands, that's exactly what life insurance is. If anything happens to Hairig, this piece of paper from America ensures that the family will not be destitute. At least that is how Hairig described it.

"It is a paper from a sultan in America," explains Mairig. "It says that Hagop's life is valuable. You can give it to the American missionary. She will keep it safe."

Iola considers this for a minute. "We who know him shall

determine his life's value, not some sultan in another sea," she says.

"Hagop would be grateful to you, Iola," says Mairig. "He would want you to do this."

"Your husband has been very good to my Demi. Give it here," Iola says, taking the scroll. "We'll give it to the American. Won't we, Demi? Now you can do a favor for me. Take this," Iola says, extending a hand out to Lucine. "Throw it in the river."

Lucine takes the dirty rag from the midwife's outstretched hand immediately and follows Mairig and Anush back toward the road.

"What is this?" she asks when they have crossed the central square. She can feel something soft and lumpy under the dirty rag.

"*Göbek bağı,* an umbilical cord," says Mairig.

"From the apothecary's son?" Anush asks.

Mairig nods.

"And why am I throwing it in the river?" asks Lucine.

"The umbilical cord has the power to influence a child's future," Mairig says. "If you bury it in the courtyard of a mosque or church, the child becomes devout. If it's buried in a school garden, the child becomes educated."

"And if you throw it in the river?" asks Lucine.

"Then the child is forced to search for his or her destiny elsewhere, far away from here."

"Do you believe in such things, Mairig?" asks Lucine.

"I believe what my Bible tells me to believe. But just in case, throw it as deep into the current as you can, my love. May the water carry it as far away from this cursed land as possible."

Lucine throws umbilical cord as far into the current as she can. "Where is my umbilical cord?" she asks.

"Under the mulberry tree, right next to Anush's and Bedros's cords," Mairig says.

Hairig's mulberry tree is the most glorious thing Lucine has ever seen. It emerges from the earth like the hand of God, fingers spread wide and reaching eagerly for every bit of sun, wind and sky. Its branches beckon the children's eager limbs and its fruit moistens their parched tongues.

"Why there?" asks Lucine.

"Because your grandmother thought it would tie you all forever to the family and its land."

"And what about Aram?" she asks.

"What about him?" says Mairig.

"What did we do with his umbilical cord?"

"Nothing," says Mairig. "We lost it."

"What?"

"One minute it was there, and the next it wasn't. That whole cord business was your grandmother's obsession. Not mine. And by the time Aram was born, she had already passed. I kept thinking we might find his cord under a cushion someday, but it never turned up."

"That's awful." Lucine imagines her own *göbek bağı,* buried deep in the hardened soil of the courtyard, and immediately feels safe again. So much better than an umbilical cord traveling down a winding river or one that's lost altogether.

When they arrive at the baths, the attendant, an unusually large woman with yellow teeth, looks unsettled by the sight of Mairig and her daughters. She sits with a burlap bag of sunflower seeds in her lap, their discarded husks at her feet. She loads one seed after another between wedged teeth, expertly cracking, stopping only long enough to say, "The hamam is full."

"We can wait," Mairig says.

Several minutes go by, filled with the attendant's steady cracking and spitting. As the mountain of husks, jagged and slimy with saliva, grows, two women exit the bathhouse.

"Surely there is room now," says Mairig.

"They were two and you are three," says the attendant.

She opens the inner door anyway and leads them into a small changing room, where all three undress. Anush and Lucine slip on their wooden bath slippers and wrap themselves in the thin cotton sheets used for bathing.

In the vast marble hall milky clouds of steam carry gossip from one group of reclining nudes to the next. Bodies, pink from rigorous scrubbing, lie languid at the foot of the massive fountain in the center of the room. Children shriek in protest under the heavy scrubbing of their mothers' arms. Lucine looks around the room for a familiar face, but there are none. They are the only Armenians foolish enough to brave a bath on this day.

Mairig leads her daughters past the others and stops in front of the private room they always use. But the measured kindness of the attendant has run out. She stands stoically in a cloud of steam and motions toward the communal room.

"Are the private rooms all occupied?" asks Mairig.

"The private rooms are for Ottomans," the attendant says.

The Melkonian women take their place on one of the divan cushions pressed against the outer wall. A Kurdish woman, seated to the right of Mairig, eyes the girls' hips with the discerning eye of a connoisseur. Anush and Lucine disrobe quickly, but the Kurd moves even quicker.

"Fine legs," she says, patting Anush's thigh appreciatively. "You'll need an Osman as strong as a lion."

Lucine and Anush ignore the muffled laughter of nearby patrons and begin unpacking. The pressed linens, bars of soap, *keses* for exfoliating, along with the glass bottle of eau-de-cologne and the silver cup for rinsing are all dutifully laid out, but the room is suddenly unnaturally quiet. Hard stares replace the familiar chiding and clicking of tongues from village women.

Lucine slips the wooden sandals off her feet. She shuts her eyes and lets the steam provide what little insulation and privacy she can get. Anush drags the *kese* down her mother's spine, letting gray curdles of dead skin drop down to the floor. It is not uncommon for women with eligible sons to ask prospective brides to scrub their backs. Lucine doesn't dare look up.

There is a melting point at which everything in this world eventually succumbs. Skin, salt, fat, tears, and laughter all meld into one. In the *hamam,* Lucine is forever suspended at this melting point. She reclines, pressing her back, buttocks, and palms into the hot stone floor. The hissing steam penetrates and escapes from every surface, seducing her skin, her muscles, and the stone into submission. Then come the organs, and despite the women ogling the productive capacity of her hips, the roundness of her breasts or the strength of her thighs, despite all this, her mind goes blank. There is always a brief period of clarity when she can hear her whispering heart.

Today she listens to the slapping noises of the fountain water, hoping it will drown out the sound of her longing and her worry. The effort is futile. The heat knocks incessantly at the door of her heart. When it finally answers, in come a bevy of images of Kemal. He smiles at her from across the courtyard. He stares with compassion at her tear-stained face and laughs uncontrollably at her anger. She doesn't know why or how, but she is sure he understands her, knows her. And this is everything.

It might be a sin against God, but God doesn't seem to be terribly concerned with her at the moment. Where was he when they took Nazareth? When they flogged the priest and robbed him of his sanity? When they took Hairig?

Hairig. The tears are just one more form of water excreted by her body.

Not here, whispers her heart. Not here.

CHAPTER 10

Bedros and the Dress

MUAMMER BEY'S VISIT comes on an especially hot day, one made for swimming and sitting under the shade of a tree. But the children are stuck inside. Anush hides in the back of the house where the governor cannot see her. Lucine and Bedros are relegated to the front parlor and instructed to be quiet. Bedros fashions a sword from a long branch and slashes the drawn curtains like a caged animal. He makes loud swishing noises, wielding the sword with one hand and holding his pants up with the other. Each time a limb from his branch nicks the lavender-colored silk, he turns his head, as if waiting for a reproach. A palm to the back of the head, a harsh word, or worse yet, that look of disappointment Mairig used to give them when they'd done something wrong.

"Stop that. You'll ruin the curtains," Lucine says, taking care to keep her voice low. "Aren't you a little too old for swordplay?" She takes the branch from him.

"Everybody wants me to be a baby again," he says.

"What are you talking about?"

"Since Hairig left, everyone wants me to be a baby again. Mairig says to try not to look so grown up."

"That's because the soldiers only take grown boys and men," she says, but Bedros doesn't seem consoled.

"Don't worry. You're way too young to be noticed," she says, putting her hands around his dwindling waist. "You're practically shrinking."

Outside, the town crier, whose voice Lucine has come to detest, repeats his now-familiar chant, "All Armenian families are to be deported into the outskirts. These measures are for your own safety. Each family will be given one oxcart for their possessions. Take only what you need. Everything will be given back to you upon your return."

"That man's a liar," says Bedros.

"He's Armenian," says Lucine.

"He's still a liar," says Bedros.

Bedros has a point. This is the same man who called Hairig to the supposed meeting.

"He tricked us," Bedros says. "Uncle Nazareth says you should confront those who taunt or trick you, but Hairig didn't confront anyone."

"He will. In his own way," says Lucine, remembering Hairig's speech about enduring.

Bedros presses his nose onto the sliver of glass where the drapes almost meet. Lucine rests her chin on the top of his head, hoping a bit of sunlight will find its way to her face. In the courtyard, bushels of wool and copper pots sit idly in the courtyard.

Beyond the family's own gated property lies the sea of flat-roofed, white-washed houses of the Armenian Quarter of Sivas. Like the Melkonian house, they have been emptied of their men. Lucine stares at the women who scurry from home to home, like chickens before the slaughter. Perhaps bed rest is a much more dignified response than running about town wringing one's hands.

"I wish I could go outside," Bedros says.

Her little brother hasn't been outside since the day Hairig left. He hasn't taken a bath, since there are no men left to take him to the *hamam*. He hasn't seen a slip of sky unless it was through a glass window.

"We'll be going away soon and then you can be outside all you want," she says, ruffling his hair.

"Even so, we've got no horse," he says. "Just a big dumb ox that clip clops like the heavy-footed farmer's wife with one thick-soled shoe." Bedros imitates the poor woman's bowlegged gait, making Lucine laugh. "What are they doing in there anyway?" he asks, gesturing toward the next room where Mairig and the governor sit.

"Mairig is going to ask Muammer Bey for help."

"I want to listen," he says. Lucine knows she should object, but the truth is she wants to listen too.

"All right, but be very quiet. We can stand outside the doorway," she whispers.

From the open doorway, Lucine stares at the back of the governor's fez with a mixture of fear and hate. She can hardly believe that this same man once amused her by making his handkerchief disappear. That was a long time ago. Before the governor started making eyes at Anush. And the last time he made something disappear it was her uncle Nazareth.

Sitting across from Mairig and Aram, balancing his haunches on the tiny European furniture of which their mother is so proud, Muammer Bey looks uncomfortable. Drops of sweat gather around his fez, trickle down the back of his thick neck and disappear into his collar. He clears his enormous throat. Lucine can hear the clink of his worry beads banging against one another under his massive fingers.

"I wonder where his magic handkerchief has gone," whispers Bedros.

"What are the charges?" Mairig asks the governor as she wrestles with Aram, who is trying to climb onto her head, his little fists pulling at her locks like ropes.

"There have been several complaints about the location of your house," the Governor says. "As you know, it should not be on higher grounds than those of your Muslim neighbors."

"And what about all the other men? Their houses are located in the valley."

"It doesn't matter. The men are accused of political agitation, but that's not the point. I warned Hagop this would happen."

"What *is* the point?" asks Mairig. "What is the point of arresting all our men?" She is beginning to sound like the chicken women on the street.

"Madam, the Ottoman Empire is at war. Try to understand," the governor says. "The Russians have crossed our borders in the eastern part of Anatolia. In the south, the British have conquered Basra and the Tigris-Euphrates delta. The Russians, French, and British, the bastards—excuse my language—are even now planning to dismember the empire bit by bit. Our courageous leaders, may Allah keep them, have wisely chosen to side with Germany."

Lucine cringes at the word *bastard,* knowing the governor would never use that language in front of her mother if Hairig were present.

Mairig lifts her palm, interrupting his current events lesson. "I hear the news, Governor, I know what is happening to the empire, but the days of the sultan are far behind us, are they not? We have a parliament and a constitution. These men are innocent." Mairig's voice trails off, making her sound as if she's pleading.

"Be that as it may, the Christian minority is considered by some to be an internal threat. The government's plan, and I think it's a fair one, is to move the Armenians south of Anatolia."

"Where are we to go exactly?" Mairig asks, her eyes scanning his face.

"To the Syrian Desert," he says.

"By oxcart?"

"You can't stay here, *hanim.* You must all go."

"And what about our men?" Mairig asks. She picks at the cross at her neck, digging one of its points into the hollow of her neck where a scar is beginning to form.

"They are being held for questioning. That is all. The men will be released later, at which point you will all be reunited."

"Like the students at Gemerek were questioned?" Mairig asks

the question in English. Her eyes dart to where Lucine and Bedros are standing, then return to the governor. She does this when she thinks the children are listening, but their English has improved. And they know about the dozen students who were killed in the town of Gemerek.

"You mustn't believe everything you hear," the governor responds in Turkish.

"And what about my brother, Nazareth? Is there any news about where he is stationed?" she asks, fingering the tiny cross at her neck again.

"No, *hanim*. I'm afraid there's very little I can do. These orders are from central government." He clicks away at the worry beads in his hand. "Unless, of course . . ."

Mairig waits.

"Your eldest daughter consented to take an oath to Allah and became my bride, then as my extended family, I could offer all of you some measure of protection."

When Mairig does not respond, the governor adds, "Please understand that I may not be in the position to make this offer again."

"Yes, yes, I understand. But it's not possible. She is betrothed to someone else," she says finally.

"Oh? To whom?"

Yes, to whom? wonders Lucine.

"Armen Haritunian, from Kharpert," Mairig answers, pressing the cross further into her skin.

Armen was a young suitor whose nose was so far up in the air that Uncle Nazareth took it upon himself to put laxatives in his *lokma*. The sounds that came out of his rear as he scurried out the door were enough to dissuade Anush from the match. The name of Armen Haritunian is always followed by peals of laughter in the family.

"I see. Well, I may be able to hide Anush and Lucine. Temporarily, of course, until things settle down."

His words sting Lucine to the core. She tightens her grip on Bedros's branch, wishing it were made of steel. Mairig must be shocked at the offer too, because she drops the tray of pastries she is about to serve. Bits of flakey dough and sugared walnuts scatter across the rug. Aram squeals with delight on her hip.

Mairig's eyes trace the path where her pastries have fallen. After a long silence, she shakes her head. "I'm sorry," she says. "It's a generous offer. I know aiding an Armenian is punishable by death and I thank you, but I don't think I can bear to leave anyone behind."

The governor nods, tucks his worry beads into his sleeve, and rises.

"I will look after your property until you return. Until then, may Allah be with you."

FOR SOMEONE WHO doesn't want to leave, Mairig moves in a frenzy. She goes from room to room, fussing over their things. She puts things inside the oxcart, then takes them out again. She has Anush and Lucine sew secret pouches into their clothing where they tuck lira, coins, and jewelry. Everything else, they will leave behind. All their treasures—the Oriental rug with red silk, the silver trays that were part of Mairig's dowry, and the dozens of books that made up the library—will be abandoned. Bedros's job is to bury some of these in the courtyard.

Mairig tucks the deed to the house inside one of Hairig's history books and asks Bedros to bury it separately. Lucine helps Bedros pick a spot in a deep but small hole under the mulberry tree where their father likes to sit. She wonders if Hairig will ever read under that tree again and if anything will ever be as it once was.

All this preparing feels useful until Lucine remembers what they're preparing for. She thinks of the chicken women wringing their hands, and the panicked look on the men's faces when they were called to the so-called meeting. She is still pondering this point when Mairig calls everyone into the sitting room. She kneels before them, holding on to Bedros's hand.

"Listen carefully," she says. "God willing, we will be back in a few short weeks, but life is unpredictable. We may not return again for a long while. I want each of you to take one thing that will remind you of this place, this house, and our lives here. It should be a small thing. Something you can hide. Something nobody can take away from you."

For herself, Mairig takes her New Testament, the one she reads from every morning, the one that can sometimes give her strength and get her out of her dark moods. Anush runs to her dowry chest, where she and Mairig have been collecting rare silks, tablecloths, silver trays, and jewels. She returns holding a small brooch with a large red stone the size of a pea in the center. It isn't the most valuable one she owns, but it belonged to their grandmother and so it is a good choice.

Lucine stands before what is left of their library, its shelves stripped of books deemed revolutionary or nationalistic. The gaps between the volumes like missing teeth. Hairig's collection punched in the mouth. Silenced. Even the poetry books are missing. Somehow Varoujan's collection with "The Longing Letter" remains exactly where Hairig left it a few days ago. Lucine quickly leafs through the trapped words before slipping Kemal's drawing between the pages and sliding it under her clothing.

As for Bedros, he knows exactly what to take. Weeks ago, when the gendarmes barged into the house looking for weapons and other "revolutionary materials," Mairig was beside herself trying to produce anything that would fit that description. In the end, she gave them Uncle Nazareth's dagger, all the kitchen knives, and Hairig's copy of *The Broken Lute* by Tevfik Fikret. She intended to include Bedros's slingshot for good measure, but he wailed and screamed until she relented. Victorious, he has been sleeping with the slingshot under his pillow ever since.

Lucine spots it tucked at the cradle of his back.

She holds out a pair of pants carefully lined with pockets of gold. "Try these on, will you?"

"What for?" he asks.

"I want to see if the coins will jingle when you walk."

"I'm not going anywhere," he says. "I'm not leaving Hairig to rot in that prison."

"We don't have a choice, little brother. And we are not letting him rot," she says, trying to soften her voice, making it sweet like milk and honey in a warm cup of tea, the way Mairig does when she's persuading Hairig of something.

"Who will bring them their food? Who will visit them and bring them news?" Bedros's lower lip starts to quiver.

Lucine moves to embrace him, but he shrugs her away, not wanting to be held like a child anymore. She reaches over and squeezes his hand instead.

"Iola and Demi will make sure they are fed. And the American missionaries will bring them news when they can," she says.

Leaving his father in the hands of the sinister Greek midwife and her half-witted son fails to comfort him, but the idea of the American missionary seems to make him feel better about leaving.

Five days later, they have all run out of things to do. The oxcart in the courtyard sags in the middle where bags of bulgur and dried fruit bear down on its axles. Lucine's heart sags too, sitting low in her rib cage, as if it has bags piled on top of it. She is playing marbles on the kitchen floor with Bedros, trying to forget the weight on her chest, when Mairig walks in. She holds up some of Lucine's old play clothes and tells Bedros to strip naked. Knowing her fragile state, Bedros obeys but keeps his eyes on her face, silently demanding an explanation. She says nothing as she tightens a head scarf around his head, disappears. When she's gone and his transformation is complete, he bursts into tears.

"Hairig said I am the man of the house now," he cries.

"You are," Lucine whispers.

"Then why am I in a dress?"

all the gold in the district and pocket the difference between the actual exchange and what we think is the current value. Sometimes they even loan it to us for higher rates."

"What does this have to do with the Melkonians?" Kemal asks.

"Nothing. Everything. The important thing is that *we* are Osmanli, Ottomans. When the Melkonians are gone, it will be our duty to continue where they left off. Who better to take over the kilim business than us? Just answer me this: do you want to be glued to that wooden loom for the rest of your life, reaping thirty, forty *paras* for a shawl or kilim?"

"No," Kemal answers him honestly.

"The Melkonians and their like will be gone soon. Driven out or worse. And there is nothing you or I can do about it. Except maybe to step into their shoes, continue the family business, so to speak."

At the word *worse,* a sulfurous pit forms at the bottom of Kemal's stomach and he closes his mouth to keep the eggplants from making a second, unwanted appearance.

"But where will they go?" he manages to ask, thinking of Nazareth.

"Who knows? Somewhere in the interior, where they won't [b]e as much trouble. Now, do you want her as a bride or not?" His [fa]ther swipes the common bowl, now empty of all its contents, [wi]th the last of his bread. Soaking up the sauces, he adds, "That [sist]er of hers is a fine catch too, with all her bows and ribbons. [Wh]o knows, maybe we can have a double wedding, eh? With the [expa]nsion of the business, I could afford a second wife!"

❦ CHAPTER 11 ❧

Infidels

THE SUN IS long gone, but the July heat circles the air, drifts through the house, and channels itself somewhere in Kemal's groin. He shifts his weight on the floor cushion and tries to pull his mind away from Lucine. For days, he can think of nothing else. Last week he sent her a drawing and the thought of her receiving it makes the heat in the room even more unbearable. He is seated near his father, in front of the *tonir* where they almost always eat their meals. The smell of garlic and fried eggplant fills the room, making his mouth water and teasing the yearning out from his loins. His grandmother is hunched over the sunken oven, pouring *imam bayïldï* into a large common bowl. It is Kemal's favorite dish, more for its colors than its taste. The dark purple eggplants stuffed with parchment-colored onions, garlic, and bloodred tomatoes. His grandmother and Emineh, who were bickering over the recipe, have been relegated to opposite corners of the room where they sit now, sulking.

"You know what *imam bayïldï* is named for?" his father asks. He has been in a jovial mood since their visit to the Melkonian house.

"It means 'the imam fainted,'" Kemal says.

"Yes, yes, but do you know why he fainted?" his father asks, wiping his mustache with the back of his hand. His eyes dance with anticipation.

"No," says Kemal.

"Let me tell you." His father leans in as if to reveal a big secret. "Legend tells of a mighty and powerful imam, who swooned with pleasure at the flavor when his wife presented the dish." He nods his head as if to illustrate the truth of the story. "Although," he continues, pausing for effect, "others say he fainted at the cost of the ingredients. You see my boy"—he laughs, slapping Kemal's back—"everything comes back to women and money."

Kemal hears a low tsk-tsk sound from his grandmother, a rare thing he recognizes as her secret laugh.

"Do you understand what I'm telling you, Kemal?" his father asks.

Kemal nods, wishing the conversation a speedy end, thinking of his sketchbook where he can retreat into a world of his own making and dream all he wants of Lucine.

"You think I'm blind, son?" he asks, shoving a handful of eggplant into his mouth.

"What?" Kemal asks.

"I said, do you think I'm blind? I see the way you look at her. The way you ran after her that morning."

"Hagop Effendi is my employer. He asked me to fetch her," Kemal says, his voice raising an octave.

"Don't be stupid, Kemal," his father continues. "The time is

ripe for the taking of an Armenian bride. You're lucky I am a modern man, not a religious zealot like our imam, may Allah bless his soul. Her uncle is gone and her father will soon disappear too. You can offer her protection and a good life. We already know almost everything about the business. And what we don't know, like where they get all that damn wool, and the formulas for the dye, we can learn from her."

"Wait, what do you mean, 'her father will soon disappear?'" Kemal asks.

"He's been arrested. Their days are numbered, boy. They are infidels, Kemal, which means not only are they not Ottoman they are morally inferior. I shouldn't have to explain all th to you."

"I don't understand," says Kemal.

"Think of the silkworms. To gather their silk, we must b cocoons whole. Before they grow wings and fly off or m you see?"

Kemal gives him a blank stare.

"We are at war and these infidel dogs have been re years," his father continues. "Always complaining rights. And when they're not rebelling they are pเ from under our feet."

"What rug?" asks Kemal.

"By Allah, you're incredibly stupid for such father says, exasperated. "What good is all yo don't know what is happening under your no

"Look at the Armenian moneylenders, fo

From her corner of the room, Emineh lets out a small shriek and storms out.

"I don't need your help. I will talk to her myself," Kemal manages to say.

His father looks up at him with suspicion. "That's not how it's done, you know that," he says. Kemal can see the plotting in his father's face as it breaks into a smile. "Suit yourself," he says, "but remember you need me. Young men are being conscripted into the army every day. You'll need someone to protect her when you're gone."

"I'm not joining any army," says Kemal.

"It isn't a choice, boy. The sultan has declared this a holy war, a jihad." His father places a palm on each knee and puffs his chest out in triumph. "You'll go when they say you'll go," he says.

CHAPTER 12

Kismet

IT IS SEVERAL hours before the rooster's crow, and one hour since Mairig's moans were silenced by exhaustion. Anush hoists the sleeping Aram onto her hip and lifts a white brick of cheese out of brine water. Lucine notices how thin Aram's once-chubby thighs look and hopes it is a sign of growth and not neglect.

"What do you suppose the governor meant when he said he would take us?" Anush asks.

Lucine rises from her seat and scoops the baby out of Anush's arms. Aram digs his knees into Lucine's chest and nestles his head into her neck without waking.

"You know what he meant," Lucine says.

"Yes, but then why the both of us? Would you be his wife too or just a servant?"

"I don't know." Trying to hide her agitation, Lucine bends over and with her free hand prepares the *tonir* for their daily bread.

"I can't imagine being married to him. Rotting teeth, old as a goat, and a Muslim to boot. I'd rather die," Anush says.

"Well, you might have to," Lucine says.

Anush looks down at the brine water but stops fussing with it. She bows her head, seasoning the cheese with her tears. "I'm sorry," Lucine whispers. "I didn't mean that. Everything will be all right, you'll see." She is stroking Anush's back when Bedros enters the room, his ill-fitting dress dyed crimson.

"What in God's name have you been doing?" asks Lucine.

"Nothing. Just trying to help," Bedros answers.

"Help with what?"

"The dyeing."

Lucine takes in his thin frame, burdened by all the loss and sorrow of the last few weeks, and she is too sad to be cross with him.

"Come here," she says. "What happened to your face?" A tear-shaped piece of singed skin glows red and purple, just under his existing scar.

"The ladle was hot," Bedros says.

"Does it hurt?"

Bedros shrugs.

"How many times do we have to tell you to stay away from the dyeing tools?" Lucine asks, dabbing his skin with her handkerchief. "It was good of you to try and help with the dyeing, but that is a man's job."

"I am the man now. Hairig said so. Besides, Kemal and Demi have been helping me."

"Kemal? What do you mean he's been helping you?"

"He came a few minutes ago. He wanted to talk to you, but I told him to get to work, which is what Hairig would have done."

"Where is he now?" Lucine asks.

"Working in the courtyard."

Lucine puts the baby back in Anush's arms and heads out. Despite the darkness, she can see the two men in the back corner of the courtyard. Kemal is hard at work pulling wet wool out of one of the cauldrons. Demi the half-wit holds the wooden stirring spoon and stares at a spot on the floor in front of him. Bedros's haphazard dyeing of the wool has obviously upset Demi, whose obsession with Hairig's dyeing started at an early age.

"We use two cups of vinegar for a pound of wool. Two cups," Demi says, holding two fingers in the air.

"Hello, Demi," Lucine says, not daring to look at Kemal.

"There are five hundred and seventeen threads of green silk," Demi responds. "That's twenty-two pounds. That's forty-four cups of vinegar," he says.

Kemal stops what he is doing and looks up at her. "Hello," he says.

"Five hundred and seventeen," Demi repeats, visibly upset.

"Bedros has hurt his face," she says, holding up her handkerchief as proof. "You shouldn't let him use the tools."

"That boy is a tyrant," Kemal says. "You should have seen him trying to stir the wool."

"What are you doing here?" she says. "The sun isn't even up yet."

"Six cups of vinegar isn't enough," Demi says, wringing the wooden spoon like a wet cloth.

"I came to talk to you," he says, lowering his voice. He rests his hands on the cauldron.

Lucine's heart begins to race.

"Only six cups. Only six," exclaims Demi.

"Sometimes I envy the silkworm," Kemal says, resting his elbows on either side of a cauldron.

"You envy the silkworm?" she asks, disappointed.

"I know it sounds funny, but think of it," he says, staring into the cauldron. "Wool starts out growing on the back of some poor sheep. It's the same thing, just displaced and altered. But silk is different. It comes from the boiled cocoons of silkworms. We clean and dye the murky cream-colored thread and weave it into the fabric of some magnificent kilim."

"Not all kilims are magnificent," says Lucine.

"Every kilim has an admirer," he says, fixing his eyes on her.

"But not all cocoons are boiled. Some silkworms become moths," says Lucine.

"That's just it. Neither, the moth nor the cocoon, has any of the properties of the silkworm. The worm stops existing all together. Either way, it transforms into something entirely different," he says, with triumph in his voice.

"So you don't envy the silkworm for its beauty," she says. "You envy its ability to transform."

"Yes. Transformation can be just as powerful as beauty," says Kemal.

"Did you get the book?" he asks.

Lucine nods.

"And the drawing?" he asks.

"Yes," she manages, trying not to look at him.

"And?" Kemal says.

"Thank you," she says, finally meeting his stare. "But . . ."

"But what?"

"The picture looks nothing like me," she says.

"Nonsense," he says.

"My hair is not that thick and long. And my mouth . . . well, you've drawn it so it's slightly open like a fish's," Lucine says.

"It's how I see you now," he says, eyes burning.

"Like a hairy fish?" she teases.

"Like a woman."

"Demi," Lucine says, peeling her eyes away from Kemal. "Go and ask Anush for a piece of fresh baked bread."

"We need thirty-eight more cups of vinegar."

"You're right, but Kemal will take care of it," Lucine says, gently prying the wooden spoon from Demi's hand.

Lucine waits until Demi is gone before turning back to Kemal.

"I don't know what to say to you," she says.

"I have more to say to you," Kemal says, stepping toward her. "Since I started to sketch you, I can sketch nothing else."

"You've been sketching me?"

Kemal nods. "I see everything differently. Everything. You've taken my eyes, my vision, captive."

Lucine stares into the objects of her thievery. Kemal's eyes are two large chestnuts, rich dark brown shells hiding something more tender and sweet inside.

She feels the warmth from his breath, but the euphoria is

immediately replaced with a sense of guilt and foreboding. Didn't Hairig say to stay away from him? *A sin against God.*

"We are being deported," she says.

"I know. I came to warn you."

"It's too late. Hairig has been arrested," she says.

Kemal's face darkens at the news. "When?" he asks.

"Yesterday."

"Sometimes I wonder if our kismet is like this wool. If God is arbitrarily dyeing it one color or the other."

Before she can ask him what he means, the sliver of silence between them is suddenly filled with the sound of shuffling feet. Kemal grabs Lucine's arm and pulls her low behind the courtyard wall.

"Who is it?" she whispers.

Kemal puts his finger to his lips. Hiding behind the climbing grape leaves, Lucine can make out a group of forty or fifty men. Arranged in a single-file line, with their hands bound in front of them, they walk with their heads bent low. The only protest comes from their feet, which they drag across the dirt path leading out of the village. The procession moves silently before the front gate. Lucine tries hard to make out their faces in the dark. Stepan the sheepherder and his young son, Gevork the apothecary, even Arzrouni the blacksmith, who has a very good relationship with the governor, are all shuffling along in silence. No one asks any questions. No one resists. They wear the shroud of being Christian and Armenian. Or maybe they are in disbelief.

At the very end of the procession, a man wearing a red fez suddenly falls to his knees. That's when she sees them: two gendarmes wielding bayonets. One picks up the fallen man by the elbow and tells him to keep moving. When the man stumbles to his feet, he turns toward the house. Lucine lets out a tiny gasp and Kemal quickly cups a hand over her mouth. Hairig's eyes are wet with grief, but he manages to keep moving. The line of men is all but gone when Lucine dares to speak again.

"Come on," she says, gathering her skirt.

"Where?" asks Kemal.

"Let's go," she says.

"Are you crazy?"

"They have my father."

"You'll get killed," Kemal says.

"Then you go," she says, pulling his hand to her cheek. "Please, for me." She knows he will not refuse.

Kemal moves quickly, trailing the men at a safe distance and staying low to the shadowed ground. Lucine slides down to the ground and presses her forehead to the earth.

A sin against God. Hairig's words come back to haunt her now. She disobeyed her fathers, both in heaven and here on earth. Her prayers come hard and fast. They pour out of her mouth and stream out of her eyes.

"*Der voghormia. Der voghormia.* Lord forgive me," she repeats over and over again, the way she has heard it repeated in the liturgy every Sunday since her birth.

SHE IS STILL there, with her forehead pressed firmly to the cool earth, when the rooster finally begins to crow and Kemal returns. He walks toward her, placing one foot before the other as if the ground beneath him is the back of a giant sorceress he doesn't wish to wake. Lucine searches his face for answers but finds a bright red scratch instead. Kemal stands dumb and mute, clutching his apron with both hands.

"What happened?" she whispers. "Did they hurt you?" She dabs his brow with her handkerchief.

"No," he says, taking it from her. His skin gleams with sweat. "I fell as I was running back."

"And Hairig? Where have they taken him?"

Kemal swallows hard, pressing his apron into a ball.

"Can you take me?" she asks.

Kemal does not answer.

"What?" she asks louder. "Tell me."

"He's . . . gone," Kemal whispers. "He's dead."

Lucine jumps to her feet. Impossible. He's mistaken. It was dark. Kemal takes her hand and pulls her body back down to the ground. Lucine wails, burying her head deeper into the folds of her skirt. She remains there, bent in half, despair pouring out of her until there are no sounds left in her throat.

"I'm sorry," Kemal whispers.

When the sun illuminates every corner of the courtyard, Kemal removes his arms from around her hunched back. He holds her head in his hands and lifts her face up to him.

A sin against God. Hairig's voice will not leave her.

"You are not safe," Kemal says. "Let me help you. I know that this is a difficult time, but it's the only time we have."

"A difficult time? We?" she asks, indignant, her hands involuntarily forming into fists. "This is no time for drawings." Lucine pulls away from him and stands up. "This is no time . . . I have no time for anything." Her voice bounces from one cauldron to the other until it fills the entire courtyard. "Don't you understand? Nazareth is gone. Anush is always crying. Mairig moves as if in a trance, and I still have Bedros and the baby to consider. And now Hairig."

"Listen to me, Lucine," Kemal interrupts. Still seated on the floor, he reaches for her hand. "You are in grave danger. It is too late to help your father, but it's not too late for you. You need to hide or go north. I can help you. If we go north, we can make it to the Black Sea."

"We'd get killed before we reached the town wall."

"Then we'll stay." He stands and moves closer to her now, placing his hand on her elbow.

"Don't. Please," she says, shrugging his hands away. Looking down, her eyes rest upon his shoes, Nazareth's old church shoes, scuffed and torn from overuse. The sight of those shoes on his feet emphasize the impossibility of what he suggests.

"There are places in the north and the west, small villages where no one cares if you are Greek, Muslim, Armenian, or Turk," Kemal says.

"You don't even have a last name," she says, remembering her father's words.

"What does that have to do with anything?" Kemal asks, withdrawing from her. "You think having a last name makes you better? More European? You are just as Ottoman as I am, Lucine. The only thing that makes us different is a few thousand lira and your mother's propensity to bow down to the missionaries."

"That's not true."

"Isn't it?" he asks.

"You want to be a hero," Lucine says, "but only to me. What about my mother, Anush, and my brothers? I am only one piece of wool. You can't just pluck me out and dye me whatever color you choose." The words catapult out of her mouth, partial truths burdened with fear and regret.

"What are you talking about?"

"Go away, Kemal. Leave me alone."

"You don't mean that."

"Please, just go," she repeats.

"No."

"Leave at once," she says, angrily.

"I will not leave," he says.

"*Deli misin*? Are you stupid?" She raises her voice and sees his eyes lower with the weight of her words.

"This is my property," she continues, "and in case you have forgotten, you work for us. The world may be turning upside down, but you are still a Turk and I am an Armenian. And if you think

I'm going to forsake my family, my religion, and my race for a measly drawing, you are out of your mind!"

Seconds later, she watches his broad back recede across her father's courtyard. The apron lies at her feet. She stands perfectly still, letting her breath out to meet his absence. A part of her wants to run after him, but the other part, the one permanently linked to those in the house, rushes back inside.

CHAPTER 13

The Whips of Satan

KEMAL HAS NEVER been more grateful for his father's donkey. Getting away from Lucine on foot, wearing these contemptible shoes, would be unbearable. He knew the moment she looked down at them that she would break him in two, but the knowing did nothing to prepare him. What does she mean by "You don't even have a last name?" Her words have conjured up a betrayal so dense he swears he can taste bile in his mouth. Her handkerchief, still wedged between his hand and the donkey's rein, burns the center of his palm. He rides the animal mercilessly, not because he's angry but because he fears in slowing down he might lose all the shattered pieces of himself. His heart, his limbs, his mind and pride, may peel away and drop to the earth, creating a trail of skin and organs that could be used to find him. And he does not want to be found.

Kemal curses his body for wanting her and his poverty for repulsing her, and rides away from the pain. This morning his heart was filled with pity and fear for her. He expected her to act shy, like a child, but she had not acted like a child at all. The Lucine who climbed trees in his shadow had vanished. In her place stood a condescending young woman whose resolute rejection of him was measured and cruel. There was no tenderness in it and no remorse. When he remembers her words, all the yearning in his heart turns to anger and rage. He suddenly understands why everyone hates the Armenians. What gives them the right to judge us? They are living in our country, living off our land. What made them think they were superior? Their god? Their ability to read? Well, he thinks, we have a god too, and anyone can learn to read.

The roads are narrower now, yet Kemal rides recklessly past the mosque and heads straight toward the town khan, a dilapidated inn populated mostly by traveling merchants and vagabonds. There he intends to get some raki to drown his sorrows.

Inside the khan's damp walls, the innkeeper is busy serving an older man in uniform. He places a small glass and a few Turkish delights on the table next to the man's fez. The soldier sits tall with his back straight, reading piles of documents and sipping his drink. At first, Kemal only sees the top half of the man's face. His eyebrows, like two fat caterpillars crawling toward one another, nearly hide his eyes.

Kemal settles at a table. "One raki," he yells out.

The soldier puts his documents aside and nods in his direction.

"A little early for raki, isn't it, son?" he says, furrowing his brow so that the caterpillars meet.

Kemal remains silent, watching the innkeeper pour a bit of raki into a tiny glass. When he adds water, the two clear liquids dance gracefully toward one another, before forming an opaque liquid that looks like a white cloud of smoke. He thinks of himself and Lucine: clear and unscathed until they try to merge.

Kemal shoots an arrow of the milky poison down his throat, letting the taste of aniseed coat his insides and burn the pit of his empty stomach.

"Another," he says. The innkeeper flashes a toothless smile and brings an entire carafe of raki to the table.

"They call it lion's milk," the soldier says, pointing to the carafe. He picks up his empty glass and his fez and takes a seat across from Kemal. "Women or money. Which is it?" he asks, helping himself to the bottle.

Kemal wants to tell the soldier to mind his own business, but the man's age and his uniform stop him. "It's nothing," he says, taking another swig. "Just a girl."

"Ah yes. Women can ruin you, if you let them. Let me guess, she represented all that is good and pure. All that is possible in the world. Am I right?"

Kemal nods. Already the raki is drifting up from his belly, past his heart, his throat, up all the way to the top of his head, where, if he closes his eyes, he can follow its ethereal dance.

"Women are the whips of Satan, my friend. And there are many to choose from," the soldier says.

"She's different," Kemal mutters, swirling the remaining contents of his glass.

"Oh? How so? Wait, don't tell me." The soldier waves an open palm in the air. "Her beauty causes the moon to blush . . . silences the nightingale. Am I right?"

Kemal pours more water on a fresh glass of raki.

"And maybe she's rich. Richer than you? Daughter of a sultan, maybe?" the soldier continues, eyeing Kemal's country clothes.

"No, it's nothing like that, " says Kemal, not wanting his problems so easily categorized.

"Then how is it? Tell me," says the soldier.

"She's no sultan's daughter." Kemal's words, burdened by raki, leave his mouth slowly and with little grace, but he continues talking nonetheless. "She's Christian. Learned. Reads like a cleric, rides like the wind," he says. "She was going to teach me my letters," he adds, though this isn't exactly true. "With her, I could be something . . . other than what I am."

"Ahh, Habib, we have a poet on our hands!" The soldier shouts to the khan keeper who flashes his toothless smile. "Well, it sounds like this little Christian girl did not see or want the poet in you. Am I right?" He slaps Kemal's back. "Or maybe she saw the poet but couldn't find the man . . . hmmm?"

Kemal nods into his glass.

"It's just like a Christian to enjoy the splendor of our land while they thumb their noses at our provinciality. It's time we take Turkey back for Turks. You know, you could show her, young . . . what did you say your name was again?"

"Kemal."

"You could show her, young Kemal. You could get out of this hamlet and see the rest of the world. You could become rich and powerful, cultured, and educated. You can become all these things without her. Despite her."

These were the thoughts circling around Kemal's foggy head when he reported to the conscription office. In the years ahead, he would think back to that moment in the damp khan and remember only two things: the unruly eyebrows of the enlisting officer and the idea of escape burning in his chest.

PART III

1990

CHAPTER 14

Selling Minds

ORHAN SETTLES HIS jet-lagged body into the starched white sheets of his hotel bed, wedging one of four pillows under his neck. The land of plenty indeed, he thinks, reaching for the phone. He calls the Tariq offices in Istanbul first. The head weaver insists his new designs are too intricate and confusing. The weavers are having a hard time telling one shade of any color from the next.

"Too same same," insists the head weaver.

"That's the point," says Orhan. He's going for incremental changes in color, so gradual that the eye and mind are softened into the transformation. Nothing abrupt, no stark contrasts. In fact, no contrasts at all. "Keep trying," he says, before hanging up.

It's two o'clock in the afternoon in Los Angeles, which makes it somewhere around 7 p.m. in Karod. Auntie Fatma will have already served his father dinner. Mustafa would be sitting in front of the television now, watching some government-sponsored program. The ringing of the phone, one of only two in the village, will startle him. It may even throw him into a rage. He might even take it out on Auntie Fatma. Orhan decides to make the call anyway. Auntie Fatma knows how to handle his father. She was always better at that than Orhan. It takes six rings for her to pick up the receiver.

"It's me," Orhan says, lighting a cigarette.

"Yes, yes. Who else would it be? My friends don't use the telephone, and your father hasn't got any friends," she says. "Have you found her?" she asks.

"Yes."

"And?"

"She's an old Armenian woman," he says. "Lives in a nursing home."

"Nursing home?" She clucks her tongue in disapproval.

Decent people don't put their loved ones in nursing homes. Even he knows that.

"Does she speak?" Auntie Fatma asks.

"No, not really," he answers, hearing her breathe a sigh of relief at the other end.

"She has no voice?" she says.

"Yes, she has a voice. But she doesn't want to speak, not to me anyway. And she understands Turkish," he adds.

"I see," says Fatma.

"She seems to be eager to get rid of me," Orhan says, exhaling a cloud of smoke through his nostrils.

"Yes, but will she sign the papers?"

"I think I've managed to entice her," he says.

"Entice her? Oh-ho! Because you have so much experience enticing women," she teases him.

"I've enticed plenty of women," he lies.

"Even so, you need to get that signature and hurry back."

"I have a feeling that getting the signature won't be a problem," he says. "But getting her to reveal her connection to Dede is another matter."

"Who cares what her connection is?"

"I care. Don't you want to know who she is?"

"She's probably some tart from his past," says Fatma.

"Doubtful," says Orhan.

"Some things are better left alone."

"I want to know why he did it."

"This is no time for fairy tales and interviews. You've got bigger problems waiting for you here."

"What are you talking about?" Orhan feels a lump forming in his throat.

"Your father is talking nonsense again. Says he's going to contest the will. He even mentioned the name of that lawyer, Hakan Celik."

"That piranha? Tell him no. I need more time. I just got here."

"This is not just about the house. You know that."

Mustafa would forcibly take the approval Dede would never give him. "I've poured my entire life into this company," he says. "All my time and attention, for years."

"By law, he is the first heir," continues Fatma. "The one who should inherit the business."

"He hasn't worked a day in his life," shouts Orhan.

"Nor will he. I imagine that will be your job."

"Did you show him Dede's letter? Did he read it?"

"Not yet, but I don't think it would change much. He's hurt. Has a right to be. Your *dede* wasn't very kind to him growing up."

"Oh, please," says Orhan. "At least Dede didn't beat him like he beat me."

He drags at his cigarette and tries to think strategically. His body aches of hunger and sleep deprivation. There will be no stopping his father once he has Celik working for him. If he wrestles the company away from Orhan, he'll sell everything Dede built and pocket it. No one knew this better than Dede. It's why he circumvented Mustafa and left everything, or almost everything, to Orhan. He has to show everyone that he has the situation under control. He has to get the old woman to give the house back immediately.

"Shit," he says. "You have to talk to him. Tell him I can fix everything. Everything will go back to the way it was before."

"You tell him," Auntie Fatma says.

"He hates me. You know that."

"He's angry and bitter, but he's not a bad man. And he's still your father."

"My father who wants to sue me," says Orhan. "Why are you always protecting him? Why can't you protect me for once?"

The question is a loaded one. Orhan was seven when the beatings began.

Auntie Fatma is silent for once.

"I just need more time," he continues. "Promise me you'll talk to him."

"I'll talk to him," she says finally, "but you know what happened when they started selling minds in the market?"

"What are you talking about?" asks Orhan.

"There were no sales. Everyone liked his own mind."

CHAPTER 15

Ani

THE ARARAT HOME is pressed under the thick gray fog of sleep, the day still tucked beneath tired lids, when Ani slips inside Seda's room, trailing the faint scent of gardenias along with her. Even with her eyes shut, Seda can sense her niece standing above her bed. Seda feels the blanket lifting but does not stir. Then Ani does something she hasn't done in a very long time: she climbs into Seda's bed, the way she used to when she was little, and wraps her arm around Seda's body, cradling it with her own.

"Meza," she whispers. Short for *mezmama,* or grandmother, it is what Seda called her own grandmother a hundred years ago in Karod.

Seda keeps her eyes shut and inhales the familiar spirit trapped in Ani's breath. When her niece was little, Seda used to place her face beneath Ani's sleeping head and inhale the oxygen leaving her nostrils. The little gust of expelled breath filled her with joy. It is the only thing she's ever taken from her niece. Ani has lost so much already. Bedros's children were conceived and born in loss. Ani (short for Anush) and Aram, both named for his dead siblings.

What right did Seda have to take anything from them? Even their names were not their own.

Once, when she was in her twenties, Ani fell in love with a Ukrainian boy named Roger. "His parents survived the Holocaust. He understands us," she told Bedros.

"He understands nothing," Bedros had shouted. "He shares his horror with the world, and the world gasps and apologizes. And what about us?" Bedros was right. The Armenians bore their loss alone. They tucked it away, like something precious, in every syllable of language taught in Saturday schools, and in the smell of dishes, and in the lament of songs. In the breath of children.

"Marry him and you finish what the Turks started," Bedros told her.

It is hard to believe that was over twenty-five years ago. They never heard much about her love life after that. If she had one, she kept it to herself. Fifty and still single, she teaches Armenian-language classes, when she's not devoting herself to her people's painful past. Seda should have said something back then, in the days of Roger.

Seda finally opens her eyes, places a hand on Ani's arm and squeezes.

"Hi," Ani whispers, smiling.

Seda takes in her niece's frizzy black bob, kohl-rimmed eyes and dark clothing. "Why do you always dress like you're in mourning?" says Seda.

"Tell me a story?" Ani says, ignoring her.

Seda clicks her tongue. "No more stories," she says.

"Oh come on. Why not?"

"Not in the mood," says Seda.

Ani starts stroking Seda's hair. "Remember when I was little, I used to sneak into your bed at night and warm my cold feet between your thighs?" she asks. "You used to tell me the craziest stories. Like the one about Aghavni Hanim who played with her breasts so much as a girl that they had grown a meter long each."

Seda smiles. "They grew so long that she had to toss each breast over a shoulder so they wouldn't knock into her knees," she says.

Ani giggles at the memory. "What was the point of that story?" she asks. "It's ridiculous."

"It was supposed to prevent masturbation," she says, struggling to sit up in bed.

"Oh my God," says Ani, laughing. "Are you serious?"

Seda shrugs.

"Why not tell a vagina story then?" she asks.

Seda gives Ani a stern look. "We don't talk about things like that. It's shameful."

"What else don't we talk about?" Ani asks, the humor in her voice gone.

Seda looks away, not knowing what to say. She has left so much unsaid.

"What's going on?" asks Ani. "Betty tells me you had a visitor yesterday."

Seda searches for an entry point to the story of her life, a life compartmentalized and safely tucked away, a life that should not have been uncovered in this way. *Damn Kemal*.

"Betty says a lot of things," she says.

"Is he from the *Armenian Herald?* They're doing a story about the survivors again. If you're going to talk to anyone, it better be me."

"Who's talking?"

"Not you," says Ani.

"That's right. Not me," says Seda, pulling the blanket back.

"But you're coming to the exhibit, right?"

"It's down the hall. I couldn't avoid it if I tried," says Seda. This exhibit is just another venue for what Ani and her generation like to call *baykar,* the struggle. Her niece had a bullhorn pressed to her lips as early as age three. Seda still has the VHS tape somewhere of Ani's first fifteen seconds of fame, courtesy of a KTLA news reporter who was covering that year's protest in front of the Turkish consulate.

"Why would you want to avoid it?" Ani asks.

"*Aman,* I'm tired of the past. I was there, remember? Once was enough."

"No, I don't remember. Because that's the one story you won't tell me."

"Your father told that story enough for the both of us," she says.

"But I want to hear your version," says Ani. "Maybe if you told me about what happened to you and Dad, I would stop harping about the past."

"You wouldn't stop. Besides, I don't remember."

"You don't remember," says Ani, her face full of skepticism.

"Old age," says Seda. "Now get out of my bed so I can start my day."

"Got a busy schedule, have you?" Ani teases.

"Very funny."

"I'll be down the hall, if you change your mind," she says from the doorway.

"If I had a mind left, I'd think about changing it," says Seda.

Alone again in her room, Seda manages to put her slippers on and lower herself onto the wheelchair. She moves her chair to the window. There was a time, not long ago, when she could have walked up to the glass. You can tell a lot about a person from his walk.

The Orhan fellow has a good walk. He is tall and lean like Kemal, but he walks differently in the world. His footsteps are more sure and his shoulders more hunched. Perhaps he gets that from his father. She wouldn't know. She left when the boy was only a small child, a halfling perpetually clinging to the hem of her skirt.

On that last morning with Mustafa, Seda woke him with her usual tenderness. His name was chosen because it meant one who has ancestral blood, an accurate description and one that would counter another word they feared would one day describe him: *bastard.* The boy reached for Seda, his plump fingers deftly searching for morning milk. She pulled away from him and produced a small tin cup filled with goat's milk.

"Anne," the child begged. "Mamma."

"No, my lion, Anne's milk is all gone," she told him, holding the tin cup to his lips. "This is Zazu's milk." Zazu was the boy's favorite goat. Seda had milked her early that morning and added a drop of honey to the cup. "It's warm and sweet," she reassured him.

She watched as the boy eyed the cup with suspicion before placing his lips on the vessel's edge and extended his sparrow's tongue toward the warm milk. She took a deep breath then, knowing the boy would eat and grow, even after she had gone. He and Fatma didn't need her anymore.

THE SOUND OF SHOES squeaking announces Betty's presence at her door. "Still crabby?" she asks.

"Always," says Seda. "I thought I told you to stay out of it."

"I did," says Betty.

"Then why is Ani asking about my visitor?"

"There's a log out front. You know that. She asked me if I'd seen him, is all. You all right?" Betty asks.

"When are you going to stop asking me that?" asks Seda.

"When you're dead," Betty says, smiling.

"More incentive to stop breathing," says Seda.

"Hush now. You got handsome young men whispering sweet nothings in your ear. If that's not a reason to live, I don't know what is. What does he want from you anyway?"

"Answers, I guess," says Seda.

"You got plenty of those," Betty says, laughing. "You gonna give him some answers Miss Seda?"

"Not if I can help it," Seda says.

"Well, either way, do me a favor. Think long and hard before signing any papers."

CHAPTER 16

Memory's Garden

ON THE DRIVE to the Ararat Home, the sun seems artificial, big and bright but without the kind of heat one would expect. Like everything else here, it surprises Orhan with its banality. This isn't what he expected from Hollywood, or *the land of the heathen,* as his father calls it. Only the palm trees zipping past his window smack of blasphemy. They don't bow their heads humbly to the sky the way most trees do. They protrude straight up, as if the landscape itself were giving Allah the finger.

Orhan puts the cigarette to his lips and fills his lungs up completely. Seda's reluctance to speak haunted Orhan throughout the night. It's clear she wants to be rid of him as quickly as possible. Getting her to reveal her connection to Dede will be tricky.

Sitting on the leather seat next to him is his satchel with the Leica, his old portfolio, and Dede's sketchbook inside it. The images of Turkey may loosen the old woman's tongue, and the camera would help him blend in with all the other visiting loved ones.

The Ararat Home entrance hall is just as it was the day before, except the receptionist doesn't look up to greet him. She pushes a clipboard for him to sign before letting him pass. Orhan walks down the hall, taking in the craft projects that litter the walls. Construction paper, glitter, and glue all competing to create the illusion of still-active lives. Resident stragglers roam around aimlessly. Mrs. Vartanian appears in the hallway. She's wearing the same dull brown house dress as yesterday, but the doll is swaddled in a pretty pink blanket. Though she can't cover much distance with her slippered feet, she shows off her impressive spitting range by launching some at Orhan's shoes. She says some words in Armenian before turning her back to him. He stands there feeling like a little boy who knows he's in trouble but isn't sure why. An old man balancing on a silver-tipped cane stands witness to his humiliation. He glares at Orhan as if pondering some accusation.

The orderly from the day before walks by, pushing a tray of breakfast foods down the hall. Orhan speeds up so he can walk with her.

"Hallo," he says.

"You're back," she says, not stopping for him.

"Yes," says Orhan, hurrying to fall in step with her. "Is Mrs. Melkonian always so quiet?" he asks.

"Quiet? Ms. Seda? No sir, but she's definitely been more cranky since she got that letter." She cocks one eyebrow at him.

Orhan's letter was as polite as could be, under the circumstances. "You have any advice for me?" he asks, ignoring her accusatory glance.

"Not really. She'll talk to you when she's ready, I guess. She does like being in the garden, though. She plants flowers when she feels like it. But stay away from the fountain. She hates that thing. Can't stand running water."

"No running water," he says. "I will remember that."

"You going over there now?"

"Yes, that is why I am here."

"Well, you may wanna wait. She's in there with Ms. Ani right now." The orderly stops her tray and looks triumphantly at him.

"Ani," Orhan repeats.

"Her niece. Visits every Wednesday. Good thing too," says the orderly. "She'll wanna know about them papers." She looks as if she's just cornered him in a chess game.

"Does Ms. Melkonian have any other family?" he asks before he can stop himself.

"No, just Ani. Sometimes her former students will visit."

"Was she a teacher?"

"Um-hm," says Betty. "Taught Armenian-language classes at one of them Armenian schools in the valley."

"No children then," says Orhan.

"Ms. Seda's never been married, if that's what you mean. Ain't got no children. Don't matter cause Ani pays close attention," she says. "And so do I, so you watch yourself, you hear?"

Orhan nods to himself. He's pretty sure the overweight orderly has just threatened him. He isn't here to hurt anyone and doesn't feel the need to defend himself.

"Ani's been organizing a commemorative event here at the home," the orderly continues, sounding like she's describing the

advanced weaponry of an opposing army. "They say the governor's gonna come," she says.

"A what event?" he asks.

"Commemorative. It means to remember," explains Betty. "Everybody here has a story about what happened in the old country," says Betty.

"It doesn't look like they need any help remembering it,"
Orhan says, eyeing the corkboard behind the orderly. It's cluttered with black-and-white photographs of Anatolian cities and
ancient family portraits. A map at the center of all this highlights
deportation routes in bright red.

"Most folks here are genocide survivors," Betty informs him.

"Bad things happen in wartime," he says. He's no extremist.
In fact, he's the first to admit the many shortcomings of Turkish
democracy, but he still can't help feeling insulted by these accusa-
tions of mass murder.

"From what I gather, these aren't just war stories," says Betty.

"That's not what I've heard," says Orhan, though the truth is he
hasn't really heard much about the Armenians of Turkey. They are
a lost footnote in the story of how the republic was established.

"I don't know about all that," says Betty. "All I know is Ani's
putting together an art exhibit. Paintings, photographs, that sort
of thing. Some of our residents will be presenting. She's trying to
get some political people to hear them stories."

Orhan nods politely, silently wondering if this niece who col-
lects stories and images would also be interested in collecting
houses.

"Well, good luck, Mr. . . . ?"

"Orhan."

"Orhan," she repeats after him, only it sounds strange in her mouth, more like "Orren."

"One question," says Orhan. "What does Mrs. Vartanian say exactly, when she points to me?"

"Do I look Armenian to you?"

"Right," he says, feeling stupid. Orhan quickens his pace.

The door to room 1203 is shut. Someone has taped a bright red flyer just under the peephole:

Bearing Witness: An Art Exhibit
for National Genocide Remembrance Day
Special Guest: Governor George Deukmejian

Orhan fixates on the word *genocide*. Massacres abound in his country's history, as they do in any nation's history. But genocide is a different accusation altogether. Why do they insist on using this word? No one would argue that a great many Christians were slaughtered in the empire during the First World War, but to claim that the Turkish government was responsible for the extermination of an entire race is something else entirely.

Orhan hears a voice through the closed door, speaking in a language he presumes to be Armenian. He presses himself against the wall, feeling somewhat like a prowler. When the voice stops, he strains himself to hear a response from Seda. Instead he is confronted by a high-pitched laugh.

Moments later, a woman with olive skin and frizzy jet-black hair walks out of Seda Melkonian's room. Her dark kohl-rimmed eyes are the only strong feature; everything from her forehead to her cheeks and lips appear blurry, and her features remind him of a collection of cushions. The confluence of dark features is exaggerated by her even blacker clothing, such that Orhan is reminded of the professional wailers at Dede's funeral. It is hard to believe that the sharp laugh he heard earlier came from her.

The niece, who looks to be in her fifties, digs in her purse, locates a bevy of keys, and heads toward the exit. She walks with hurried steps toward the dining room. Orhan stands there a long while, following her with his gaze, wondering if she already knows about the inheritance. God knows how this Ani woman, who clings to her people's grief, who dwells in loss and mourning—embodies it even—will react to the news. She'll get a lawyer, that's for sure. She might even tell the governor of California, for all he knows.

When he enters her room, Seda is seated in a wheelchair near a window facing the garden. He can see only the back of her head, damp, he assumes, from a morning bath. She is wearing the same dark blue cardigan, this time with a canary-colored silk scarf at her neck. The pale cream walls of the room are made yellow by the fluorescent lighting. And this saddens him; there are few things worse than bad lighting. Her single bed is pushed up against a wall. Next to it is a chest of drawers whose surface is almost entirely covered in a beige needlepoint, reminding him of the doilies of Karod. An old framed photo of the niece is displayed prominently in the center. In it she is much younger, wearing a blue cap and gown and holding a diploma. A golden sash draped across her chest hints of special honors. Above the chest of drawers is a generic landscape scene framed in dark wood. The only other furniture in the room is a tall bookcase whose shelves are crammed with books, both vertically and horizontally until there isn't an unoccupied inch. He is about to approach the bookcase to take a glimpse at the titles, when Seda turns her wheelchair around and faces him.

"Good morning," he says.

The old woman clears her throat but remains silent.

"I hope you don't mind me visiting so early in the day," he says, speaking into the silence that still hangs between them. "I was here earlier, but you had a visitor. I didn't want to interrupt."

"My niece," she says.

"Does she know about the will?" The question, out before he can restrain himself, embarrasses him. The fact that he asks it while still standing is somehow even more embarrassing.

Seda shakes her head. "No," she says.

"It's so sunny here," he says, trying to change the subject. "Back home, it is raining. I live in Istanbul now, but I was in Berlin for several years. September can be a very cold month, not like here," he says, settling into a chair next to her.

The old woman's eyes follow him into the chair. Orhan knows she wants to be rid of him, but he goes on anyway. "I moved to Germany in 1981. I had some trouble in Turkey." It's more than he's told his closest friends in Istanbul about that time. And he wonders why he finds it so easy to allude to it here, in front of this woman. "Anyway," he continues, "I moved back home a few years ago and have lived in Istanbul ever since." The one-sided conversation makes him feel silly, reminding him of a chatty blind date he once had. Now this old woman knows more about him than all his friends in Istanbul put together.

"I wish you would talk to me," he says suddenly.

"There's nothing to say," she says, turning away from him.

Orhan follows her gaze back out the window where a bright bougainvillea bush is the star of the show. Its pink flowers are so vibrant they seem artificial, like the California sun. The composition reminds him of a photograph he once took.

"I'm not such a bastard, you know," he says.

"I never said you were a bastard," she says. "You're a businessman, aren't you?"

"I am," he says.

"Businessmen care about results. They don't ask why."

He pauses, not knowing what to say to that. He starts reaching for the legal papers he's brought for her to sign and glimpses his portfolio in the satchel.

"I was a photographer once," he says on impulse. There is something unconvincing in the way he says the words, like he is trying to make them true.

"Oh?" she says, not sounding the least bit interested.

"I was exiled." It is a simple declaration, consisting of just three relatively simple words, but Orhan feels as though he's just given birth to a hairy mammal through his mouth. *I was exiled.* How many times had he tried and failed to say those words to Hülya?

Orhan was only nineteen when he photographed a group of Kurdish villagers in traditional dress. It was the sharp contrast of colors and textures that interested him. He had no idea that the stout bearded fellow standing in the back corner of the frame was a notorious insurgent. How could he know that a group of Kurdish villagers in traditional dress would be so offensive to the Turkish state?

The photograph was exhibited in a gallery in Istanbul, where it attracted the attention of the new government, which made all sorts of connections between his motley crew of creative acquaintances and the national security of the state. Within days, he was proclaimed a communist and imprisoned. That photograph earned him twenty-three days of "interrogation" by the Turkish police. They beat the light out of his eyes in that cold, soot-covered cell. He said good-bye to his youth and to all its dreaming then. There were no more photographs after that.

"Exile? Exiled for what?" she asks, coughing into a handkerchief.

"For 'denigrating Turkishness and insulting the state.'"

"With your photos," she says, one eyebrow cocked.

"Yes."

"And were you?"

"Was I what?"

"Insulting the state?"

"I was trying to understand the world through a lens," he says more to himself than to her. "I was offering some kind of description. I guess I was framing the world in a specific way that pissed the government off."

"And now?" she asks.

Now I make and sell kilims, thinks Orhan. "I don't do that anymore," he says.

"You don't do what? Take photographs or understand the world?" she asks.

"Both, I suppose," he says. Now that the words have escaped him, his insides feel like a cavern. Did he really understand the world back then?

"The truth is I was never really that political. Not intentionally. I have some of my earliest work here with me, if you're interested," he says, reaching into his satchel.

"I don't want to see any more pictures of that house," she says.

"Most of these are of Istanbul," Orhan says, ignoring her.

He pries the thing open. The first image is a black-and-white photo of a horse-drawn wagon loaded with heavy burlap sacks in what looks like Taksim Square in Istanbul. The wagon has stalled in the middle of the street and behind it a man in a Mercedes-Benz is shouting out of the car window. The man and his wagon look as if some time machine accidentally spit them out into a modern city square. Orhan remembers the colorful insults the man in the Mercedes was shouting on that day. He remembers the light and the deep ache he felt in his heart for the old man trying to survive in a time and space he wasn't equipped for.

Seda turns the pages slowly, giving each photograph its due respect. Orhan hasn't seen the photos in years. The memories come flooding back. Each image is a living, breathing moment of his life laid bare before him. Watching her watching him as he once watched the world makes him feel transparent.

The faces in his compositions are intentionally blurred. No human expression. All eyes are turned away from the camera. All faces obscured. The black-and-white images depict a city riddled with contradiction. Crowded and forlorn, ancient yet modern. So many of the photos are architectural, devoid of their human subjects. Doors, arches, minarets, alleyways, and fountains appear against the dark sky. The few people captured in the frame are fractured somehow, blending into the structure of his compositions. Orhan realizes, perhaps for the first time, that the true subject of these photos is the melancholy that lurks mysteriously in each and every image. There, in the spaces between darkness and light, a sadness hangs in the air, invisible to the human eye yet heavy on the heart.

Then the photographs change dramatically, the monochromatic cityscapes being replaced by colorful images of village life. There is a series of photos dedicated to *tavli* players, old men wearing skullcaps and newsboy hats, bent over the backgammon table in their button-down shirts, smoking. Orhan can still hear the sound of die smacking the side of the backgammon board and someone yelling *"shesh, besh!"* above the clamor. Unlike chess, *tavli* is a game in which your kismet plays a much larger role than strategy.

"In these, I began focusing on what I called the 'other Turkey,'" he says. "The part we don't always like to think about. The part no tourist would want to visit. It is the Turkey of my childhood."

"Anatolia," she says, looking up at him.

"Yes," says Orhan. "Anatolia."

The old woman turns the final page of the album, where a group of peasant women sit weaving before a giant wooden loom. They are seated in a small courtyard where a rainbow of wool strings hang from hooks in a weathered wall. She stares at their hunched backs, bowing before the colorful altar, and strokes their curved spines with her index finger.

"You look as if you're willing them to turn around," he says, in what he hopes is a light conversational tone, but his words snap the old woman out of her revelry. She shuts the album and hands it back to him.

"You don't take pictures anymore?" she asks.

"No," says Orhan.

She nods her head in acknowledgment. "You want to avoid being political," she says.

"I've been focusing on the family business."

"Everything we do is political," she says. "Even the things we choose not to do."

Orhan remains silent.

"Do you have those papers for me to sign?" she asks him abruptly.

"Yes," he says, "but I was hoping we could talk for a little bit. Would you like to go to the garden? I could get us some tea."

"A cup of coffee commits one to forty years of friendship," she says, reciting the proverb in Turkish.

Orhan gives her his best smile.

"It wouldn't be so bad," he says, suddenly longing for a cigarette. "We could enjoy the good weather."

"Here's fine," she says. "I don't want anyone interfering."

"I saw your niece head for the exit, if that is what you mean. It'll be fine. I promise."

The old woman sighs, clearly irritated. "Fine," she says. "Just make it quick."

Outside, Orhan pushes her chair along a meandering pathway. The sidewalk beneath his feet is covered with words. Etched into the concrete is a timeline of Armenian historical and cultural dates commencing with the Bronze Age in the year 3000 BCE and continuing to the present. What kind of a people is this? he wonders. So obsessed with their past that they etch it into the very ground beneath their feet. Orhan pushes Seda slowly toward 1982, skimming bits and pieces of history as he approaches the visitors' courtyard and the circular fountain. The spouts emerging from the mouths of several cherubs are dry and the water in the circular pool is completely still. Just behind the fountain is a massive map made of marble. Under it a plaque reads HISTORIC ARMENIA. His own hometown, located in the province of Sivas, is included in the borders of what is labeled as BYZANTIUM ARMENIA. He stands there dumbfounded. Theirs is an entirely different version of history.

The sound of crunching leaves brings him back to the present.

Seda is rolling her wheelchair toward a mulberry tree under which sits a lone wooden bench. Unlike the tree back home, this one displays thick succulent leaves, punctuated with berries drooping down in clusters. Orhan takes a seat on the bench next to her and lights a cigarette, letting another awkward silence hang between them.

The woman before him is like an ancient tapestry whose tightly woven threads could tell quite a tale, if he only knew how to unravel them. One loose thread and the whole thing could come tumbling out of her pursed lips.

CHAPTER 17

The Fountain

SEDA WATCHES HIM light a cigarette. She knows where this is going, this path of shared photos and garden chats. It's called intimacy and she must avoid it. She lets him take two long drags before speaking again.

"Not everyone would want me to sign those papers, you know," she says finally. "There are plenty of people around here who wouldn't. Plenty of people who would fight for that land." She watches his face for any sign of worry.

"I know," says Orhan. "And I'm grateful to you. But I don't want to leave here without knowing why my grandfather did this. I'm sure you can understand that."

You can never understand why people do what they do, thinks Seda. What's the point in trying? It's like trying to explain the world with a handful of photographs.

"I have something else to show you," he says.

"I don't want to see any more pictures," she says, her voice firm.

He smiles at her again, revealing two sets of parentheses at the corners of his mouth. "This was one of my grandfather's sketch-books," he says, pulling a tattered tomb from his backpack.

Seda's heart stops. Looking at the photographs was hard enough. Seeing Kemal's drawings might be more than she could bear. Seda stares at the tattered black cover in Orhan's hands, where the last traces of Kemal's fingertips remain. Before she can form another thought, her bent fingers reach for the sketchbook, drawing it to her and peeling the cloth cover open.

Seda is transfixed by the very first drawing. Fleshy dark mulberries dot a landscape of textured leaves thick enough to make a silkworm's mouth water. And Seda is pinned like a butterfly. At first she can only see the sweeping gray of graphite covering all but slivers of the creamy paper. She flips through the sketchbook, trying in vain to weaken its power over her. In the drawings that follow, the tree loses its fruit, its leaves, and ultimately many of its branches, until it looks more like a lonely stump. The entire sketch pad is dedicated to the mulberry tree in Karod. Kemal has captured every corner and inch of their courtyard from its infancy to its ultimate decay.

Their laughter as children is trapped in the crux of a branch, where the imprint of her backside remains from when they climbed that very limb, the one with the eye of some forest djinn encapsulated inside it, forever glaring.

There is an image of the tree bearing fruit and offering shade, before all the lamenting began. Even then, Kemal has cleverly alluded to their impending tears, collected in the marrow that fills the cauldrons nearby. It is all there. The gray, black, and dark blue of their longing and sorrow.

On one page toward the middle, Kemal's drawing reveals the cavity of the tree, the light gray living tissue of inner bark hidden beneath the hardened outer bark. The rendering is so close, it transforms the bark's ridges into a topographical map. Here is a metaphysical fingerprint, a small indecipherable indication of the Creator's existence and identity.

Seda extends her own knobby index finger, itself riddled with sloping lines and hardened bone, over an area of the drawing covered in cross-hatching, where Kemal's pinky must have glided across the space as he drew. Like the djinn in the tree, Kemal is trapped here too. His whole life and her life with him is entombed in these pages.

"Are you okay?" Orhan asks her, his hand on her right shoulder now. Seda can not even look up at him, this young stranger, this bearer of her past. She covers her face with the hanky to hide the tears that won't obey.

"I'll get you some tea," he says. She waves him away, too upset to respond. Alone with the last of Kemal's drawings, she shuts the sketchbook, hoping to trap the mourning emanating from its pages. But the past and all its horrors have already escaped.

Seda's eyes dart to and fro, searching for an escape, when she is confronted by a red-vented bulbul perched on a branch of the mulberry tree above her.

It is so like the tree of her childhood. It may be the same tree, even the same bulbul, a bird-ghost from her childhood, a phantom that flew out of Kemal's sketchbook and into this Los Angeles garden.

And this is when she begins to hear it: the wind sifting through the tree's branches, the river curdling and bubbling toward her. It gargles as it advances, spitting out blood. She tries to breathe, but her mouth and nose are full of water. Gasping, she drops the album and turns in her wheelchair. The custodian behind her is watering some bushes and the dreaded fountain has started working. Seda commands her mind to recognize these basic facts, but her heart is racing outside the reach of reason, and her body trembles and shakes. All she can see is the river screaming at her. Its liquid jaws swallow Aram's face whole, again and again. She does not yell or move but watches in silence, as she did all those years ago. Murderess. Another whisper in her ear. Her eyes roll back into her head and everything darkens.

WHEN SHE COMES TO, the first thing Seda notices is the spicy scent of cinnamon and cigarettes. She realizes she is being carried, her body draped like a delicate tablecloth on Orhan's forearms. She can hear his quickened steps and his panting. The citrine fluorescent light of the nursing home beats down upon them both as she hears him say, "Help me, please."

"What happened?" Seda can hear Betty Shields squeaking across the linoleum.

"I don't know. She fell or . . . passed out. I was getting some tea," he tries to explain.

"I thought I told you not to let her near running water." Seda can hear the anger in the orderly's voice. It's the same tone she uses when old Mr. Kalustian soils himself in the dining room.

"The fountain was off. There was no water. I don't understand," he says, carrying her into her room.

"There's water everywhere, Mr. Orren," Betty interrupts. "Do you know how I got to bathe her?" Betty asks as Orhan hoists Seda onto her bed. Seda keeps her eyes shut, silently wishing Betty would go away, but the orderly's voice, shrill and full of reproach, keeps pounding on. "I got to let the water run with the door closed, shut it off, *then* bring her inside."

"I don't understand," he says.

"There's nothing to understand, Mr. Orren," Betty interrupts. "She's ninety. You can't be upsetting her like this. You better go home now, Mr. Orren. That's enough excitement for the day," she says, checking Seda's body for bruising.

Seda opens her eyes wide and grips Betty's forearm in protest.

"All right." Betty lets out a big sigh. "But he's got to leave soon. I don't want you getting sick from this mess," she says. "You holler if you need me," she adds.

When Betty is gone, Seda turns her eyes to Orhan, who is hovering above her. Desperate as he is, he has been nothing but kind and patient. She lifts her head to say something, to calm his worried face, but Orhan places his palm on her shoulder and gently pushes her back onto her pillow.

"It's all right. You don't have to say anything. I am sorry. I am so very sorry," he says.

Seda holds his green-gray eyes in her stare and sighs. A lifetime of silence is suddenly weighing upon her chest and she wants to be rid of it, to cast it off, throw it into the phantom river haunting her. She reaches to him and grasps his hand.

"I killed him," she whispers.

Orhan stands there bent over her bed, mouth agape, saying nothing.

"He didn't fall. I threw him in," she says.

"Who?" he asks, but Seda puts her fingers to his lips.

"It is my turn now," she says.

PART IV

1915

CHAPTER 18

The Pretty Ones

WITHIN HOURS, LUCINE'S world and everything in it turns to dust. Sound is the first thing that deserts them. The clamor of Sivas, its people and animals, the clang of its copper pots and tin coffee trays, grows faint with each step they take, until all that is left is the creaking of wagon wheels and the shuffling of feet. The paved roads slip away, stone by stone. Storied structures give way to small wooden abodes, until they too are sparse. And the deportees, their lips locked against the grimy air, have lost their tongues. In the six hours since they began marching, the family has exchanged few words. Only the baby, nestled deep in Mairig's bosom, peppers the silence with random noises.

Anush, whose cream-colored bonnet hides a head of optimistic ribbons, is tucked deep in the back of the covered wagon with Mairig and Aram. She sings a ditty about a little partridge, cooing at Aram's broad, smiling face.

"*Gagavik, gagavik,*" she croons.

Lucine walks in front of the wagon, where she can be sure to see everything. She holds the missionary book with Kemal's drawing tucked inside. It reminds her that somewhere under this same hot sun is an ordered world of books, and schools and libraries, a world where a boy can draw pictures for a girl. The smell of lemons and perspiration from the coachman, Firat, drifts backward and into the wagon's cavity, but no one complains. He is a Muslim man, a talisman of sorts. There is safety in that body, in that smell. The Kurd has placed Bedros at his side, and now and then, when the road is smooth, he lifts the boy's spirits by giving him the reins. He listens to Bedros boast about his skill with the slingshot and smiles, revealing teeth like yellow chicks in the nest of his scraggly beard.

The caravan of villagers—some two thousand souls—stretches out for several kilometers before her, reminding Lucine of a serpent twisting and turning its body up and down the dusty road. When an oxcart stalls or a family slows down for an elderly loved one, the slender bodied snake looks as if it has just swallowed a mouse. Lucine knows that she too is a part of this snake, but she tries to imagine herself as an insect on its back, able to fly away on a whim. The terrain is mostly flat until noon, when, just as the sun is at its cruelest, they are forced to start an uphill trek. Lucine hears the groans of those without oxcarts. Acquaintances, friends, and strangers march ahead like a band of gypsies. She tries to console herself with the idea that soon they will be marching downhill. She fixes her eyes upon the next hill and resolves not to ask for food until they reach the top, where she hopes the gendarmes will let them rest.

A spattering of men, too old to imprison and too young to

conscript, accompany their families. Lucine makes a game of counting them, stopping at seven. The father of Gevork the apothecary walks behind his wife and daughter-in-law who take turns carrying the newborn. Lucine wonders how far the baby's *göbek bağı* has traveled down the river. She wonders what the old man's done with that silly white robe that belonged to his son. Everything that seemed so important days ago is now as worthless as a pebble.

A few meters to the left, the pregnant Arsineh walks slowly beside her husband, Vartan Berberian, the butcher known to trade a prime choice of meat for a quick glance at a girl's feet. (It was the delicate fold where ankle met heel that he couldn't resist, not that the Melkonian girls ever complied.) He pants under the weight of two large sacks carried on each shoulder. By the pungent smell of things, the sacks contain links of *sujouk* and *basterma,* the preserved meats and sausages that will sustain him and Arsineh on the journey ahead.

The governor has allowed a few men to accompany their families as a gesture intended for the benefit of Miss Graffam and the foreign missionaries who, everyone knows, correspond with the West. Miss Graffam stunned Muammer Bey when she announced she would be "braving the journey with these good Christians." Every so often, Lucine turns her head toward the tail end of the caravan, where Miss Graffam follows them in her smart hat and sturdy gait. Her presence is a kind of declaration, that their lives matter, that Hairig's life mattered.

Lucine's own men are lost somewhere where she can never

reach them. Hairig in a shallow mass grave she hasn't told anyone about, Uncle Nazareth in a labor camp or worse, and Kemal in a cloud of rage and rejection. When Lucine thinks about how she hurt him, it's not so much pity that she feels, but shame. Kemal is not like other men. He is soft and gentle, fragile even. She knows she's crushed him, but there was no other way to say no to him. When a gentle never-ending stream flows down toward you, slow and persistent, there is only one way to stop it, with a strong, resolute barrier like a dam, something that does not permeate or negotiate. She built a dam right there in the courtyard.

The sun ducks behind the distant hills and the sky darkens. The marching slows to a halt, and though they are too far to be heard, Lucine assumes the gendarmes have ordered them to stop. There are six soldiers in all, meant to escort and perhaps even protect the two thousand deportees. The two who ride horseback have colorful patches sewn onto their coats and must be officers. They wear proper uniforms made of khaki cloth, caps made of closely curled gray fur and sturdy boots that ride all the way up to their calves. They hold themselves erect in their saddles, punctuating both ends of the long line of marchers.

The other four have no horse or proper uniform to speak of. Their dusty coats hang loose about the shoulders and their trousers sag heavily in the middle. They curse as they hold their weapons at the ready, fingering them with self-importance. Rumor is that these four are not gendarmes at all, but a ragtag bunch of criminals newly released.

Clusters of families squat down to rest in the human chain that stretches across the plain. The Melkonians are near the end of this long line of displaced families, flanked on both sides by familiar faces from their village. Where once they shared a pot of tea or a choice piece of gossip, now their only commonality is the concern for survival. The gendarmes on horseback dismount and tie their animals to a pair of thin pomegranate trees that would serve better as whips than posts. If they were so inclined, the horses could easily walk away with the saplings in tow. Lucine wonders if it is fear and obedience that makes them stay, or exhaustion? She wonders the same thing about the deportees, who are busy building makeshift camps with the last rays of the setting sun.

Shrouds of dignity muffle complaints about hunger, but thirst is another matter. The missionary passes her goatskin to any who ask. Mairig's god would like that. And though he has been anything but kind, Lucine thinks it smart to appease him just now. She has no goatskin, only a clay jug more fit for a formal meal. She pours water into cupped palms, and her heart grows heavier with each pouring.

While the two ranking officers rest, the other four gendarmes march off to the east of the encampment, goatskins in hand. On their way back, they use both hands to carry their vessels, now heavy with water. Lucine carries her own empty jug to Firat, knowing the officers wouldn't deny a Muslim man some water. Firat is resting behind the oxcart, far enough from the family to allow for privacy but close enough to offer protection. He has taken off his vest and shoes and is prostrating himself in the direction of Mecca. When his incantations cease, Lucine clears her throat. She extends the empty jugs toward him.

"At your service, *hanim,*" he says, taking the jug and bowing his head.

"There seems to be a spring or fountain to the east of that little hill. It isn't far," she adds, by way of apology for disrupting him.

"Of course. Should I take Bedros along?" he asks.

"No." Mairig's voice comes from behind Lucine. How long has she been standing there?

Mother and daughter watch as Firat marches up the little hill. "Let's hope he returns," Mairig says.

"He will," Lucine says.

"He'll have to answer to your father if he doesn't." There is power in Mairig's voice, a certainty that comes from knowing Hairig would do anything to protect them. Lucine considers telling Mairig the awful news. That Hairig is dead, buried somewhere with other men of the village, that he isn't coming and won't be reprimanding or protecting anyone. But the words will not form themselves in her mouth.

She stands near Mairig, watching Firat walking against the pale orange color of dusk. He moves briskly past the gendarme's camp, but one of the soldiers stands up and follows him. It is one of the lower-ranking, bootless men. Lucine recognizes him: a young thick-lipped gendarme, prone to screaming obscenities at lagging elderly marchers. He says something to Firat they can't quite make out, something about "helping those dogs." Whatever it is, it makes the others erupt in laughter. Two more soldiers head toward Firat and soon all three are slapping and kicking him. The water jug crashes to the ground and a soldier crushes it with his foot. The gendarmes step away from Firat's crouched body. One gives him a final kick in the groin. In the next instant, Firat is hobbling away, holding his abdomen with both arms. He doesn't look back at his assailants, the crushed water jug, or the two women he swore to protect. He simply disappears.

Mairig tries to usher Lucine back to camp, but she stands perfectly still, watching the spot where Firat once was. She should never have asked him to get the water.

"Don't worry," she says. "He'll be fine. And your father should be coming along soon with more provisions."

The neat French twist of hair at the back of Mairig's neck has come undone, wisps of stray hair float about her temples. She smells of day old milk and dry earth.

"He isn't coming," Lucine says.

"Of course he is coming. As soon as they release him."

Lucine shakes her head no.

"He's not like the others, Lucine. He's got connections. He will bribe the governor . . ." Mairig's mouth is active, but her eyes go blank. They sink deeper into their sockets, retracting from the world.

"Kemal saw it." It is all Lucine can manage, but it is enough.

Mairig does not wail or moan. She does not scream or ask

questions. She simply stares, slack-jawed, into Lucine's face. Three sharp exhales escape her parted lips, as if an invisible djinn is pumping the very life out of her body. And just like that, Mairig's spirit is back in her bed, refusing to get up.

THAT NIGHT, MAIRIG sits motionless at their makeshift camp, holding the now useless silver cup. Anush spreads a *yorgan* on the floor and gives each of them a generous portion of dried figs and cheese. Lucine is trying in vain to swaddle Aram when she spies the silver vessel in Mairig's hand. It is a ridiculous bit of finery for those who sleep in the dirt and don't even own a water jug.

Bedros pulls at the fabric of his already-loose dress and wedges a piece of cheese into his mouth. The rest of the men in her life have disappeared overnight and now, little by little, Bedros is disappearing as well, by a few kilos a week. Seeing the morsel slide down her younger brother's throat gives Lucine some comfort.

"Where are we going?" Bedros, scowling, directs his question to Mairig.

"I don't know," she answers, her eyes looking past him.

"Will we have proper quarters soon?" Anush asks.

"I don't know."

"Why do I have to be in a dress?"

"I don't know. I don't know. I don't know!" Mairig's voice pierces the night air and attracts the attention of the thick-lipped gendarme who takes large, authoritative steps toward them. Soon he is standing above the family with his bayonet pointing down.

His lower lip hangs fat and low, like a hound's. Mairig tucks her chin into her chest and goes quiet.

"Shut her face or I'll shut it for you," the hound says to no one in particular. His glance is met by the only pair of eyes willing to look up. The gendarme, whose hair is still wet from his visit to the spring, uses the tip of his weapon to raise Lucine's chin up.

"Well, well, what is this?" he says, panting.

There is a long and uncomfortable silence, when no one is willing or able to answer him. Finally, Berberian the butcher, the lover of feet, wedges himself between the sisters and addresses the soldier.

"So sorry, effendi. She is just tired," he says, crouching between Anush and Lucine.

The hound uses his bayonet to peel wisps of Lucine's hair away from her face.

"You think you are better than us, *gâvur*? With your tasseled oxcart and your servants?"

"No, no, effendi," answers Mr. Berberian, placing a protective arm around each girl. "I will see to it that things stay quiet," he adds, looking up at the uniformed young man whose mouth is ajar and whose eyes remain on Lucine's face.

"Next time you need water, you get it yourself and only with my permission," he says, lowering his bayonet and walking away.

"Thank you," Lucine whispers. Mr. Berberian nods at her before returning to his wife. They stay quiet after that. Cloaked in stillness brought on by fear, even the ox yields to the night.

The family has never slept outdoors before, and Lucine is

surprised at how easy it is. Sometimes, on hot summer nights, the children would observe the rest of the villagers sleeping on their flat roofs and beg and plead with Mairig to let them do the same, but she would never allow it, saying, "We are not animals, and besides, our roof is not flat." Lucine looks at her family now lying on the cold ground, wrapped in shawls and thickly woven *yorgan*s and wonders how many nights they will spend under the stars. Bedros, whose angular bones are visible even under the woolen folds of his blanket, stares back at her, his eyes a pair of burning coals. She silently wills him to fall asleep and he does, the permanent scowl still on his face. In contrast, Aram's sleeping face cracks open in the kind of smile that Iola says means he's conversing with angels.

"Tell Hairig to help us," she whispers in his ear.

EARLY THE NEXT morning, Lucine lies on her back, watching clusters of stars disappear, much like her world, a little at a time. Anush rises with the sun and offers apples for breakfast. When Bedros refuses them, their big sister cocks her head to one side, saying, "You know, Bedros, if you don't stop scowling, we will never find you a handsome husband." She laughs at the joke, leaving Lucine to marvel at her sister's frivolity.

Anush's laughter irks Mairig. She spills some of their remaining water onto the dry dirt and starts rubbing the thick mud paste into Lucine's cheeks.

"Come here. You too," she says to Anush, but her older daughter shrinks away from her.

"Come here now," Mairig commands, tousling up Anush's hair and pulling out her modest ribbons before smearing her face with mud.

"What are you doing?" Anush says.

"They take the pretty ones," Mairig says.

CHAPTER 19

The Road to Kangal

WHEN THE GENDARMES give the marching orders on the third morning of the journey, it is with a great deal of cursing and yelling. Perhaps they too wish to be anywhere but here. As for the deportees, they look more and more like sheep, walking one after the other, their arms hanging like wet wool at their sides. Aram lies listless on the wagon bed. Lucine and Anush sit near him, their thrice-shielded faces covered by soil, bonnets, and the shelter of the oxcart.

Bedros sits tall in Firat's old seat, the oxcart's reins held in each hand. Mairig slouches next to him, and his left shoulder is a shelf for her head. The scorching sun beats down, amplifying the deep creases in her brow and cheeks. Hers is a face made for the indoors, for piano recitals and books of poetry. What would Hairig do if he saw her like this, looking more and more like a sheepherder's wife, her Parisian face cream abandoned in one corner of the house? *She looks like all the rest.* All the things that made her float above everyone else in Sivas have disappeared, eroded by the instinct of survival. Lucine looks away, choosing instead to count the sacks of bulgur in their cart. If they eat only a handful a day, they can survive for a week, maybe more.

The landscape unfolding before them is a glorious reminder of lighter days. The rolling hills are like yards of amber and jade silk draped over a voluptuous body. Patches of purple flowers decorate the tops of rounded peaks, and a carpet of honey-colored grass covers most of the earth, so the marchers are no longer immersed in dust. The farmers among them agree that where there is grass, there is irrigation and possibly a village or town.

"It is the road to Kangal," says Arsineh, the butcher's wife, pressing a palm to her swollen belly. She speaks of the large family she has there, of their wealth and generosity. This lifts the spirit of all those within hearing distance and they pass the good news down the long line of marchers. Perhaps water and warm food will be available for them there. Some dream of a khan where beds of straw and hay might be found. Others ready their hidden coins for bribing and a bit of trade at the local bazaar. But instead of following the main route into the town, the gendarmes lead them into the hills outside its periphery. The road to Kangal disappears like a tight seam in the landscape.

The deportees' spirits sink to a new low. Lucine looks down at her book. She cracks it open and, hoping for comfort, begins deciphering the English words. There are words about spreading God's word to the four corners of the world, letters and short articles about different schools where his message is taught,

alongside algebra and home economics. She hopes the people
who wrote the book, the same ones who sent Miss Graffam, will
soon send food and water.

Lucine removes Kemal's drawing from the book and studies
it anew. The river and moon are rendered microscopically in the
irises of her eyes. She notices a cluster of mulberries tucked behind the waves of her hair. There is so much here she didn't see
before. Lucine folds the paper again and again until it is small
enough to tuck near her breastbone, away from the world and
all its miseries.

The sun dips down behind the mountains and the road seems
more endless than it did before. It slopes upward moderately, but
enough for Lucine to see the apothecary's father fall behind, his
wife and daughter-in-law too busy with the infant to notice. He
trails farther and farther behind, until there are a good ten meters
between him and the last of the deportees from Sivas. The gendarme assigned to the end of the line marches behind him. He is
shorter than the rest, with a narrow protruding nose that reminds
Lucine of a parrot's beak. He's wrapped a big white cloth around
his head to shelter himself from the sun. It makes him look less
official, more like an Arab than a Turkish soldier. The officer on
horseback is farther behind him. He rides a good distance away,
his job to protect the flock from raiding Kurds and villagers.

Lucine watches the turbaned gendarme nudge the old man
with the butt of his rifle. The apothecary's father is old and frail.
He has endured more misery in the last few days than in all his
other days combined. Still, he has his grandchild to consider. The

old man picks up his pace, but this only heightens his exhaustion. He collapses onto his palms and knees, a four-legged animal wheezing and gulping in air.

The gendarme looks impatient. He too is on foot, enduring the heat and exhaustion, far away from the glory of battle, doing shepherd's work.

"Get up." His voice is angrier than before. He takes this opportunity to adjust the makeshift turban, unfolding and refolding it tighter around his head. This is when Lucine realizes that it is not a shirt at all but the coveted apothecary's coat.

The old man stays down, still wheezing.

"Fine, stay then," he says. He picks up his weapon and lodges a single bullet into the old man's back. The sound stops everyone. The old man's wife screams in protest. "*Aman Asdvaz eem!* My God." She hobbles back toward him, but the officer on horseback gets there first.

"*Mee nayeek,* don't look," orders Mairig, but Lucine climbs out of the wagon anyway. It is the first time she has witnessed a murder. Her eyes go from the old man's splayed body, to the assassin's face, above which the crumpled white coat of the apothecary sits like a crown.

The officer dismounts his horse, calling the turbaned gendarme to attention. He stands erect, just like he did in his saddle, a full head taller than his subordinate.

"You idiot," he barks. Spit flies out of his neat mustache and lands on the nose of the turbaned one. "Who told you to waste a bullet on this dog when we have so few? Next time use this," the officer says, grabbing the gendarme's bayonet and shoving him with it.

The old man lies facedown, staining the grass with his blood. The apothecary's mother falls to her knees beside her husband. The officer ignores her and remounts his horse.

"Keep walking, all of you," he shouts to the spectators.

They leave the old man face down in his open grave, his left ear and cheek pressed to the earth, listening for God's apology.

"Where is your Christian god now?" the turbaned assassin shouts. Lucine thinks it is a good question. Not one person answers him. Not Mairig and not the missionary. Perhaps they sense what Lucine already knows, that if God is indeed anywhere, he is not here.

Farther down the road, with the memory of the old man's murder festering like an open wound, the deportees come to a company of old women, from the town of Tokat. They say they have been without food or water for three days. Robbed of everything, their bare feet weeping pus, they beg to join the caravan from Sivas. The gendarmes agree, but only after a bribe is conferred by the butcher Berberian, who seems to be carrying more than just sausages in those sacks. But after what they have just witnessed with the old man, the group sees that the price of an Armenian life is not negotiable. The Tokat women speak of a valley nearby filled entirely with corpses and point to a flock of birds circling above. They think nothing of crouching before a pile of ox excrement and picking at the visible grains. Lucine wonders if the bread they are given is an act of charity or just a clever way of stopping their mouths.

She walks slowly, keeping her eyes lowered to the dry earth. Determined to ignore the moaning and shuffling sounds of the company, Lucine focuses on her shoes instead. They are sturdy shoes, with leather soles she knows will take her far. She can depend on them like she can depend on little else. Her eyes rest on the scuff of her right toe, where the soft brown leather is stripped, exposing a lighter, more vulnerable layer.

But the shoes, her own and everyone else's, are a comfort. Brown, black, heeled, and flat with an occasional sturdy boot—all proceed before her. Constant, tangible and oh so reassuring, less worn than their spirits and limbs. If she keeps her vision focused on just this one article of clothing, Lucine can pretend to ignore the fear that creeps up and overwhelms her.

Anush's shoes, in particular, are a lovely sight. She wears a brilliant pair of dark blue suede shoes with a large silver buckle that gleams in the sun. As she walks, the sunlight kisses the sweet little buckle now and then, shooting sparks of light into the dusty air. Lucine's eyes chase these sparks, irregular and unexpected as they are, and her spirit soars with each whimsical, short-lived dance. Her attention is so fixed that at first she does not hear the sound of galloping hooves. But the sound crescendos until both Anush and Lucine are engulfed in a dust.

"*Asdvaz!* Dear God!" Mairig wields her voice like a sword through the air, but the sisters are hidden in a dirt chamber.

Lucine sees nothing but a uniformed arm reach down. Thick fingers clamp down on Anush's braids, pulling at them like ropes. Anush screams, holding the side of her head where the hair is being torn out. Before Lucine can react, the great arm scoops Anush's tiny waist up. Lucine catches a glimpse of the man's face. She sees the hard eyes and familiar mustache of the captain who doesn't believe in wasting bullets. Anush lunges forward, arms stretching toward Lucine, but the uniformed arm cinches like a tight belt at her waist. Lucine holds her sister's terrified gaze for a fleeting moment before it recedes with the sound of the hooves. She is left standing only a few feet from where Anush was a moment ago, a cloud of dust settling back at her feet.

When she looks down, one dark blue shoe lies on its side, its shiny silver buckle hiding from the sun. Mairig runs up behind her with such force that they both tumble to the ground. "*Aman aman . . .*" Mairig screams, tearing at her hair, wailing at her deaf mute god. Lucine swallows her tears. She turns around, staring ahead back toward the road that brought them here. It is empty and nondescript. Nothing about it, not the few discarded articles on the ground nor the absence of the gendarme on horseback, hints at what has happened here.

"Get up! Keep moving!" The turbaned gendarme is yelling again. He kicks the ground and a fresh batch of dust circles the air. Lucine looks ahead for the horse-backed officer, but he has vanished.

Bedros comes running from behind, carrying baby Aram. He has left the oxcart with all their remaining provisions behind.

"Mairig, Mairig," he calls, holding the baby out to her.

Mairig stands but does not reach for the bundled infant. She drags her feet forward in a stupor. It is Lucine who must take the baby from Bedros. She places Aram into the crook of one arm and squeezes Bedros's hand.

"You stay close to me," she says, looking him in the face. "Do you understand?" Her voice is louder and angrier than she intends it to be and Bedros whimpers. But Lucine is too broken to apologize or comfort him. She keeps her grip tight and wills herself to walk on.

CHAPTER 20

Empty Prayers

LUCINE TURNS HER head back again and again, scanning the line of deportees for Anush. She reminds herself repeatedly that girls who are violated in the night are sometimes returned. They weep and hide their faces in shame, but they return. The thought of Anush's thick brown braids and warm embrace make Lucine's insides weak. If only Uncle Nazareth or Hairig were here, things would be different. They would find Anush and get them all out of this misery. They would show that gendarme where to stick his bayonet.

Mairig, who insists on walking, shows no interest in taking Aram from Lucine. Tucked under the soft folds of her brother's swaddling clothes, below the faint scent of breast milk, is a velvet pouch containing Mairig's hidden treasures: two gold bangles, meant for her daughters when they marry; an emerald brooch in the shape of a cross that belonged to their grandmother; and the ruby ring Hairig had recently given her. Local merchants keep approaching the caravan, selling a handful of almonds for a gold ring or six dried figs for a silver spoon. So far Mairig has kept her treasure to herself. She didn't reach into it, even when the old women from Tokat needed to bribe the gendarmes. And it's a good thing, because they may need Mairig's treasure to rescue Anush.

Now and then, Lucine can hear Mairig catapulting a prayer or two to the heavens in a low angry voice. She uses words that she's never used before, words that curse and damn things, words that she would have pulled Lucine's ear for, if she ever used them. Mairig's eyes have lost their focus; Lucine wishes she would stop looking past them. Not even Aram's crying can claim her attention.

Yesterday the gendarmes led supervised trips to a public well, but by the time their turn came the soldiers had grown tired of the task. Lucine wonders if the others are as thirsty as she. If only she were bigger and less afraid, she would swallow her beating heart, which seems to be lodged in her swollen tongue. She would put it back in her breast where it belongs and find a way to protect the people she loves. That is what Hairig would have wanted. But swallowing anything, much less the lead ball lodged in the middle of her mouth, is impossible. Sometimes, if she locates her fear somewhere specific, like in the face of the thick-lipped gendarme or the uniformed arm of the man who took Anush, her fear grows smaller but more potent. It transforms into something else entirely: a hate so pure that it sustains, even nourishes, her.

When the sun starts to set, the gendarmes order the deportees to stop marching. The relief at the prospect of a few hours of rest is short-lived, for a cold desert wind begins to whip at their backs. Lucine huddles close to Bedros and Mairig in their makeshift tent. Mairig doesn't say a word. She turns her back to them and falls asleep. Perhaps she's right to do it. A rescue plan is better executed after a good night's sleep.

Lucine vows to stay awake in case Anush returns in the night. She peeks at Bedros, who is also still awake.

"How can it be so cold at night when we are boiling in the day?" he asks, picking at the tear-shaped scab on his left cheek.

"The weather is fickle," Lucine says. "Stop picking. You don't want another scar on your face, do you?"

Bedros shrugs. "Girls worry about the strangest things."

"Get some rest," Lucine tells him.

Despite her fatigue, Lucine finds it easy to stay awake. Thirst attacks the remainder of her body, traveling down from her throat to cramp her abdomen and legs. Her mind drifts back to the night Uncle Nazareth was taken. She sees herself standing before Governor Muammer, like David before Goliath, aiming Bedros's slingshot straight for the man's forehead. Next, she strangles the potbellied fool with those yellow-and-brown marble prayer beads he's always carrying around. Numerous versions of this heroic vignette play over and over in Lucine's mind until her lids grow heavy with satisfaction and sleep.

She awakens in the middle of the night to screaming women and the furious pounding of hooves. There is so much dust and so little moonlight that she wonders if this too could be a dream. In the faint orange glow of the moon, four expert horsemen ride toward the caravan. They are dressed in large fringed turbans and tribal *şalvar*, pants so baggy and wide they look like inflated balloons. The horsemen open their mouths and let out a piercing tribal scream in a language that's neither Turkish nor Armenian. They swarm like hornets toward the caravan.

"Bastards!" she hears someone shout in the darkness.

The few remaining oxcarts are plundered. One of the horsemen is dragging a young girl by the hair. Lucine runs in the opposite direction. She cannot see the totality of what is happening but recognizes the backside of a lumbering ox and runs toward it. The animal moves quicker than it ever did when Bedros was driving it. *Damn ox.* In her haste, she trips over something or someone. It is Bedros, kneeling next to a broken wooden crate, desperately trying to put something back in it.

"Are you all right?" she asks him, forgetting about the ox.

He shakes his head in response. "Our oxcart is gone."

"I know."

"They've taken our pot and the ladle but left all our grain," he says.

"Kurds," says Lucine, her eyes searching the ground. "It is against their custom to take our food."

Lucine stares into the wooden crate where Bedros has managed to collect two sackcloths of bulgur grain and one plum. *What kind of custom allows you to take a girl but not her bulgur?*

That is when she remembers Mairig. Only after she has surveyed the remaining food supply.

"Mairig!" she yells, ignoring her burning throat. "Mairig!" Lucine runs toward bodies rising from their crouched positions. She scans their grimy, stunned faces. Tearless, because their bodies are just as parched as their souls.

She finds Stepan the sheepherder flat on his back, his hands still folded together in sleep. Lucine touches his peaceful face with the lids sealed shut and decides to wake him before seeing the wound at the side of his skull where an animal has trampled him. Lucine remembers the heavy-footed ox clamoring for safety and feels strangely responsible for Stepan's fate. This thought and the blood, so dark and sweet smelling, make her fall to her hands and knees, heaving.

This is how Bedros finds her. "Come, she's here," he says, leading her by the elbow to a wooded area. "She's over here."

Mairig sits with her back against a tree, her legs spread wider than Lucine has ever seen them. Aram lies squirming beside her, his swaddling clothes loosened. Mairig is holding something tight in her two hands, but Lucine cannot see what. Lucine stands before Mairig in the darkness, taking in her matted hair and sunken eyes. She shudders at the sight of this stranger who has replaced her mother.

"Did they take our water?" asks Mairig, pushing the words past her parched lips.

Lucine does not know how to respond. They have had no water since the incident with Firat and the broken jug. Bedros runs before her and wraps his arms around Mairig's shoulders.

"Listen," says Mairig, pushing Bedros away from her. "You

should leave now. Let me rest. Take good care of the baby. I will catch up later."

"Catch up? When?" asks Lucine.

"In a little while. Or you can return for me when you find some water. That would be better."

Bedros looks to Lucine. They both know she isn't making any sense.

Mairig reaches into her bosom where a few gold coins are hidden. "Here. Take it. The rest is with the baby."

"We should stay together," Lucine insists.

Mairig shakes her head. Then she does something she's done before. She closes her mind to the world and to her children who remain in it.

"What will you eat?" Lucine whimpers.

"This," says Mairig, looking down at her hands. In the moonlight, Bedros sees the New Testament open in her palms. Mairig's delicate fingers lift a page and rip it loose, releasing a sound like a slap in God's face. She crumples the page into a tiny ball and, lifting it up to her lips, presses it into her mouth.

"What are you staring at?" she snaps. "If God will not eat his words, then I will do it for him. Now go. And take Aram with you."

CHAPTER 21

God's Will, *Inşallah*

LUCINE LEAVES MAIRIG on the open road, under the eye of a merciless god. She leaves her own heart there too. It lies beating in the cradle of Mairig's cupped palms. She tells herself that the heart is a burdensome organ and leaving it behind is the best thing to do. The rest of her body moves forward, following the hunched backs of other deportees but her thoughts are like a whirlwind, circular and fierce. She's glad *The Missionary Herald* is gone. She was stupid to take it in the first place. What good did she think it would do her on the march? For that matter, what good will Kemal's drawing do, still tucked inside her dress? Where would Aram and Bedros be now if she had listened to him?

She carries herself, head heavy, reluctant lids lowered.

When she does look around, Lucine sees everything differently now. Everywhere she looks, in every face and every pebble, is an opportunity for death or survival. Bedros and Aram are no exception. She sees hope's ghost circling around their shrunken faces. Every now and then, Bedros tries to pry his hand from hers, but she only squeezes harder. Aram is fastened to her back now, wrapped and propped up by their only blanket. Two long sticks protrude from of the blanket, parallel to the ground. She plans to use them to hold up the blanket, transforming it into a shield against the biting desert wind. Two largish leaves are pressed flat against her belly. She can use them to clean the baby when they finally rest. Eyes shrunken, lips dry, she isn't sure if he will survive.

Bedros does not ask for water. He does not ask her when they will go back for Mairig. He does not ask her anything and for this she is most grateful. His silence is so merciful that if she had a heart left, there would be tenderness in it.

One of the old women from Tokat walks beside them. Lucine keeps her eyes fastened to the earth and does her best to discourage conversation. "Daughter, water," the woman says, extending an open palm.

Lucine shakes her head and looks away. *I am no one's daughter now.*

A man she does not recognize, one of the few male deportees left, turns around.

"There is no water yet, Auntie," he says. "But we are soon approaching the Tokma Su River. There will be water there."

"Eh, *Inşallah*," she responds with a sigh. "May God will it."

God's will. *Inşallah*. The phrase rings in Lucine's ears like a familiar and angry bell. This mysterious and vengeful god and his unpredictable will have been evoked every day of her life. In moments of grief and exaltation, in casual comments exchanged without much thought, and in solemn whispers uttered every evening in the Lord's Prayer. Lucine hears it whispered to her as an infant. *May she be a lucky child, Inşallah.* And it continues from there, every day, until this dirty miserable day when she is walking hungry and desperate with no parents and two younger siblings, the sun at her back and dust at her feet. Suddenly she is swollen with anger. If God's will materialized as a pitcher of water, she would throw it back up to the sky. Wasn't it his will that placed her here? His will that killed Hairig? His will that took Anush, broke Mairig's spirit, and caused her to give up? No, Lucine will no longer pay any attention to him or his will. She discards his will, exhaling it out of her body in the form of her breath. She drops it to the earth and steps over it, feeling lighter and more in control.

The caravan from Sivas follows a narrow bend in the road that widens suddenly, revealing the bridge at Tokma Su and the vast plain beyond. A slow-moving line of oxcarts as far as the eye can see proceeds before them. Lucine thinks longingly of their own dumb animal, whose burden she now carries herself. The people with oxcarts are members of an earlier flock, deportees from some other province of Turkey who share the same fate. As they approach the bridge, Lucine begins to see the bodies of those who came before them, who succumbed to hunger or thirst and now lie dying or dead on the side of the road.

To her immediate right, a pair of vultures pulls at the intestines of a woman's body. The larger one is perched on the woman's chest, his black tail feathers batting at what was once her chin. Lucine places a hand over Bedros's eyes.

Neither one of them mentions Mairig, but the image of her is there before them, perched under a tree, an open invitation to friend and foe alike. *Perhaps Hairig's ghost will hide her.* It is a comforting thought and one Lucine holds on to. His words drift back to her now: *Sometimes we have to be like a riverbank, twisting and turning along with the earth, withstanding swells and currents. Enduring.*

The plain on either side of the bridge is dotted with villagers, their white *şalvar* pants blowing in the wind. Some launch insults and stones. The more ambitious pick at the bodies of those not yet dead. Two village women, their heads covered in piety, think nothing of stripping a fallen deportee of her clothing. The younger of the two does the stripping, while the older one checks for hidden seams and pockets filled with loot.

Lucine removes Aram from his place on her back and presses him to her chest, her arms forming a makeshift fence around him.

Miss Graffam runs up and down the bridge, trying to make sure no one is badly hurt. She looks and behaves so differently than she did in Lucine's classroom; gone are her pressed skirts and even more pressed manners. The calm authority of her once-serene face is replaced by wild eyes. The only thing familiar about her now is the big hat on her head. It impresses a handful of Kurdish villagers enough to sell her some water, which she offers to her former students. Lucine accepts without a word. Putting the wet ladle to her lips brings forth a kind of anticipation akin to joy, but her swollen tongue lets in only a mouthful of water at a time.

It's as if her throat forgot how to swallow. Lucine does her best to drink what she can, taking care not to make eye contact. The days when she strove to catch her teacher's eye are gone. Now she wishes only to be invisible.

She dips the corner of Aram's swaddling cloth in the water and puts it in his mouth. Aram's chapped lips suck urgently at the wet cloth for a few moments but his face, full of anticipation, goes red when there is no milk to be had. He turns left, then right, his head thrashing, lips searching for sustenance. Within seconds, he moves from a state of anxiety to anger. He cries with his mouth wide open, exposing the flashing red ball hanging at the back of his throat. There are no tears, no snot. Not a drop of liquid from his body. Lucine doesn't bother rocking him or singing a lullaby, as Anush would have done. She simply moves forward, one foot in front of the other, eyes scanning the road ahead. Her body stays true to this linear trajectory while her mind turns around and around in her skull, like a whirling dervish.

Arsineh, the butcher's wife, doubles over in pain. Her water broke this morning, but no one seems to care. She is squatting down now and wailing between breaths. Butcher Berberian is stooping at her side, minus his sack of dried meat, which disappeared in the night along with almost everything else. The years of severing animal limbs have not prepared him for this, a woman's job. The deportees stop marching. Standing, Berberian looks around in vain for Iola or Mairig or any woman willing to help. Lucine averts her eyes from him.

The gendarme closest to them approaches. He nudges the

butcher with the butt of his rifle to keep moving. Without a word, Berberian refuses. He stands with his body facing the gendarme and his eyes still on the crouching Arsineh. The gendarme whistles to his companion who is walking on the other side of the caravan.

"Hey, girl or boy?" he asks.

"Who the fuck cares?" his friend answers.

"I'll give you three *paras* if you guess right."

His companion smiles broadly. "A wager then," he says. "Boy."

The two gendarmes stand above Arsineh, who is breathing harder than ever. She grunts long and hard. She grasps her knees and then gets on all fours, like an animal. Berberian runs to the back of the caravan, toward Miss Graffam, to get some help.

The gendarme leans against his rifle and waits for the results.

"What is the hold up back there?" the commander on horseback yells from the front of the line.

The gendarme does not respond.

"Hurry up, you bitch," his companion says to Arsineh.

She lets out a long wail, raking the dry earth with the fingernails of her left hand. Then silence as she keeps pushing. Five minutes go by, then ten. Intervals of grunting and silence, all while the entire world waits. In the distance, the commander's horse neighs as he makes a sharp turn toward the commotion.

The gendarme places the flat part of his foot on Arsineh's shoulder and pushes her onto her back. She pulls her knees up in defense, but it is not enough to stop his bayonet from piercing her stomach and slicing it like a ripe piece of fruit.

Though there is blood everywhere, no sound escapes from Arsineh's lips. Her eyes remain open as the blood seeps out of her.

"You owe me three *paras*," says the gendarme.

Just then Berberian arrives with Miss Graffam at his heels. He screams and rushes toward the gendarme, knocking him on his back, not far away from the dying Arsineh and her unborn son. Berberian's meaty fists pound into the gendarme's face. Over and over again, until a single bullet, launched from the gun of the commander on horseback, plunges into the butcher's neck.

Lucine presses Bedros and Aram's faces to her chest and squeezes her own eyes shut. She doesn't want to see where Berberian will land when he falls. She doesn't want to see anything ever again.

"WE ARE GOING to be flies, Bedros," Lucine whispers to Bedros. "Do you want to be a fly?"

"A fly?" asks Bedros.

"Yes. We're going to pretend that this long line of marchers is a slow-moving serpent and we three are flies on its back. Soon we will fly away. Do you think you can do that?"

"Yes," he says simply. It is all she needs.

They come to the end of the bridge, where the rest of the company of Sivas is gathered near the river. Groups of people from Amasia and Samsun are also waiting there. A young woman with one long, unruly braid rushes toward the river only to be intercepted by a gendarme.

"Keep away. All of you," he shouts to the deportees.

Miss Graffam, who has been bandaging someone's leg, stands up to confront him. He sees her quick steps and points his bayonet in her direction.

"You, no more," he says.

"The river is only a few meters away," she insists. "We will go single file." She says the last two words in English, holding up her finger to signify one person.

The gendarme interprets the gesture as an insult to his manhood. He says something about not being one of her students. He curses with gusto, stopping only when his commanding officer approaches.

"What's the problem here?" the commander asks.

"Your man won't let us drink," Miss Graffam says. Her hands do not rest on her hips the way they did when children disobeyed her at the school. They hang low at her sides in what Lucine interprets as exhaustion and defeat.

"I believe your pitcher is full, madam."

"Yes, but one pitcher is hardly enough for everyone."

"It is for their own protection," the commander says.

"For their protection," repeats Miss Graffam.

"Young ladies in the previous caravan were deliberately drowning themselves in the river," he says. "We can't have that, can we? Our job is to protect you, all of you."

"*Protection* is not the word I'd use to describe what has been happening here," she says. Her teacher's hands are at her hips again. It is a mistake and Lucine wishes she could warn her.

"I do not condone what happened earlier," he says, pointing

back to where Arsineh and her family now lie. "But the truth is, they would have died eventually anyway."

"You do not condone?" Miss Graffam raises her voice.

"We are doing our best, madam," the commander says, his face reddening. "I have one man for every five hundred deportees."

"Yes, and why is that?"

"Why?" The commander raises his voice above hers. "Because we are at war, that is why. We are soldiers, not mother hens." He steps closer, his face centimeters away from Miss Graffam.

"Do you think I want to be escorting this heaping pile of shit you call your flock? We are being attacked on every front by people who worship your god, their god." He keeps his eyes on her, but his finger points at the deportees. "If you hadn't filled their minds with all sorts of ideas, they wouldn't be in this mess." Lucine wonders if this is true. There are rumors that those who convert to Islam will go unharmed.

"This has nothing to do with God," Miss Graffam whispers. "Let me remind you that Germany, your ally in this war, is a Christian nation. Please, let them have a little water."

"You're right, this has nothing to do with God. These people attack us from within our own borders. Collecting arms and waiting patiently to join the Russians and the English when they invade our borders. Every country has the right to do away with traitors."

"These people are not revolutionaries—"

"Enough," he interrupts, shouting. "In this country, madam, we do not discuss politics with women." Then, composing himself, adds, "Tonight you will come to Malatya with me. The governor of the province has requested your presence."

"I will do no such thing," says Miss Graffam.

"You can and you will," he states simply.

"Who will escort these people when you leave?"

"Others. Replacements." He shrugs, walking away from her.

"Perhaps I will tell the governor of our treatment here," she threatens at his back.

"As you wish, madam," he says, an almost imperceptible smile creeping across his face. "We leave in less than an hour."

Miss Graffam leads the last of the hopeful in an impromptu prayer. Lucine stands outside the group and waits patiently for the celestial entreaties to come to an end.

"You didn't join the prayer," Miss Graffam says to her finally.

"I don't need prayer," says Lucine.

"Everyone needs prayer, Lucine."

"Not me. I came to ask you for a favor."

"Anything."

"My father's insurance papers. Can I have them?" asks Lucine.

"They are back in Sivas."

"Then will you take the horses?"

"The horses?" her teacher asks.

"Tell them you can't walk. Make them take both horses. Please."

Miss Graffam's sad eyes drift toward the sleeping infant in

Lucine's arms and then back to Lucine. "All right," she says, nodding her head slowly.

The missionary leaves early that evening, accompanied by the commanding officer and a gendarme, all on horseback. Miss Graffam's big cream-colored hat recedes away from the river. Another trusted adult disappears from her life, but this time it is a gift.

"Where is she going?" Bedros asks.

"Malatya."

"Will she get help?"

"She will try."

"Are we going to be flies and follow her?"

"No, Bedros, where she is going there will be soldiers, and you and I need to stay away from people for a while. We will follow the river down as close as we can, staying close to nature," she says.

"So we won't get swatted," he reasons.

She smiles, surprised at his cleverness and at her ability to smile at it.

"But we're going back for Mairig, right? And Anush?" he asks.

Lucine pretends not to hear him. The four remaining gendarmes issue no new orders. With their commander gone, they disrobe and reward themselves with an impromptu bath in the river. The deportees huddle closer together, turning their backs to the river both from modesty and from envy.

"It'd be nice to bathe with a beauty," the thick-lipped gendarme barks at their backs.

"Anyone who wants to bathe with a beauty won't be bathing

with the likes of you," says a fresh-faced soldier, laughing. He reminds Lucine of a Greek boy who once courted Anush. Earlier in the journey, this soldier seemed kinder than the others, but soon he was just as cross as the rest of them.

Lucine waits until all four are up to their necks in river water. "It's time," she whispers to Bedros. "You walk along the caravan on the side of the river. I will do the same on the other side. Stop along the way, just like a fly would, going from one group of people to the next. Make as if you are searching for family members. When you get to the end of the caravan, make your way to the brush. Aram and I will be there, waiting for you."

"How will I find you?" he asks.

"Don't worry, I will find you."

She waits for the bony mass of his back to recede, then makes her own way to the wild uncultivated bush that dots the road all the way back to the bridge. She sticks her pinky finger into Aram's mouth. He slurps and sucks on the makeshift nipple in relative silence. Very few people raise their heads when she approaches. Everyone is concerned with themselves and what's left of their own. When she gets to the last cluster of deportees, she walks behind the nearest bush and squats as if answering nature's call. The sky goes from blue to gray, deepening until it resembles one of Hairig's fabric dyes. Lucine imagines him standing in his leather apron up in the clouds, stirring the colors of the sky until they are dark enough to protect his loved ones. *Protect me, Hairig. Hide my body from the wolves and vultures.*

She scans the groups of deportees for Bedros. The gendarmes

are out of sight, but she can hear them swimming in the river. A branch snaps behind her and her heart leaps into her mouth. Could Bedros have made it to the bush before her? She remains completely motionless, frozen in her squatting position.

"Don't move." She recognizes the voice as well as the deep, openmouthed breathing of the thick-lipped gendarme. "Don't move and you won't be hurt," he says from behind her. He is closer now, his breath heavy. "Bend over." He wraps one arm around her waist and pushes her neck down with the other until her knees buckle and her forehead hits the ground. Aram squirms on the ground between her elbows and knees.

The gendarme's boot grazes Lucine's calf. He lifts her skirt and rips the bloomers off her backside. Exposed, prostrate, she is too shocked to cry. A bead of water or sweat from above drips down her back. *Dear God.* A prayer bubbles to the surface, but she bites her lip. She will not plead with him. Not with God and not with this bastard. She has never been more afraid. She closes her eyes.

He places his hands on her hips and pulls them to him. But something stops him. Lucine hears a loud thud, like the sound of an empty bucket falling in a deep well. He collapses on top of her, his heavy breathing stopped. She bears the dead weight of his head and torso to protect Aram who is trapped underneath. He slips off her back, and his body lands, like a sack of bulgur, on the ground beside her. From his slack-jawed face a pair of startled eyes stare back at her. When she looks back, Bedros is standing there, a large rock in his hand. Without dropping it, he extends his other hand out to her. It is the same little hand she's been holding all along. She weeps but says nothing.

They walk swiftly, side by side. Lucine wraps the sleeping Aram in his blue swaddling cloth and places him on her back. Empowered by fear, arms swinging, she takes one long stride after another, still holding her brother's hand. As they walk away from the river and toward the mountains, her eyes and ears scan the earth for predators, soldiers, villagers, anything that may come between them and survival.

✒ CHAPTER 22 ✒

Eagle Eye

SOMETHING ABOUT THE tip of the gun embarrasses Kemal, makes him want to cover it up or stand in front of it. Perhaps it is the sharp bayonet poking out at the very end. Kemal knows he is blessed to have it. There are rumors that soldiers all over the empire are without guns. Still, if he could get rid of that bayonet at the end, he would. The other trainees lunge forward, thrusting their bayonets into imaginary abdomens. They whirl like dervishes and strike down hard on the rifle with their left hand, pretending to disembowel their victims.

Only Tekin, the burly one, does not practice. He sits nearby, his uniform straining against the bulk of his body, whittling away at what looks like a small piece of pinewood. Kemal does his own lame dance with the bayonet at a safe distance from the rest of the division before sitting down not far from Tekin. He takes Lucine's handkerchief from his breast pocket and presses it to his nose, letting her lavender smell wash over him. It has been a constant companion, this little pale blue kerchief consecrated with his blood, a reminder of the wound that led him here. He strains his neck toward Tekin, trying to recognize the shape emerging between the man's fingers.

"A finch," says Tekin, his steel-gray eyes glued to the pine and blade. It's the same blade he uses to trim his beard. He is easily a foot taller than all the rest, and much broader, so gets to do as he wants. The perpetual scowl he wears on his face contradicts the smooth, broad brow and straight nose that would otherwise render him handsome. Kemal wonders if Lucine would refuse a specimen of manhood such as Tekin, before remembering that he hasn't got a last name either.

"For my son," Tekin says.

Kemal nods, embarrassed of his thoughts. "Sorry. Didn't mean to pry," he says.

"Damn eunuch," Tekin says.

"Pardon?" asks Kemal.

"You heard me," he says. He stops whittling and turns his eyes to Kemal. "If you're going to apologize every time you fart, burp, or try to kill someone, you're just as worthless as the rest of them." He nods to the group of men dancing with their bayonets.

Sorry, Kemal thinks. "Are you a professional soldier?" he asks.

"No, I'm a professional survivor," says Tekin. "Now if you'll fuck off, I've got some whittling to do."

Kemal wonders how much of the man's temperament is due to hunger. It has been almost two days since their last ration. Even then, there was only one wagon of food for the 370 trainees.

Nurredin Pasha, the officer in charge of their training and transport, is constantly promising more bread, but the mess hall is more or less empty.

When he was first conscripted, Kemal had only his despair to keep him company. He imagined the army would be a haven of adventure and sport. It would pick him up like a gust of wind and throw him to the four corners of the empire. But mostly he hoped it would erase her from his memory and transform him into something new and unrecognizable. At first, it didn't disappoint.

Though the training camp was only sixty kilometers from his home, to him it felt completely foreign. Here he could become whoever he wanted. After an embarrassing medical exam, during which he stripped naked for a man with a peculiar accent and spectacles, Kemal was given his very own uniform: a fez, a jacket, pants, a pair of woolen socks, a water canteen, rawhide sandals, and a pair of puttees—strips of cloth that wrap around his ankle to his knee. All six items were his and his alone, and they gave him a new sense of ownership and importance. But the thrill of being in full uniform disappeared when he remembered she would never see it. Now the uniform only makes the heat more unbearable. Where it once fit snugly around his shoulders and middle, it now hangs loose.

Competing with the heat and hunger is a third discomfort characteristic of his new life: monotony. Morning drills are almost always preceded by a breakfast of weak tea. Bayonet drills and rifle marksmanship take up his afternoons, and evening drills are only rarely interrupted by immunizations and the rare first-aid lesson. And of course, there is the marching. Every time an officer wishes to take a nap or go to the coffee house, the trainees are asked to march. Marching, it seems, is the Ottoman army's answer to everything.

"Damn it!" Tekin's massive hands have accidentally clipped the finch's wings with the carving knife. Grunting, he throws the pine bird into a nearby bush and walks away.

The wingless bird falls from one branch to another until it lands in the mud. The trainees leave for yet another marching drill, but Kemal does not join them. He picks up the wooden creature, tracing his fingers over its crudely carved body. Tiny slashes imitating feathers cover the entire surface, but its eyes and beak are barely visible. Kemal takes a pencil from his breast pocket. He cleans the dust and debris off with the linen; then using his pencil, he begins to revive the pathetic bird. First, he works on the creature's eyes, creating an expression of such fragile beauty that the more difficult task of refashioning its wings becomes a necessity. He ignores the break in the wood where the wings once were and decides to render the bird at rest instead of in midflight. Soon a pair of wings graces the sides of its breast, and expertly drawn tail feathers are etched in its rump.

"Get up, boy." His commanding officer, Nurredin Pasha, stands against a cloudless sky with Lieutenant Hikmet at his side. Kemal stands up, looking straight ahead, back straight, arms at his side, the finch in one hand and the pencil in the other.

"What are you doing here, soldier?" Nurredin asks.

Kemal knows not to answer.

"Why are you not marching with the rest? Who do you think this training is for?"

Kemal says nothing.

"He has a pencil in his hand, sir," Hikmet says. "And a kerchief."

Nurredin snatches Lucine's kerchief from Kemal's hand. He turns it over with disinterest, then throws it back at Kemal.

"A peasant with a pencil," Nureddin says. "Interesting."

"Like a woman with a sword." Hikmet chuckles.

"Tomorrow you will report to the officer's tent for a literacy test," Nurredin says. "But for now, a lesson in obedience. Whip him," he tells Hikmet.

When the first blow lands on his bare back, it makes a noise that rings in his ears and vibrates all the way down his spine. Kemal winces but does not scream. Each time the leather belt lands on his skin, he squeezes the bird in the palm of his hand. And when the thrashing is over, Kemal suddenly decides it will not go to waste. He swipes his fingers across his lower back and spreads the warm red liquid of his insides all over the finch's belly.

Kemal limps to the barracks, carrying the red bird over to the straw mat where Tekin is resting.

"What the hell happened to you?" Tekin asks.

"For your son," replies Kemal, handing him the red-bellied bird.

Tekin stares at Kemal, then at the bird in disbelief. "How?" he begins but does not finish. "Thank you," he says finally cradling the bird in one massive palm.

That evening, Tekin strokes the wooden finch as they listen to the other men talk. In the cover of darkness, Kemal tries to forget his stinging back. He holds Lucine's kerchief to his nose. The faint smell of lavender is all but gone, replaced by the smell of his own sweat.

Hüsnü, a merchant from Istanbul, who on the first day naively demanded sugar with his tea, is complaining again. "How do they expect us to learn how to fight on an empty stomach?" he asks.

"What's a little hunger when you are doing God's work?" Mehmet the Babe, so called for his childlike face and small frame, answers him. "Soon the Prophet himself will open the gates of heaven and present us with seventy-two virgins."

"You can keep your virgins. I'll take a good whore and a long life," Hüsnü says. Peals of laughter rip through the room.

"The keys to paradise are no laughing matter," Mehmet says. "We took an oath of martyrdom on the Koran. We are guaranteed a victory by Allah himself and will be rewarded accordingly."

"Yes, and what will you do with that reward, Mehmet?" Hüsnü asks. "You wouldn't know what to do with one virgin, never mind seventy-two."

Tekin laughs.

"I know plenty," Mehmet says.

"Really? Well, then let's talk about this, shall we?" says Hüsnü, and he begins a graphic discussion of the pleasures of heaven, with heavy emphasis on dark-eyed houris.

Kemal smiles to himself. They are a sorry bunch, as far as soldiers go, but brave. Like him, their training consists mainly of marching under the Anatolian sun, but in their company he goes from being an only son to a brother. Here he is one of 370 conscripts, all born at the tail end of the nineteenth century, to one father, the Ottoman nation. Three hundred seventy young men sleeping in one barrack, eating in one mess hall, training and marching endlessly as one. And though the heat, exhaustion, and monotony are sometimes unbearable, Kemal is cured of his loneliness.

Six weeks later, Kemal is riding a train toward Aleppo and then Baghdad. They are to fight in the Mesopotamian campaign against the British and British India. At certain points on the road, their paths run alongside the deportees, who are being driven to the Syrian Desert. The sight of this collection of displaced humanity, whatever their crime might be, causes Kemal's stomach to turn. He scans the slow-moving crowd, looking from one hollowed-out face to the next. Dirty rags hang like wet laundry from their bones, and their vacant eyes look for death or mercy. He takes comfort in the knowledge that Lucine would not be among them. Her family has money and plenty of connections. Even so, the sight of one woman in particular, her hair tied in a style he recognizes to be a familiar French twist, reminds him of Mrs. Melkonian. Though the woman is a stranger and not his former employer, the sight of her tattered European dress causes Kemal to vomit his breakfast of black bread and tea. He bends over, but the crammed quarters of the railcar make discretion impossible.

"Donkey fucker!" Hüsnü says, shoving him a little. "Get away from my boots."

"See something you can't handle?" says Tekin.

Kemal wipes his mouth with his sleeve but says nothing.

"Before you cry for the Armenian," Tekin continues, "remember he would gladly hand a Russian the knife to slit your throat. The only reason they're out there and you're in here is because we beat them to it."

"It's true," Mehmet adds. "They say hundreds of Armenians have joined the Russians in the eastern province of Van. They store guns and celebrate every time we lose a battle. They even shed Muslim blood on our streets."

Kemal takes another look at the people on foot. There seem to be a thousand or more, mostly women and children, huddled together. Walking against the wind, their backs hunched under bundles, they look more like burdened mules than revolutionaries. He tells himself that the Melkonians are no revolutionaries. Lucine is probably somewhere in the West by now, practicing her English with a prissy young man, someone with new boots and a last name. Suddenly Kemal realizes what the enemy is truly after. If we don't stop them, he thinks, the West will take away more than just our land. They will take our women and our pride, our mosques and our manhood.

Kemal turns his gaze away from the deportees. He studies the uniformed men around him like he would a landscape or tapestry, with an eye toward detail. He notices Hüsnü's clipped fingernails and pomaded mustache, and the way Tekin's face softens whenever he's whittling. He sees Mehmet's grip tighten on his bayonet whenever he speaks of the enemy or death. White knuckles on brown wood grain.

The details give Kemal an insight into the most tender parts of his new friends. His heart aches for them and for himself, and there is a part of him that hopes this war is truly holy and sanctioned by Allah, because how else can they bear it, really?

THE BATTLE IS to take place in Ctesiphon, which lies on the left bank of the Tigris River in the barren Mesopotamian desert, about sixteen miles southeast of Baghdad. Nurredin Pasha, whose hatred for the Greeks and Armenians, any Christians really, will prove to be useful in battle, now commands two other divisions, but they consist mostly of Arabs. Together his men number over eighteen thousand strong. The Arab soldiers are more seasoned. They eye Kemal and the other conscripts with a palpable contempt. Commander Nurredin speaks to the Arabs in their own tongue, which impresses Kemal. He will never reconcile the man's intelligence with his brutality. It is the first time Kemal has ever seen those qualities contained within a single man.

Kemal follows every order, listens much, and speaks little. He scans faces and landscapes, taking notes and measuring the frailty of friend and foe alike. His eyes, which once only searched for beauty, can now see a target from miles away. The men take to calling him Eagle Eye. When Nurredin Pasha hears of this, he calls Kemal to a private meeting and hands him a Mauser. Unlike the standard issue Turkish rifle and bayonet, it incorporates the clip and magazine into a single detachable mechanism, and although it is unsuited for rapid-fire warfare, the fitted optical sight piece makes it ideal for sniping. It is the only one of its kind in the division, and Kemal promises the pasha he will put it to good use. Secretly, he says a prayer of gratitude, relieved that his hands at least will not be stained with a stranger's blood. He will not have to hear a man groan or meet his last gaze.

In Ctesiphon, the 130-degree heat of the Mesopotamian desert gives way to the torrential rains of the fall season. Soldiers who for months prayed for water and shade now strive to keep everything from washing away. The men dig from dusk until dawn, creating a continuous embankment along the trenches of the riverbank. Sand bags are piled twelve feet high and moats are dug around each and every tent in camp.

Kemal is stationed three miles south of the main line in an ancient fortress, with a giant arch at its center. Rumored to be the remains of a Parthian capital, it now serves as an observation post. He spends hours, days, and weeks patiently looking through his scope. He imagines a line, smooth and obedient, stretching from his eye to the tip of the Mauser and eventually to the target.

Mehmet the Babe is given the task of positioning an old fez in multiple locations along where the enemy is expected. Kemal blinks, holds his breath, and only when he is sure the bullet is ready, and the line will be drawn perfectly, does he release both his breath and the bullet. Kemal discovers he can make a bullet do things others cannot. The fez is transformed into a mutilated red rag in a matter of minutes. Kemal is told to target the birds instead.

The first time he kills, Kemal weeps over the body of his victim, a yellow-breasted bulbul. He holds the bird in his palm, its one eye staring up at him.

"What in Allah's name are you crying about?" Tekin asks. "What did you think you were conscripted for?"

Kemal turns away, suppressing his tears.

"What? Did you think you would be immune to tragedy in that big safe arch of yours?"

"He was innocent," Kemal says, wiping his face.

"We are all innocent," says Tekin. "Stand up." His voice is more gentle than usual. "Put the bird down," he says, placing his hands on Kemal's shoulders.

"I'd give my left arm to be stationed in that throne of safety you call an observation post. You don't have to smell and taste death, like the rest of us. But you're still here to do the same job. Understand?"

Kemal says nothing.

"Do you believe the bit about the virgins?" Tekin asks.

"I'm not sure," replies Kemal.

Tekin nods. "Well, what about your mother? You are eager to get back to her, am I right?"

Kemal thinks about this. He tries to recall an image of his mother, but she died so long ago. All he sees is his grandmother competing at the loom with Emineh.

"Never mind that. What about a woman? Have you got your eye on a woman?"

Kemal's face flushes as he remembers Hüsnü's detailed description of a woman's body. He thinks of his own innocent sketches of Lucine, of all the parts of her he never knew. The thought makes his chest hurt and his eyes sting. He shrugs Tekin's hands off his shoulders. "No. There's no woman," he says.

"Then why so angry all of a sudden?"

"I'm not angry," says Kemal.

"The hell you're not."

"Fuck off, Tekin."

Tekin laughs deeply, from his belly. "Fine, I'll fuck off. You can forget the woman or not, it's none of my business, but let me tell you something. Here, you are Eagle Eye. You have a job to do and that is to survive."

I am Eagle Eye, Kemal tells himself, so that one day he can abandon the name and the scope and return to being Kemal again.

Ctesiphon

THE BRITISH ATTACK begins on an especially clear evening in the middle of November, with the kind of night sky made for stargazing. Nurredin Pasha orders the men to form two well-camouflaged lines of trenches crossing the Tigris River. The more seasoned Arab soldiers are placed on the east bank, where the brown water is already rising to meet the land. His friends in the Forty-fifth Division are stationed somewhere on the west bank. But this isn't the time to think of them.

Eagle Eye is lying flat, with his chest, stomach, knees and feet immersed in the runny shit-colored mud of the earth. His body and rifle are covered entirely by leaves and branches. When he stays motionless, as he is now, even his comrades have trouble finding him. Behind him the din of machine guns and artillery rifles rip through sky, earth and limbs.

He shuts his eyes and listens to his breath. It travels up his chest, to his neck, then back again, until finally it reaches his right index finger. He opens his eyes again. His breath, vision, and rifle become one. Through his scope, he sees two enemy officers standing beside a low table near a mud-covered tent. He knows from the missionaries what a European man looks like, but these men look nothing like what he expected. They are dark-skinned and sport large curving mustaches. Nurredin calls these brown men who are British subjects "Indyan." The older one wears a turban on his head like those who've visited the haj. Any minute now they may place a prayer rug in the direction of Mecca. Nothing about this war makes sense. How can this be a holy war if our allies pray to the Christian god and our enemies look as if they carry prayer rugs? He remembers Tekin's words. He has a job to do, to survive, and these two would stop him if they could.

The one with the turban points down at what Eagle assumes is a map. They think they are safe. They are not. They stand on a mound of elevated mud, 150 meters away from where he is, and though his rifle is only capable of launching a bullet three hundred or four hundred feet, Eagle isn't worried. He doesn't think about the thirty-degree angle of elevation he's supposed to assume to maximize the distance of his bullets. He doesn't pay any attention to the kinds of calculations they taught him during training. He simply closes his eye, steadies his breath, and draws a line. A clean line from his eye, to the tip of his rifle, and beyond. Not a straight line but an arc, lovely and pure, only it ends in death.

Eagle releases breath and bullet. The turbaned one doing all the pointing drops to the floor, a privilege due to his higher ranking. There is very little blood. Eagle makes sure of it. The other soldier ducks behind a boulder. He looks around but sees nothing. Eagle stays still. This one will live. He will go back to France or

England or wherever his dark-skinned people live, never knowing that a man called Eagle Eye, who once was Kemal, who once loved Lucine, considered killing him.

He continues this way until nightfall, remembering the face of every man he kills, trying hard not to think about who they are or aren't. More than once, he envies his friends in the trenches. How wrong he had been to think of sniping as a gentler brand of killing. In the trenches, men engage in dozens of fifteen-minute offensives, with every weapon in the division firing collectively in the general direction of the enemy. No one can be certain of the trajectory of his own bullet. And their shared shame or glory is, in Kemal's view, a much lighter burden to bear.

The brown British advance slowly up the river. The mud rises to their knees, making easy targets of all but the most careful ones. Kemal likens their clumsy bodies to flightless ducks. He marvels at the congruence of ingenuity and idiocy of this race. How can these men, who can't even navigate their bodies safely across the water, be responsible for the massive battleships and gunboats that float down the river? How have these fools, who call everyone on the Turkish side "Abdul," managed to build air vessels that glide across the sky, laying explosive eggs all over the land?

Thankfully, their gunboats explode in puffs of dark smoke, eliminated by carefully laid mines in the river. And Kemal is grateful that he need only face these men and not their machines. Though the enemy manages somehow to capture the first line of trenches, it is a small victory. Their dead litter the banks of the Tigris.

Kemal shivers as an errant drop of rainwater trickles down his neck. He wiggles his toes, numb and wet in their ill-fitting army boots. Through his scope, he spots Hüsnü and Tekin. His friends are safe.

He turns around to find the enemy, but they are out of range, moving closer to the river, no doubt in search of water. Dozens are busy loading the wounded onto springless carts. The cartloads of tattered bodies will be bumped to death or killed by the fresh downpour that will inevitably rain on their open wounds, but what is it to him? The enemy is retreating or else taking a much-deserved break.

THE NEXT DAY, Kemal is sleeping in a trench when the sun beats down on his head and wakes him. The familiar call of the bugle is missing, and the screaming sirens of death have gone silent.

"They're gone," says Mehmet the Babe. He is washing himself with a British helmet filled with water.

"Have we won?" asks Kemal, removing a branch from his back.

"Glory be to God. Nurredin was about to call a retreat, but it looks like we'll be chasing the infidels to Kut now."

"Kut?"

"Toward Baghdad."

Survival is a strange thing, he thinks. Not as triumphant as he had imagined. Not a thing separate from death but akin to it. And though Kemal is still living, death permeates his every breath. Death floats in the material world, hiding in every sight, sound and smell, until everything is perceived in relation to it.

"Where's Tekin?" Kemal asks.

Mehmet says nothing.

"Hüsnü?" asks Kemal.

Mehmet points toward the river. "He's probably combing through the sea of corpses for a new pair of boots," he says.

Kemal struggles to his feet, still carrying his coat of leaves and branches. Everywhere the ground is covered by bodies fossilized in the mud. Vagrant limbs stick out like weeds. A swarm of flies descends upon friend and foe alike, but the sight is nothing compared to the stench.

Kemal weaves through the mud, taking care not to look down at the human debris, lest his nausea gets the better of him. He presses Lucine's pale blue handkerchief to his nose, but the smell gets stronger as he nears the river. Suddenly he doubles over, vomiting over his own boots.

"You look like a vomiting bush," a humorless voice says. Kemal looks up to find Hüsnü standing over him.

"Glad to see you too," Kemal says.

"Seen Tekin?" asks Hüsnü. His eyes continue scanning the ground.

"No, I just woke up. Mehmet hasn't seen him either."

"Humph! Of course he hasn't. That little pussy lice has been prostrating himself before Allah all morning. He doesn't even pause to help me look for Tekin."

"He was washing himself, not praying," Kemal says.

"That's the only other thing that ass giver is good for: ablution."

"That's not true. He's a brave fighter. We all are," Kemal says.

"Go and join him then if you're so fond of him. I'm looking for Tekin."

Kemal does not respond. "The last time I saw him, it was through my scope. He was right over there. In fact, you both were."

"Yeah? What the hell were you doing staring at us when you're supposed to be shooting at them?" Hüsnü steps toward him, his eyes seething with anger. "It must be nice to shoot the enemy from three hundred yards away, hiding in a bush, while the rest of us fight tooth to tooth."

The bastard. "You know what's nice? What's nice is shooting blindly into the dusty unknown, with your comrades flanked on both sides, so no one need take responsibility for ending a life. That's what's nice." Kemal presses his finger into Hüsnü's chest.

"Fuck responsibility," Hüsnü says, stepping forward so that some of his spittle lands on Kemal's chin. "We're the ones who get shot back at while you hide in a bush."

"You're the only brave soldier. Is that it, Hüsnü?" says Kemal. "Brave Hüsnü, who kills the British but fails to save his friends."

"Shut up, " says Hüsnü, shoving Kemal back with both palms.

"No, you shut up," Kemal pushes him back. His hands land higher on Hüsnü's body, near his neck, and with greater impact than he intended. Hüsnü falls backward before springing back up. Once on his feet, he swings at Kemal's jaw. Kemal feels nothing except rage. He strikes at Hüsnü's ear and knees him in the groin.

Hüsnü stays on his knees panting, then lunges at Kemal's calves and wrestles him to the ground. The two soldiers are soon covered in mud, their arms and legs struggling against being pinned by the other. Kemal ducks his head from under Hüsnü's arm and manages to pull away. They continue panting for breath a few feet from one another. Kemal eventually lies down on his back. Gulping for air, he turns to Hüsnü who is holding a hand to his bloody ear.

"The rest of us are shit, right?" Kemal says. "Mehmet for his prayers and me for my tears. Ass givers and donkey fuckers."

There is a long pause as Hüsnü stares at him with a blank look on his face. "And pussy lice," he says finally, his upper lip curving mischievously the way it does just before he smiles.

The two lock eyes, then burst out into laughter.

"Let's go find Tekin," says Hüsnü, extending his hand.

Kemal nods and makes to get to his feet when he sees Mehmet the Babe approaching.

"There is no need to find Tekin," says Mehmet.

"Why? Have you found him?"

Mehmet nods his head. "I've just come back from the infirmary," he says. He does not look at either one of them.

"Is he badly hurt?" asks Hüsnü.

Mehmet the Babe looks past Hüsnü, directly at Kemal. "No," he says. "He is not hurt. He's gone to be with his maker."

Kemal feels as if he's swallowed a piece of shrapnel. His tears, so often shed for paltry birds and strangers, are no longer at the ready. It is Hüsnü who breaks down, hiding his face in his sleeve.

The three friends carry Tekin's body to a hilltop facing the arch of Ctesiphon. The imam is nowhere to be found so Mehmet directs the cleansing of the body and wraps it in a shroud made from the shirts of fallen soldiers. It is the best they can do in these circumstances. Kemal tucks the wooden finch meant for his son in Tekin's lifeless hands. These are hands that killed the enemy and also whittled a toy bird for his child, he thinks.

"*Inna lillahi wa inna ilayhi raji'un,*" Mehmet chants in Arabic. "To Allah we belong and to him we shall return."

Kemal listens as Mehmet's voice washes over Tekin's body before being carried away by the wind. The words speak of the same god who sanctioned this war, this war that took away Nazareth and then Lucine. This war that has now claimed Tekin and is slowly claiming bits of Kemal's own soul. And for what? For some pasha or war minister they've never even seen and for some god whose identity and nature no one can agree upon. Kemal is now certain there is no truth or beauty in this god, just as there is no truth or beauty in this war.

CHAPTER 24

Place of Sin

"HOW MANY?" FATMA asks. The boy, Ahmet, grunts in response.

"How many today?" Fatma demands to know.

"Three," the boy answers.

"And is he among them?"

They begin every morning in this fashion. Fatma asks the first question and quickly follows it with the second. When the troops were first garrisoned in Malatya, Fatma saw it as a sign of God's mercy. The Almighty had taken her husband, taken her parents, and left her with an invalid mother-in-law whose dependence on her was continually increasing. Desperate for money, she had gone to the lieutenant governor of Malatya to offer the troops lodging and meals. Nabi Bey had a reputation for being a just and moral man. The rumor was that he had initially defied the deportation orders, sparing hundreds of Armenian women and children. Fatma, who had expected a portly, balding man, was taken aback by the lieutenant governor's bright green eyes and freshly pomaded hair. For his part, Nabi Bey took one look at Fatma's black curls and full lips and appointed her innkeeper of an abandoned khan just outside the city proper, with only her mother-in-law and a boy named Ahmet as helpers. The troops arrived shortly thereafter, which is also precisely when Nabi Bey began his daily visits. Being married did not slow down the lieutenant governor's courting of Fatma. A courting that began on his first visit, to which he brought with him a sack of pistachios and asked only for tea, and ended a few visits later, when he gifted Fatma with two herrings and a gilded hand mirror in exchange for her body's warmth.

At first, her mother-in-law treated the lieutenant like a proper suitor, hoping against hope that the widow girl, who had brought her nothing but bad luck, was finally going to be useful. And though Fatma could sense her mother-in-law's disapproval, she also noticed that the old woman's moral outrage didn't prevent her from enjoying the herring. All the snorts and grimaces stopped with the arrival of deportees from the eastern provinces, the sight of them reminding the old lady that as Kurds their loyalty could also be questioned. The deportees marched through town like the walking dead, clothed in rags, stinking so badly that the old woman put carbolic acid on the windowsill to keep the stench away. Dogs and birds followed them wherever they went, tracking the scent of death. Bodies were carted away in the darkness, buried, their possessions burned or stolen. The people of Malatya looked on in horror or hate, feeling better about their own lot. A few risked their lives to save a child here, feed a mother there, but soon they returned to the business of their own survival.

When Fatma finally relented to her suitor's wishes, Nabi Bey suddenly insisted upon paying her for what she had already given him more or less freely. He placed three *para*s on the indentation of the mattress where his body had lain. Fatma stared at the coins for a few moments, knowing their power over her life, before curling her fingers around them. Soon after, in a moment of despair, after another one of his visits procured barely enough to feed a mouse, Fatma told the bey that any soldier willing to pay was welcome to her services. Her mother-in-law, who until then needed bread more than she needed a chaste daughter-in-law, expressed her disapproval by practically climbing into her burial shroud and dying.

For her part, Fatma now thinks of her sex as a cabinet of sorts. Men open and shut its doors, putting things in and taking things out. When the cabinet between her legs hums and gyrates in response to a rough caress or a slow kneading, she tells herself that it is separate from her. Inside her but separate, like a piece of furniture she's inadvertently swallowed. She gets up, determined to see if Nabi Bey is among the three waiting for her. She feels drawn to him despite how he has treated her. He is one of only two men who have ever piqued her interest. The first turned her into a widow; the second, into a whore.

Drawing her shoulders back and donning a haughty expression, she walks into the main room where, indeed, Nabi Bey is seated across from two other rather scrawny-looking soldiers leaning against the wall. Upon seeing her, he rises from the divan. But Fatma strides right past him, extending her hand to one of the young soldiers in the back of the room. Nabi Bey stands red-faced while the soldiers mumble something about not minding the wait.

Fatma claps her hands at the boy, saying, "Come, come. Neither God nor the devil recognizes rank in these walls."

When his turn finally comes, Nabi Bey is more interested in giving Fatma a lashing than receiving any pleasure from her.

"You ungrateful whore! What kind of pleasure do you get from belittling me, huh?"

"I wasn't a whore until I met you," Fatma says.

"That's true. You were a lowly Kurdish cunt leaching off your dead husband's mother. Without me, you'd be starving or dead. Do you know what is happening right now to thousands like you?"

It is a rhetorical question. She is no Christian and he knows it. Still, Fatma is determined to find out more about what is happening in the world. The troops of the Tenth Army Corps, who started as her guests and became her clients, have provided Fatma with a great deal of information. Bit by bit, as men dropped their pants, prodded her with their fingers, or reached into their pockets for a few *para*s, she's learned about Malatya and the empire. But she can no longer stay in the little house blind and dumb to what is happening outside, spreading her legs by day and sniffing her dead husband's ghost by night. For now, she concentrates on making Nabi Bey forget her offenses and remember her many "virtues." She leans back on her divan, exaggerating the arch in her back and letting her heavy breasts go their separate ways on her torso.

Nabi Bey lowers himself on top of her. She lies inert, letting his considerable weight press her back deeper and deeper into the straw mat until she can feel the stalks pressing into her flesh. The straw is bothersome, as is the moistness that turns his body into a slippery whale of a fish. But what is intolerable is the scent that accompanies the ordeal. The man's gastro-intestinal adventures waft out of his pores and into Fatma's flared nostrils. Garlic, pistachio, and cured meat. *Aman Allah*. Dear God.

Her sight is the only one of her senses that dances to the rhythm of a distant harmonious melody, far away from here. She fixes her eyes upon a spot in the ceiling. It looks like an oil stain just above the bed. *Now how did an oil stain make its way up there?* If a splotch of oil could find its way up seven feet and lodge itself permanently to a ceiling, then surely Fatma could find herself far away from this room—in an equally unpredictable spot in the universe.

Hours later, with her customers all gone, Fatma sits on the floor, away from the dreaded divan where she spends her days. She places the basin between her spread legs and begins her nightly cleansing ritual. She spends every evening like this, cleaning her place of sin. As a child, she hadn't noticed the mystery in between her thighs. She skipped and climbed trees with all the other girls and boys, but then the two dark cherries on her chest grew into apricots, then melons. She was covered in a head scarf and hidden, forbidden to play and told she was shameful. She hated that place between her legs until Ibrahim, her husband, came to worship there nightly.

Now she hunches over herself, carefully cleaning the folds of delicate skin that make men weep and quiver, and keep her alive and well. She pays it its proper respects but knows that like everything else it mustn't be overused. When the ritual is over, Fatma remains seated on the floor, contemplating her trip to the Armenian Quarter, or what is left of it. Those who left with nothing more than an oxcart are said to have buried their gold in courtyards and orchards. There, in the abandoned homes of her former neighbors, she might find some hidden treasure that will help her escape this life.

Given the climate in the village, Fatma has left the inn only twice in the past year, once to the mosque and once to the *hamam*. Both times she took care to cover herself and was accompanied by her mother-in-law. At the *hamam,* the village women had taken pleasure in taunting her. A few refused to share the bathhouse with that *orospu,* dirty whore.

Her husband had been the only son of the town butcher. When his father died, the mothers and aunties of the village paraded their daughters around him expectantly, but it was far too late. By then Ibrahim had fallen under the spell of his youngest and toughest customer. He liked to say it was Fatma's haggling tongue that did him in, but Fatma suspected it was the way she let her head scarf drop every time she smiled at him. His mother's illness gave Fatma a rare opportunity to rule the house. Where other young brides bowed their heads in submission to their husbands and mothers-in-law, Fatma made decisions and gave her opinion freely. Outside the house, she shrugged off the insults.

Ignoring the jeers and hisses from the villagers, she laughed her loud laugh and spat at those who dared cross her. When confronted about his wife's behavior, Ibrahim only smiled and encouraged anyone who disapproved to take their oxcart to the only other butcher in the region, located some twenty kilometers to the east.

It has been two years since Ibrahim left for the Balkan front and two months since Fatma buried her mother-in-law. If Ibrahim appeared to her now, she would beg his forgiveness. She pulls her veil down, making sure the dark wool covers her entire face and body. She extends her hand, pretending to reach for something and notices that this exposes a sliver of skin where her hand meets her wrist. The fabric, concealing everything but her kohl-rimmed eyes, is meant to provide a measure of modesty but covering herself always gives Fatma a surge of power. Under its folds, her past is erased and her sins absolved. Besides, these days there is nothing modest about her. Like the veil, which separates her body from the world, she exists now only in the in-between places. Between modesty and seduction, damnation and deliverance.

Once on the street, Fatma keeps her eyes lowered and her steps quick. Using her sense of smell to guide her, she strides past the scent of dead skin and soap outside the *hamam* and through the back alleys of the spice market where the smell of mint and garlic almost makes her stop. When she reaches the merchant's stalls that mark the beginning of the Armenian Quarter,

Fatma thinks that perhaps her trusty nose has finally betrayed her. Where once the blacksmiths, cobblers, and tinsmiths released clouds of copper, sulfur, and leather dye into the dusty air of Malatya, Fatma now smells something entirely different. She is sure the devil himself has vomited onto the earth's crust, producing an odor so vile and permeable that it burns her eyes and throat.

Gone too are the sounds of clanging metal, the scraping of soft bristles on leather, and the excitement of human voices straining above the clamor of the once-bustling market. Fruit flies swarm past her, swooping up before her eyes, daring her to look up. The shock is not in what she sees but what she doesn't see. The merchants are all gone, their overturned stalls and broken windows offering silent testimony of hasty departures. The door of the Armenian Church is splintered, as though some demonic animal with large horns has pummeled through it. *Someone must have tried to take shelter here.* She says a silent prayer even though she is quite convinced by now that there is no god, not in heaven and certainly not here in Anatolia.

She places an acid-soaked handkerchief to her nose and quickens her steps, veering as far away from the river as possible, thinking only of survival. A sea of twinkling stars, blasphemous in their majesty, illuminates the dark night. How dare they shine on so much suffering? And then it occurs to her that these stars have borne witness.

"What have you seen?" she whispers, looking up. She is half

waiting for an answer when her foot collides with something and her body falls to the ground. It is a body, sickly smelling but not yet ripe with death. Fatma rolls away at once. The body groans. It turns on its side, away from her, clutching what looks like an infant's swaddling cloth. From the long wild mane, she knows it is a girl.

CHAPTER 25

Rebirth

THE DRY DIRT of the desert covers the open sores on her feet. Huddled in one corner of the abandoned shed, Lucine shuts her eyes and tries to pray, but the words, so carefully etched into her mind by Mairig and their priest, have escaped her. Fragments and short phrases from ancient prayers rise above the fog, empty and impotent: the crazed ramblings of a misguided race. She pushes the words aside and presses Aram's blue swaddling cloth to her chest instead. The smell of Mairig's milk is long gone, but inside its soft folds she can still smell the sweetness of him. She burrows her face in the tattered blue wool of his swaddling cloth, sniffing at the lingering scent of his sweat and licking its center where she still tastes the salt of his tears or hers, she isn't sure. Soon his screams, long melodic wails, followed by a staccato of angry reprieves, fill the empty shed, and she is glad. She will do nothing to stop them this time.

A dusty beam of daylight filters through the small crack in the back wall through which her keeper, the plump woman, regularly wedges small pieces of cured lamb and bread. Lucine tries to relieve herself as far away from this opening as she can, but the chamber pot sits festering in the opposite corner. The excrement, like so much suffering, is ongoing and unpredictable. It leaves her as Mairig and Anush and Bedros left her, permanently and without warning. In her arms, a silent witness to all this exorcism, Aram's ghost gives up his screaming and sucks impatiently at her breast, the only part of her body incapable of excretion.

At nightfall, the plump one arrives carrying her stale bread. She talks about how the gendarmes liked to lick her back and pull her hair as they thrust themselves in and out of her.

"How are you today?" she asks Lucine, but Lucine does not answer. She hasn't spoken since the river.

"How is the child?" the woman tries again.

Lucine continues rocking the phantom Aram.

"What does he eat?" the woman asks.

Lucine lays a hand on her concave chest.

The woman sings, *"Dandini, dandini danalı bebek. Elleri kolları kinalı bebek."* It is a lullaby to an infant resting in a secret hiding place. When the infant dies, its mother goes mad and buries it in a golden cradle, then offers herself to the waves. A fitting ditty, only this wasn't the exact order of things.

Some days later, when the plump one is once again delivering her bread, Aram is gone. His screams recede from her ears to the back of her head, like church bells in a dream. The swaddling cloth lies weightless on her lap. Lucine is searching its folds for any evidence of him: a hair, a stain, but all that remains is the smell of her own vomit and shit. Still, she searches for his spirit in the now-coarse fabric of the swaddling cloth. The plump one finally pries the blue wool out of Lucine's hands.

"You can come out now," she says. "You'll live with me. I've arranged it."

Lucine cries out at the words *you'll live.* A hot liquid anger courses through her veins. She strikes the woman over and over again, in the face, shoulders and chest. The woman wraps her plump arms around Lucine's body and squeezes. She writhes and thrashes until her strength gives out and her limbs go limp with grief. There, with her head pressed into the woman's ample bosom, and her arms pinned to her sides, Lucine succumbs to life and to living. She slides down to the earth with the woman's arms wrapped around her.

"We are not what is done to us," she whispers in Lucine's ear. She pulls something silver and smooth from the pocket of her dress. Lucine stares at the blade with relief, thinking the woman will now end all her suffering. Lucine tilts her head back, offering her exposed neck to the stranger.

"My name is Fatma and Allah has placed you in my protection," she says. "Gold doesn't lose its value by falling into the mud," she mutters to herself, scraping the flat, cool blade against Lucine's scalp. Clumps of hair, like small rat's nests, fall to the ground and soon she can feel the wind prickling the back of her head.

"Now we burn these rags," Fatma says, peeling the tattered dress off Lucine's body. She gives her a smock to cover her nakedness and burns the dress right there on the spot. Lucine thinks of the lice in her hair and in her clothing burning to their deaths.

Perhaps this was how God sent death to our door, without a single thought.

Dressed in the plain smock, her feet bare, Lucine's apparel is a far cry from the rustling dresses Mairig forced upon her. Fatma wraps a dark head scarf around her bald scalp and face.

"You need a Turkish name," she says. "From now on you will answer to Seda. It means 'echo,' so that you may find your voice again."

Lucine chews the pair of unfamiliar syllables in between her teeth and in the space between the roof of her mouth and the tip of her tongue. The name, like her silence, is comforting. It allows her to disappear from a world where children die and mothers lose their minds, where the sun continues to climb the sky and the rooster's screech still grates against morning sleep. And for this and only this, she is most grateful. Everything else, from the head scarf to the breath going in and out of her lungs, is unwanted. All these she would gladly give back, but the name is different. The name she keeps, along with her silence.

She follows Fatma into the moonlit night. They walk out of the orchard that housed the shed, and past a field, then into a courtyard. A boy, only a few years older than Bedros, is lying on the floor with nothing but a *yorgan* to keep him warm.

"That is Ahmet," says Fatma. "He takes care of the animals of our guests." The boy looks at her without turning his head. His eyes are dull like an old man's.

The khan is a dark building made of stone and timber. Fatma

walks around the main entrance and leads her to a small room in the back of the building.

"This is where you will spend your days, " she says, opening the little door. The lilt in her accent reveals that she is Kurdish. "Through that door is the main chamber, where the men eat their meals and drink their raki. You must never go into that room. They can't know you are here. I'm risking my life by keeping you here. Understand?"

Seda understands. *They* are the soldiers, the ones who mix suffering with sport. The Kurdish woman could be hanged for helping her. The room is no bigger than a closet. A *tonir,* just like Mairig's, sits at the center of the floor, except its open mouth threatens to swallow her whole. There is a small wooden table and a single chair facing a paneless window that looks more like a hole than a proper opening. Under the table is a wooden crate. It holds two knives, a ladle, four pots of varying sizes, and clay jars of pickled cabbage. Sacks of wheat, rice, and bulgur lean against the remaining three walls. A wooden ladder rests against an opening in the ceiling.

"Up there is my room," says Fatma. "At night, when a soldier is visiting, you stay away. In the morning, when he's gone, I'll knock on the opening four times. You can come up then and clean or put away the bedding. The bedding has to be cleaned every few days. You will also be in charge of the meals. Ahmet and I will serve them, but you must prepare them.

"Can you cook?" Fatma asks.

Lucine has never cooked a meal all by herself. She has shelled peas, dried figs, and salted meat but doesn't know what comes before or after any of these steps. These things were relegated to the servant, Ayse, and sometimes to Anush and Mairig and to all the other women whom she has loved and lost. But Lucine remembers that she is Seda now and nods her head yes.

In the days and weeks that follow, Seda follows Fatma closely, does what she is told. She cleans. She cooks. She delouses *yorgans*. She waits for death to visit her in the night. All the while Aram's wailing rings in her ears. The sight of his flailing arms, Anush's waist cinched by a uniformed arm, Bedros lying prostrate on the grass, and Mairig with her crumpled Bible pages, all these she sees in the daily wash and at the bottom of the barley soup.

Twice a week, she climbs up the stairs to the three little rooms on the second floor but only after Fatma gives her the signal. These are the rooms where Fatma entertains the gendarmes and her bey and where a wandering traveler will stay for more than one night.

Soldiers, merchants, and the occasional missionary travel through these walls without ever seeing her. She is a spirit—a ghost—soundless and practically invisible. Existing only in the in-between spaces—between daylight and darkness, in the narrow wall between the main mess hall and the inner chambers. And though they cannot see her, she sees them.

She sees merchants eating their watery porridge, their cunning eyes darting from one side of the room to the other. They rarely ever sleep indoors, preferring to stay with their animals and goods. The soldiers are an entirely different matter. Most are officers who, tired of the earth and sun, crave the comforts of a clean *yorgan* and a hot meal. She does her best to avoid them. Even when they are asleep or unconscious, they make her wild with fear and hate. She wants to cram their discarded shits back into their postcoital slack-jawed mouths.

The American missionaries politely sip their tea, not knowing that hiding in the shadows is someone who can hear and understand the insults they lob at Turkish soldiers in hushed English whispers. At night, she presses her ear to the curtained wall of their chambers, drinking in the sounds of their English words. They speak and pray. They liken what is happening in Anatolia to hell. This almost makes her laugh. What do they know of hell? Hell is to witness all this and still soak the cracked wheat in water, to empty the chamber pots of fools and murderers. She wants to scream at them, Your mighty god is a joke, but to do this she would have to give up her silence. And that she will never do.

CHAPTER 26

Altar of Contrition

EARLY EVERY MORNING, Ahmet goes to the well to fetch water. He leaves well before the cock crows, before the women of the village trickle down from the valley. When he comes to Seda's little room to fetch the water pails, he makes a point of waking her with his noise.

"This is women's work," he complains.

Seda does not rise or respond. She does not tell him how the well beckons to her, how when she wakens in the middle of the night, cursing the breath that enters her lungs, it is the well's promise of solace that soothes her. How she regularly imagines slipping out of her room, bare feet on wet grass, past the orchard, climbing the low stone wall and falling into the depth of water until it fills her lungs. She tells him none of this.

She turns to the cooking, instead. Beneath the cauldron, flames lick the weathered cast iron, heating the water until it scalds the cabbage leaves, releasing a putrid smell. Pungent. Not like burning flesh. No, not like that. Seda lifts the wooden spoon and places the boiled cabbage leaves, piled one on top of the other, in one corner of the tray. She lifts one, with her fingers, letting the steam prick her fingertips. The hot leaf, its translucent skin the color of rain, gives her the gift of pain, of feeling. She flattens the leaf, then places her burned fingertips in the cool mixture of the filling, but it offers her no pleasure.

There is always plenty to eat here. Fatma's bey makes sure of it. And though Seda spends almost all her time in this little room that is half oven, she eats little or nothing. She sees no reason to sustain this body, prolong this life.

Sometimes the baby still visits her. She cradles him, soft and pink, inside her arms. But when she opens her mouth to sing him a lullaby, nothing comes out. Her mouth is no longer a portal. Nothing but breath comes out and very little goes in.

A few morsels slide down her throat but only when Fatma insists upon watching.

"Don't you dare bring that back up," she says, waving a stout finger in her face. "There are people starving everywhere."

I know. I know. I know.

The third winter of her visit has come and gone. They say the war will soon come to an end. And yet she has hardly enough on her bones to distinguish her as female. The head scarf is the only thing that gives her away. Not that it is necessary. She is almost always hidden. A ghost vanishing into the stone walls and hidden chambers of the ancient inn. Her body receding, her voice gone.

Hairig, I would give all my teeth and fingernails to see you again. It would be a small price.

And he does come. Not in her sleep, like she would prefer,

but while she is awake, chopping the parsley or beating the wool. He whispers in her left ear. Always the left. But instead of solace, he brings her more worry for he speaks in the foreign tongue of the dead.

What are you saying? Please, please, tell me what you are saying. Say it in Armenian, Hairig. I would do anything to hear it in Armenian.

On more than one occasion, Fatma has witnessed her silent begging. "Do not spend your time with ghosts. Trust me, I know what I'm talking about." But what does she know? The closest thing she's come to a man like Hairig is her bey, that patron saint of whores and sinners.

Nabi Bey, who thinks she's a poor Kurd, pays no attention to her. She is like the mule in the stable, the pail in the well, a useful thing to be tolerated. He forgets she is there. Or so she thinks.

She is standing at the table, adding onions to the pot, on the day he enters her little room. His smell, a mixture of pistachios and cured meat, fills the air between them. The stuffed cabbage leaves lay steaming on the tray. He looks around at her world before leaning against the table and picking up the tin cup she uses for measuring. He turns it around in his hand, studying it like it's a rare thing, before putting it down. He picks up one of her rolled cabbage leaves, blows on it at length, before placing it into his mouth. He does this slowly, his eyes pinned to her face.

Seda pours barley into the pot with the onions and, turning her back to him, takes it to the fire. He will think it rude, disrespectful, but she cannot stand him looking at her. She stirs the barley until it turns into mush. Fatma will be unhappy. Seda can hear the rustling of his pants as he shifts his weight. She knows those pants. The dark fabric of an Ottoman soldier's uniform. Only Nabi Bey's pants are not torn or crumpled, not stained with sweat or blood. They are always clean, always pressed, a severe line of demarcation running down the front of both his legs. Who put them there so dutifully? Not Fatma, but some other woman. Someone he calls wife. Someone who's borne him three daughters and no sons.

"Turn around," he says. And she obeys.

"How long have you lived here?" he asks.

Seda lifts her right hand and shows him three fingers. One for each year.

"You live because I allow it," he says finally. "Remember that."

Seda stays right where she is, bracing herself for him to approach, remembering that other time, when Bedros stood above her exposed body, holding a giant rock. But within seconds she hears the door slam shut and he is gone.

Fatma enters soon after that. In her hand, she carries two nails and a metal latch.

"Give me your rolling pin," she says, and Seda obeys.

Fatma pounds the nails into the door and wall, creating a makeshift lock from the inside.

"Use it every day. In the morning and at night. Whenever possible."

Seda furrows her brow, demanding further explanation.

"Nabi Bey thinks you should start earning your keep." Fatma's eyes glide over Seda's body.

Seda understands. She places the blade of a knife at her wrist.

"Don't be dramatic. I didn't save your life to offer you up like a platter of cheese."

Why did you save my life? Am I an offering on your altar of contrition?

"I told him you were diseased. God knows you look it. But you'll have to be more careful. I don't know how I'm going to protect you."

It is true that Fatma is protecting her, but it is also true that, in her own way, Fatma loves her bey. Seda has seen the way she sniffs at his collar when serving him his soup. The way she insists the sheets stay unwashed after one of his visits.

"I don't suppose you have any people left," Fatma says.

Seda shakes her head no. Everyone is dead and gone. Hairig's older brother may be somewhere in Constantinople, selling his textiles, cloth that was once meant for Mairig's trip to Paris. But that was a long time ago, an entire dream ago. Besides, what would she tell him if she found him? Where would she begin accounting for all the dead? No, better to remain here, slowly disappearing.

"I have enough troubles of my own," Fatma says, handing Seda the rolling pin and collapsing onto the floor cushion. She is always tired lately, and her breasts are more swollen than usual. She has taken to wearing a flowing robe of brown wool that wraps around her thickening middle.

Seda feels a pang of worry. She takes two steps toward Fatma and, kneeling, gently places a hand on her stomach. Fatma looks straight into her eyes and sighs.

"At least there is no danger of you telling anyone," she says and then, "It is the bey's doing. I am sure of it." She brushes the hair away from Seda's forehead. "He doesn't know. Thank God. He won't marry me, of course. Calls me a whore. If it's a girl, he will discard me. If it is a son, he will surely take him from me. Either way, I will be destroyed. And you along with me. The quality of gold is distinguished by flames and the quality of humans through misfortune. You and I are made of solid gold.

"He will be traveling to Sivas next month for a meeting of some sort. That will give me time to think of a plan."

Seda gasps at the mention of her birthplace. Her hand flies to her mouth.

"What is it, child? Don't worry. I will think of something," she says, caressing Seda's worried face. "For now, just keep away from him. Use the lock. Understand?"

Seda nods. That is when the thought comes to her, like a fly buzzing in her ear. The bey is going to Sivas. If she went with him, she may find Nazareth or Bedros or Kemal . . . She may yet go back to being Lucine. But the thought instantly vanishes.

"Fatma, bring me some porridge." The bey's voice comes booming through the thick walls of the inn. Seda shoos her thoughts away and ladles a healthy portion into a large clay bowl. She holds it before the sitting Fatma, but before handing it to her she bends her head into the steaming porridge and, keeping her eyes fixed on Fatma's face, spits into it.

Fatma laughs her hearty laugh. And Seda is surprised at her own pleasure in hearing it. It must be hard to please others for a living, she thinks, to be a source of pleasure and hate all at once.

⊶CHAPTER 27⊷

Spilled Porridge

THERE ARE RUMORS that Ahmet is an orphaned boy, another victim of the deportations, hiding behind a new Muslim name. There is a new name for survivors like Seda and Ahmet. They are now known throughout Turkey as "remnants of the sword." Seda once heard the bey use the term when he was telling Fatma not to take in any more strays. Whatever his story, the stable boy is trapped in his own world. He rarely speaks to Seda and, then, only when it's absolutely necessary. They have an unspoken pact to manage their miseries separately and with silence.

The boy is sick today. He refuses to fetch water or tend to the animals. He refuses to get up at all. Fatma asks Seda to tend to him, and to everything else. To do so, she will have to leave her modest room. Her hair is longer now and her body more shapely than it has ever been. She must take care to cover herself, especially on a day like today, when she is free to walk through the courtyard. In her hands, she carries a bowl of porridge, lumpy but warm, with which to comfort Ahmet. She aims to nurture the boy and cheer him up. God knows, he can do with some kindness. Seda suspects he is not sick at all, but weary. Of life and of death.

The air is stiff. It bites her exposed ankles. Her bare feet grip the packed earth. Cool and moist, the sensation is foreign to her. It's as if her feet still remember that other time, of lace-trimmed stockings and suede shoes.

Ahmet is lying on the floor, huddled near the solitary bundle of hay that awaits any visiting horses. Seda would give up a day's bread ration to see a horse in the stable. Ahmet's head rests in the crook of his elbow, facing the back wall. His eyes bore into the stonework the way old fortune-tellers stare into coffee grounds. Seda stands above him in her familiar silence. If she had words, she would use them now to console him. Whatever it is, it's in the past, she would say. Forget it.

She lays the bowl of porridge at his feet, hoping the gods of memory will leave him alone. Ahmet doesn't look away from the spot on his wall. He stretches a bent knee and gives the bowl a good stiff kick. The porridge spills out of the bowl, splaying across the hay and part of the wall. Annoyed, Seda places her hands on her hips and stomps her foot, only to be ignored by Ahmet. She may be a mute maidservant, but he is only a stable boy. How dare he? She turns quickly to fetch the broom and some water but collides face-first into a body. There is no mistake about it, her nose is pressed up against the ironed uniform on Nabi Bey's chest. The smell of pistachios and cured meat coats her face like a shroud. Despite the eye-watering odor, Seda stands perfectly still, holding her breath.

The bey grips her arms, pins them to her sides, and throws her down. Seda's head lands in the warm porridge, somewhere between Ahmet's curled body and the wall he faces. She looks up at the boy in alarm, but his eyes continue to decipher something in the stone wall. He doesn't say a thing. Nor does the bey, whose hands move quickly. He lifts her apron, followed by her skirt. He pants a strange pant and through it Seda is transported to that other time. She waits for Bedros and his large rock, for the bey to slump down onto the ground the way the gendarme did, a gaping hole in his skull. But there is no Bedros and no rock, only the strange scent of pistachios and garlic, the sound of panting and the urgency of a pair of probing hands. Seda turns her head and bites her lip. The bey rams himself into her. A scalding steel spoon scraping what little is left inside. He scrapes once, then twice more. And it is over before she can remember to scream.

The bey stands before her, buckling his belt.

Seda presses her thighs together and places a protective hand in between her legs. She is like the porridge on the floor, only dirtier. There is a sensation that the bey has forgotten his spoon inside her. Like maybe it is still lodged there, where it might sit and fester, where Fatma might see it and feel betrayed.

Nabi Bey bends down, offering his hand, and without thinking, Seda takes it. He helps her up. Then, as if in retrospect, he glares at the spilled porridge at his feet. He nudges Ahmet in the calves with the front of his boot. "Clean this up," he says before leaving.

So, it is simple as that. Spilled porridge, a push, a shove, a steel rod penetrating her middle, and the necessity to clean it all up, to move on. Seda is lowering the back of her bloodstained dress with her trembling hands, while Ahmet fetches the broom and rag in silence. As for the filth and shame left inside Seda, that Ahmet ignores.

CHAPTER 28

Ghosts

KEMAL AND HÜSNÜ collapse onto the cushion along the back wall of the khan, their wearied bodies colliding at the shoulders. They have been dreaming of this khan since the border town of Gaziantep where a goat herder poured encouraging words into their desperate ears. He promised they would find warm food and, for the right price, the soothing embrace of a woman's arms. This last vision alone was responsible for Hüsnü's unyielding pace in the past two days.

Hüsnü does not hesitate to pull his tattered boots from his feet, dropping them to the floor like stones. This act alone is a luxury. As soldiers, they almost always kept their boots on, in defense against cold and theft. But Kemal stays as still as possible, his eyes fixed upon the officer seated at the back of the room. For a moment, he is Eagle Eye again, scoping out danger. Even in the dim light, he can make out the officer's starched uniform and pomaded mustache. The man sits erect with only his head bent slightly before a steaming bowl of broth. He lifts the bowl to his lips and buries his mustache in the warm liquid. It has been weeks since Kemal has had something warm dance upon his tongue and years since he's seen a creased uniform. Suddenly he is acutely aware of the stench of his body, his torn trousers and the abhorrent condition of his boots. The coarse hair of his beard itches with lice.

A portly woman, her thick hair loose beneath the head scarf, comes toward them.

"*Merhaba.* What's your pleasure?"

Hüsnü's face lights up, but Kemal keeps his eyes upon the officer and his soup. The man's gray temples flinch at the sound of the woman's voice.

"*Çorba,* if you have it," says Hüsnü, flashing his best smile.

The woman nods and disappears behind a small wooden door in the far corner of the room.

"God, I hope the rumors are true," says Hüsnü. "Did you see how round her back side was? Like two watermelons cooling in a brook."

Kemal can sense the old officer listening. "Not now," he whispers.

"Not now?" exclaims Hüsnü, loud enough that the stable boy might hear. "Then when? When I'm dead?"

The portly one comes back, balancing a pair of bowls on a large rusty tray.

"I like women. Is that a crime?" Hüsnü's voice is jovial. He is asking Kemal but looking at the woman. "But my friend here, he's like a cleric." He clamps a hand down on Kemal's shoulder.

"Maybe he likes boys," says the woman, raising an eyebrow. "Or goats."

The officer with the starched uniform clears his throat.

Kemal feels his face reddening. "We need a room for a night or two," he says, ignoring her.

The woman nods. "You can stay as long as your pockets allow. My name is Fatma and the boy outside is named Ahmet."

"We have no use for the boy," Kemal blurts out. "Just the room."

"I wouldn't give him to you anyway. The boy is for fetching water and taking care of animals."

"No one said anything about wanting a boy," Kemal says, exasperated.

"Easy, friend," says Hüsnü. "The *hanim* here is simply clarifying things. Aren't you, Fatma dear?"

At this, the starched officer heaves himself off of his cushion, leaving his empty bowl on the floor where his feet once were. He takes careful measured steps toward the two friends.

"You boys have papers?" he asks, looking down at them.

Hüsnü stands up. Reaching in his breast pocket, he produces the corrugated piece of parchment with their signed release.

The officer's eyes scan the page and rest upon the seal at the very bottom. "I'll take this for now," he says. "If everything checks out, I'll return it to you by sundown tomorrow."

"But, sir, the war is over," Hüsnü begins to protest. "We've served the better part of three years in the army and have been lawfully dismissed."

"You have an objection?" the officer asks, the question more of a dare.

"No, not at all," says Hüsnü, suddenly cowed. They've been through this before. Every village has an *ağa,* or chieftain, intent upon demonstrating his power. This bey is no different.

"All my friend wants to know is, whom do we have the honor of waiting upon tomorrow?" Kemal asks.

"It is not your place to ask questions, soldier. That privilege is all mine." The officer leaves them sitting before their now-lukewarm porridge.

"Oh, don't look so forlorn," says Fatma Hanim. "That is Nabi Bey, the governor, and he is more or less harmless. He's leaving for Sivas soon anyway. Eat your soup," she says, turning her backside to them.

"What about the room?" asks Kemal.

"And the . . . company?" asks Hüsnü.

Fatma clucks her tongue with amusement. "Like chickens before the grain," she mutters.

SEDA LIES DOWN on her cot, drinking in the darkness, too tired to turn her stiffened body. Though the images of her life are happily lost in the darkness, sleep continues to evade her. Tonight it is sounds that come to torment her. She hears their voices, every one. Nazareth's hearty laugh silenced by the clicking of Muammer Bey's worry beads. Kemal's soulful voice accusing her of stealing his vision. The sound of Nabi Bey's grunts plays over and over again in her head.

The bark of the sheepherder's dog interrupts the symphony and pulls her back into the present. She is here, unharmed, mind more or less intact, breathing in a dark khan where no one remembers her name. What happened in the stable is already forgotten, relegated to the past, like everything else. Still, she has been extra careful to avoid the bey not only for her own sake but also for Fatma's.

From her paneless window, Seda can see the sun rising up again, its orange light chasing away all the sounds in her head. She stands up, reaching for her apron and tucks her hair beneath her head scarf. The apron is key, because she sleeps and works in the same dress, her only one. She thinks of her nightgown, lying next to Anush's in a drawer somewhere in Sivas.

Three knocks come from above her head, where the ladder meets the ceiling, Fatma's signal for Seda to ascend the ladder and erase the sins of the night. She climbs the ladder and enters the empty room. A drained bottle of raki, Fatma's antidote for ambitious clients, lies on the floor, spent. It loosens more than their tongues, she likes to say. The divan has been stripped of its *yorgan*. A trick Fatma uses to lessen the washing of the week. Seda can smell the bedpan full of urine, sitting at the foot of the bed. On the tiny desk in the corner is a basin with soapy water, an empty pitcher as its only company. The desk is also where Fatma keeps her hand mirror. Seda goes to the mirror first, fingering its wooden handle.

One year after her arrival, Seda spent a night doubled over with stomach pains. The next morning she bled all over her only dress, convinced that death had finally caught up to her. Fatma invited her into this room. She pressed a washcloth in between Seda's thighs and slowly, gently, parted her legs. Holding the small mirror in between her thighs, Fatma forced her to look. Seda had looked away in shame, but Fatma turned her chin back to the bloody flesh wound in the mirror.

"This is where all life begins and ends," Fatma said. "You are not dying. Only beginning."

I don't want another beginning, she remembers thinking.

"This is life happening, despite you," continues Fatma. "Independent of you. This here is what fascinates and scares them. You must know it better than they do."

Seda blushes at the memory of this speech. What would Mairig say to such a thing? Fatma warned her that now more than ever she must stay out of sight, confining herself to the small room, back doors, and hallways. If she doesn't, men will claim her for themselves.

Seda places one hand on her belly, wondering if the mirror could help her see if the bey's spoon has planted a seed. She puts the mirror back, reflective side down, closing the portal to the place that threatens to trap her, that has already trapped Fatma. She walks toward the divan and picks up the bedpan full of urine. When she turns around, she is confronted by a bearded soldier in the doorway. Fear rushes through her entire body. He is holding a pair of boots in his hand and staring at her like a dumb ox. How long has he been standing there?

Seda turns her back to him immediately, her face close to the

wall, chin tucked in so that her forehead brushes against the lime-
stone. She stays perfectly still, willing her body to evaporate into
the stone, the smell of urine from the bedpan filling her nostrils.

"I'm sorry . . ." he stammers, his voice barely audible. "I was
looking for my friend." Then silence. His voice lingers, its familiarity hanging in the air. The voice calls forth a yearning in her
belly, fear mixed with longing.

Seda turns around slowly, forcing herself to look, but he is
gone. Has she seen another ghost? If she were sane, she would
not hear these voices and see these visions. She would not wake
cradling her *yorgan* and pressing a phantom baby brother to her
chest. She would not liken bearded soldiers to her Kemal.

She opens the latch and quickly climbs the ladder back down
to her room. The room appears smaller than usual, its walls closing in on her. She has been found out. Whatever, whoever, he is,
he has seen her. But instead of pursuing her, he fled. Thank God,
he fled.

If he gains his courage and comes looking for me, I will kill him.

Once downstairs, Seda throws the contents of the bedpan out
of the window and sticks her head into the cold morning air of
the courtyard. There are different forms of death. Not everyone
dies of disease or hunger. Perhaps the fates have reserved something different for her. A kind of madness designed to blur her
reality. Dreams and nightmares blending into one long sorrowful path. Was the bearded soldier really there? Had he spoken in
Kemal's voice or was she finally going mad? Either way, he must
be forgotten or destroyed.

Ahmet approaches the window. He avoids her eyes, as he's done every day since the incident in the stables.

"Need an extra pail," he says to her.

Seda waits for more.

"Guests," the boy offers. "Two of them. Soldiers."

So she is sane after all. The soldier was real, the familiarity of his voice an aberration. Not the first time the real and unreal danced in her head. Seda ducks back indoors to give Ahmet what he wants. She wants to ask who they are, where they are from, and how long they will be staying, but this would require speaking. She unlocks the door to the courtyard, the pail too big to fit through the window.

"Leave it unlocked, will you?" Ahmet asks, grabbing the pail. "I'll be right back."

Seda says nothing. She turns to the dough resting beneath a square of muslin, intended for *ekmek* bread. Like her visions and ghosts, it has risen up and grown in the night. She is pounding at air bubbles trapped in dough when the door swings open.

There, with the sunlight at his back, is the bearded soldier from the morning. Seda moves quickly. She picks up a cast-iron pot and swings it at his head. The soldier ducks, barely avoiding the pot. He takes two large steps toward her. Seda backs up into the table, knocking over a sack of flour. Puffs of flour rise up at the man's feet, making him look like a demon rising from a cloud. He clamps his hands around her wrists and pins her to the wall. The soldier's face is only inches from Seda's, but she keeps her head turned to the left and her eyes squeezed shut. Her panting is the only thing between them. She opens her mouth to scream, but the voice she has neglected for so long has now turned its back on her. She twists her wrists, but his grip only grows stronger.

"Stop," he whispers. "Stop. Please."

She keeps her face turned, her eyes glued shut.

"It's me." He is whispering again, his breath warming her right ear.

"Lucine." He whispers her name like a desperate prayer. It is an incantation that pulls her all the way back to that other life.

CHAPTER 29

Resurrection

KEMAL'S HEART FINALLY begins beating again. He lets the air into his lungs in one loud gulp and holds it there, afraid to let it go. He had thought nothing of walking into the room, and even less of interrupting the girl. Until she turned her head. Beneath the head scarf were the gray eyes and proud chin. There was surprise and terror in her face but no recognition. He knew her immediately. And in that moment, he forgot to breathe. His mind and body disconnected, pulling apart like threads of yarn. Now his hands are wrapped around her wrists and his body is pressing her against the wall.

She stops struggling, but the fear is like a third body wedged between them. She keeps her head turned away from him, pressing her right cheek into the wall. Her head scarf has come undone, and he can see that her dark hair is much shorter than before. She is gaunt, like so many these days. Her eye sockets recede into the cave of her face.

"Am I hurting you?" he asks.

She shuts her eyes tighter and thrashes her head back and forth, right to left. Again and again.

"Stop. Please. It's me. It's Kemal."

But the thrashing does not stop.

"Lucine," he repeats again. This time she stops, but still will not look at him.

"I'm going to let you go now. Please don't hit me or run away."

She makes no reply to this.

"Will you promise?" he asks.

Her eyes remain shut, but there is a faint nod. He loosens his hold on her wrists. He lets them slide down from the wall until they hang at her sides. He pulls away from her slowly, in small increments. It is like pulling away from the sun.

"Have I hurt you?" he asks.

She shakes her head no.

"Will you open your eyes now? Please."

She does this. Her eyelashes part and her eyes settle on a spot to the right of his feet. Then, bit by bit, they come closer to the middle where he stands. They settle on his boots, then climb their way slowly up to his calves, knees, and waist. Kemal blushes, feeling exposed. She looks higher up, at his chest, then at the hollow where his chest meets his neck, where she stops.

Kemal waits an eternity for her eyes to reach his face. Her eyelashes quiver with hesitation and fear. Silently, he wills her to look at him. Just once. So that the spell of fear can be broken.

"I'm going to touch your chin now," he says. His hand floats up to her face. He places his thumb on her chin and slips his fore-finger underneath its soft underbelly. He is holding her chin now like a delicate flower. He only needs to lift it a few inches until she can face him, but those few inches span a lifetime and several continents. And he cannot do it. Does not want to. She must lift her chin herself, of her own free will.

"Please look at me," he says. Once again he is pleading with her: to see him, to love him.

CHAPTER 30

The Handmaid

"IT IS ME," he repeats over and over again, like the words are some sort of salve.

And what if it is you? Then what? You with your man's beard and soldier's uniform. You, who calls me by that other name. You may be you, but I am another matter. I am no longer.

"Where is everyone else?" he asks.

Gone. They are all gone, she thinks, still staring at his khaki uniformed chest.

"I'm sorry," he says.

She makes her eyes smaller with hate and fixes them on the epaulet on his chest, a signifier of death and killing. She throws her head back and spits straight at the brass medal. He flinches but doesn't move, allowing her saliva to linger on its target, then dribble down over a buttonhole.

"I was conscripted. I've been fighting in the south. I have had nothing to do with the deportations. I am not ashamed. Nor proud. I did it because I had to."

His hand reaches into his coat pocket.

"I have something of yours," he says. He is holding a pale blue fabric in the palm of his hand. He holds it out to her. The linen is soft and worn from a thousand uses, but she recognizes her initials embroidered in Armenian in one corner. It is the kerchief she gave him the night he followed Hairig, the night she refused him.

Seda feels her chin releasing. He is waiting for her to meet his stare. It is a small thing, this thing he wants. When she finally looks up into his face, something inside her breaks. Her body relaxes and she crumbles into him. She buries her face into his chest and cries, silently, with her open mouth resting against his beating heart. He strokes her quivering back like he once did by the river all those years ago.

Seda pours all her agony into him. He is an empty vessel, a container for her grief. Whoever he is—Kemal, soldier, ghost—the apparition tries to comfort her. He tells her to hush. And she does, eventually, pulling herself away from him.

His choices are deplorable, but then so are hers. The Lucine he wants is dead and gone. Now there is only Seda, the handmaid.

Seda squats down to the floor, scooping what is left of the flour into a single mound. With her finger, she spells her new name, Seda, and then with her eyes locked on Kemal, she points to herself.

"You've changed your name?" he asks.

She nods. He pauses, as if he's trying to understand the meaning of this.

"You want me to call you Seda?"

She nods again.

"An ironic name for one without a voice, don't you think?"

She underlines the name in flour.

"All right," he says. "But why won't you speak to me?"

There is no way to answer this question. To tell him that all the words in the world have betrayed her and she in turn has turned her back on them is impossible. She wants to tell him that though she cannot control her own actions or the actions of others, she has complete control of the little piece of flesh that lies dormant, housed in her mouth full of teeth.

"Has something happened to your tongue? Your throat?"

She shakes her head no.

"Then perhaps I can coax your voice to come out again." He steps closer to her.

He understands nothing. This Kemal is just like the other, full of impossible dreams. Still, when he looks at her in that way, her body feels boneless and weak. She walks to the wooden door that leads to the courtyard and opens it.

"You want me to leave?"

She holds the door open in confirmation.

"All right. But can I come back tonight?" he asks at the door.

She says nothing.

"I will come when Hüsnü is with the woman Fatma," he says before disappearing.

CHAPTER 31

Finding Faith

SEDA WAITS FOR Kemal in the dark. It has been so long since she's waited for anything. Waiting is a luxury only those with desires and expectations can indulge in. When he whispered her name, the dead crow inside her awakened. Black feathers fluttering, sharp beak pecking painfully at her organs. There is a part of her that wants that bird dead and gone. Then there is the her waiting in this room in the dark.

She is standing when Kemal pushes the door open. He is still wearing the dreaded uniform, coat and all. The soldier's hat is perched on his head, his beard is combed clean and his boots polished. He stares at her awkwardly before taking a seat on her cot. His stare is unwavering and full of intention. It makes her feel as though she is made out of liquid. She must sit, but there is nothing to sit on besides the cot, so she remains standing. Then the black crow takes over her body. She places her hands on her hips the way she used to, as if to ask him what he wants, why he is here. A kind of protest against this clandestine courting ritual.

He smiles at her. "Everything and nothing has changed," he says.

She thinks about this, resisting the comfort the words give her.

"Have you got any tea?" he asks.

She turns to boil the water.

"You were always the one who spoke while I listened," he says to her back. This is a lie. She spoke but never to him. She spoke to Uncle Nazareth, Anush and Bedros, to all of them, but hardly ever to him. When she turns around, his hat is no longer on his head. He turns it around and around in his hands nervously. He bites his lower lip so that there is only a line in his beard where his mouth should be. She keeps her eyes on his soldier's hat. It disturbs and distracts her, reminding her of all the cruelty that comes with it. She removes it from his fidgeting hands, placing it on the table for kneading dough.

"We are not all monsters, you know," he says.

Her mind fixes on the word *we*.

"I have nothing else to wear," he says.

She lowers her eyes in sympathy.

Kemal extends his hand out to her. His index finger slides down from her knuckle to the tip of her finger, gently hooking it with his.

"Sit with me," he says, and he is that other Kemal, the quiet boy with the shy glances. Only in that other life, he would never have dared to hold her hand.

His skin is dry and cool to the touch. His fingers do not tremble the way hers do. Outside, an emaciated crescent moon dips into the frame of her tiny window, the only other witness to his presence.

"I don't really believe in God anymore," he says. "I'm not sure I ever did. But finding you here is a blessing from God. *You* are a blessing from God." He is still holding her hand.

Seda turns her head away from him and shuts her eyes tight. *I am no blessing. I am hateful and selfish.*

"You are everything that is good in the world," he is saying now, and she can't bear his words any longer. *No, no.* Seda is shaking her head. Her palm, the one he's not holding, comes down hard on her forehead, then again onto the crown of her head. Once. Then twice. Harder now.

"Stop." Kemal grabs her other hand. "Stop it." He is holding them both in a tight grip on her lap.

Seda can hear her own whimpering like a riverbank running below his words. But she doesn't stop it. She lets her tears pour out in place of words. The muffled sounds escape her like the first steams of a teakettle.

"I don't care what's happened. Whatever happened to them, Nazareth, Anush, your mother, your brothers. It wasn't our fault. Not yours and not mine." Kemal's voice is desperate and pleading. "They were lucky. Did you hear? Lucky."

Seda has heard stories about Der Zor, the Syrian Desert where the surviving deportees ended up. The people are described as diseased animals forgotten by man and God. Left to die. They say there is an entire desert littered with the bones of her people.

"They didn't have to live like you, Lucine," Kemal continues. "Carrying all their deaths around on your shoulders."

Maybe he is right. Maybe they were spared and she is left here to suffer their loss. This is her cross to bear. It is all their crosses really. Kemal's and Fatma's and every neighbor and gendarme that did or did not have a cruel word or thought or deed. They would bear this cross eternally, together with their children and their children's children.

"I have learned not to ask any questions," Kemal says. "In this war, the answers are never pleasant. I will not ask you any more questions. But there is one thing I need you to do for me.

"Will you look at me with fresh eyes? Not with the eyes of the past or of the future. Just stay with me in the present, here and now. And I will do the same."

It is such a strange request. If she could only oblige him, she would never have to think about the questions that plague her every breath. She will never be asked why she didn't go back for Mairig, why she no longer had Aram.

"The past is full of sorrow and the future laden with worry," he continues. "They are two weights that will surely drown us. I don't want to drown. Do you?"

That is another question entirely. Which should she answer, the first or the second? Seda chooses to answer the first and ignore the second. Drowning would be too good for her anyway. She looks into his eyes, the same warm chestnut brown orbs he once accused her of stealing, and shakes her head.

"Good," Kemal says. "Let us strip ourselves from time."

With that, he begins to speak. He speaks to her of the souks in Baghdad, the spice market where one could find spices of every color imaginable, plus four or five more. He talks to her of the rug merchant who taught him the principles of perspective. He tells her about Tekin and Mehmet and eventually Hüsnü, who is just now fondling Fatma above their heads. Gaining her confidence inch by inch with every word until her hand no longer trembles and her lips form themselves into a forgotten line of a smile.

HE COMES TO her nightly, and always when the moon appears in her window. On that first night, the moon was nothing but a curved line, bent and thin, like a fingernail, on the verge of disappearing. But every night since, Seda listens as Kemal feeds the moon with his words until it is swollen and round. It burns bright, penetrating the dullness inside her chest where her heart used to be.

"Are you even listening?" he asks her now in the third week of their visits.

She gives him a slight smile. He has changed too. He looks less like a soldier and more like the boy she once knew. Last week, she held the mirror as he shaved his beard, leaving a neat little mustache behind. He wiped his newly shaven face with her pale blue kerchief. He asked if he could keep it and she acquiesced. The truth is his words are all she longs for throughout the endless days. If only she could give him a few in return. A syllable or two. But her tongue has forgotten what her mind clings to.

I dream of dark things, she wants to tell him.

"Hüsnü wants to leave," Kemal says suddenly. "I can't ask him to stay any longer. I'm afraid he tired of your friend days ago."

Seda isn't surprised. Fatma tired of Hüsnü before he even bedded her. She will be happy to be rid of him before her bey returns.

"He's going to Istanbul, where his father's a merchant."

He is blabbering. Giving her needless details. Is he going with his friend or not?

"Don't scowl," he says, holding her chin in his hand. "Why are you scowling?" He laughs. "I didn't say I was going with him. Do you want me to stay? All you have to do is ask me to stay, Lucine."

There it is again. The name he called her when he first returned. The name he refuses to forget. She says nothing.

"You are a stubborn girl, Lucine Melkonian," he says, his eyes shining.

Seda gives him a sharp look. Call me Seda, she wants to scream.

"Before we came here, our plan was to go to Istanbul and start a kilim or rug business. With my understanding of the artistry and Hüsnü's father's support, we could set up a stall, maybe even a small factory. Remember the rug merchant I told you about, the one in Baghdad?"

Seda nods.

"Well, he gave me a name. A contact, who will help me get started. Istanbul is teeming with foreigners. The money will be good. A fresh start for all of us. You too, maybe." He hesitates, then says, "If you'll wait for me."

There is a long silence, in which Seda remembers the last time he asked her to go away with him. The sight of his slumped shoulders when she refused him. There was so much else to consider back then. Now there is nothing. Not a single thing.

She fixes her eyes upon his face and nods her head just once.

"No. No more nodding. Tell me yes or tell me no, but *tell* me."

Seda rolls her tongue to the roof of her mouth, but it remains dormant in its cave. *Evet,* yes. Her tongue refuses to release the two little syllables so powerful, they could whisk her away from here, to the majestic city where her parents first met.

But Seda can be no one's wife or mother. She is a ghost, a remnant of the sword. She shifts her weight on the cot, where they are both nestled. She leans into him. His eyes are darting from one feature of her face to another. She gets close enough to lose them and, shutting her own, places her lips on his. They lie there, two pairs of lips heaped on top of one another like a collection of pillows. Neither one moves. Then, slowly, gently, Kemal takes her lower lip into his own. She hears her father's voice then. *A sin against God.*

What sin? What god? No more, Hairig, No more. Hush now. Please, Hairig. Hush.

Kemal kisses her eyes first. His lips rest on one eyelid, then the other, stamping each with the warmth of his love. He cradles her face in his hands and kisses her lips. In response, Seda's lips seek him out. They part and let him in. She takes a deep breath, taking in the scent of his body and his breath all at once. Then, tilting her head back, she offers her neck to him. Kemal moves slowly, unwrapping this gift, sacred and sensual all at once. Her hands move down from the back of his neck to his shoulder blades, then lower to his back. Before he enters her, she holds him in her gaze and between her legs. Holding all of him. Limbs, thoughts, and unspoken prayers all find shelter in that embrace. When he thrusts, an unexpected current of warmth and pleasure moves through her. Her body feels as though it's swallowed the sun. She takes him in, again and again, each time with new hunger. Seda opens her mouth and lets out a moan. Kemal cries out then and collapses onto her. Seda presses her nose into his neck, wraps her arms around his middle, and weeps. The moan is gone and the heat that filled her body, that made her feel whole just for a moment, that too is slowly disappearing.

The next thought that comes to her is unexpected and obscene, for at that moment, she thinks that perhaps, maybe, there really is a god.

PART V

1990

CHAPTER 32

Exile

THE SOUND OF Seda's breath rises and falls, gentle and melodic, in sharp contrast to Orhan's own frantic heart. Did the old woman just confess to murder? And if so, whose? He leans his body closer, taking in the contours of Seda's sleeping face. He can see the still straight and narrow Roman nose, the almond-shaped eyes as they must have been before the upper lids lowered with age. Suddenly Orhan is certain that this is the woman in Dede's black sketchbooks. Where does the chain link of this woman's harrowed past attach itself to his own family history?

Seda opens her eyes slowly, smiling when she sees him.

"White days," she whispers.

"Yes," he says. "A white day sheds light."

"Not always," Seda says. She closes her eyes and takes a deep breath, pulling the bedsheet up under her chin. Orhan pours water from the pitcher on her bedside table into a cup and offers it to her. She purses her lips and drinks from it with her eyes closed. When she opens her eyes again, they are fixed, trancelike, on the opposite wall.

"I too lived in Karod once." Her Turkish is old and rusty, but the dialect of the interior, rural and rugged, is unmistakable. She is from that "other Turkey." His Turkey. "Until recently, I could remember very little from that time. I spent a lifetime forgetting it."

This information does not surprise him. Where else would she have met Dede? As far as Orhan knew, Dede left Turkey only once, in World War I, when he fought as an Ottoman soldier in Baghdad.

"Maybe that is why I hate it here," she says.

"Here?" he asks.

"The nursing home. It's everywhere. They won't let you forget it. It's in the music, the damn sculpture in the garden, in schools and living rooms. You can't open a book or sip a cup of coffee without confronting it."

"Confronting what?" Orhan asks.

"The past." The word comes out like an ancient curse. "Everything is soaked and mired in its bitter liquid. Our young people want us to live in it. They can't get enough of it. Where did you come from? How old were you? How did you survive? They make you tell it over and over again, write it, record it, make videos. It's exhausting," she says. And he believes her. She looks thoroughly exhausted.

"Maybe they think it's therapeutic," Seda continues, "this sharing of past horrors. But not for me. I don't want them poking their fingers into my wounds." She jabs a finger into the air. "All these years, I was praying for a scab, a hardened piece on dull skin that would cover it all up. But I'm ninety years old, and still the thing festers like an open wound in my chest."

Orhan thinks of his own past, the photographs and his time in exile, hidden under some hardened scab he has no intention of picking.

"I thought I could put it away," Seda continues. "Abandon it like I abandoned everything else. But then here you are."

"A scab is much better than an open wound," he says, thinking about his own past. His memories of prison are never visual. They always begin with the feeling of being cold and naked in an all-encompassing darkness; a feeling of despair that lodges in his chest and stops his breathing. He was blindfolded within minutes of entering the police station and remained that way for the rest of his three-week stay. Remaining in complete darkness, without light, without the ability to see, let alone capture anything.

The first few beatings were painful but unimaginative. They quickly gave way to more sinister kinds of torture designed to entertain the guards and strip him of his dignity. They hung him backward, with his wrists tied together behind and above his head for hours. It was a special torture known as a "Palestinian hanging," the entire body's weight resting on the shoulders, causing them to dislocate. Questions about the Kurdistan Workers' Party, or the PKK, and its members were wielded his way, followed by electric shocks to the groin, the tongue, and the buttocks. Someone kept calling him an "ass licker for the PKK" and demanding a confession. That last beating entered his body and lies there still, dormant, nestled in his blood cells, muscles and organs, materializing unexpectedly for the rest of his life. These days, it is not an image or a memory that drags him back to that cell, but a feeling.

The last thing Orhan remembers about his time in custody is screaming in agony and soiling himself. He discovered later that he suffered from five broken ribs, a bruised kidney, and a collapsed lung. His face and head were so badly beaten that Dede had trouble identifying him.

Orhan was labeled a political activist, an honor he never sought and didn't think he deserved, before Dede managed to put him on a plane to Germany.

Propping herself up in bed, Seda turns her head toward the window, where the California sun is finally descending.

"Shameless," she says.

"Pardon?" asks Orhan.

"Shameless," she repeats. "The sun. It is shameless. Like everything else here, it has no modesty. Always parading around like a harlot, regardless of the time of day or season."

"I'm sorry it offends you," says Orhan, smiling warily and thinking he's going to need another cigarette before defending the virtues of the sun.

Seda gives him an amused smile.

"I am so sorry about earlier," he says.

"Never mind that. You don't have to apologize. You're a good boy. I can tell," she says, tapping her index finger to her temple. "Your name is Orhan?" Her question sounds like a demand.

"Yes," he answers.

"Do you like Turkey, Mr. Orhan?" she asks.

"Yes, very much."

"What do you like about it?"

"Nothing and everything," Orhan says, smiling sheepishly.

"Like what nothings? What everythings?" she asks.

"Like the taste of hand-picked apricots in the spring. And the bulbul's birdsong," he answers.

"I remember. Like she is happy and suspicious all at once," she says.

"Yes. Like that," he says.

"But you didn't fly all this way to talk about birds singing in trees, did you, Orhan?" she says finally.

"No," says Orhan. "My grandfather was my hero. I came to make things right and to understand why he did this."

"Then what? You'll go back to your kilim business?"

"Yes," he says.

"And your photography?" she asks.

"I haven't taken a photo in years."

"Yet there's a camera hanging from your neck," she says.

"It is complicated," he says.

"All extraordinary things are complicated."

"You do not understand," he begins.

"I understand more than you know," she says. "Places and things stay with us, and sometimes we stay with them. I left Turkey de-cades ago, but my *göbek bağı,* and with it my spirit, is still buried in Karod. You see?"

Orhan says nothing.

"How much do you know about your history, young Orhan?"

"I know my mother died of childbirth," he answers.

"No, not that history. I'm talking about Turkey. How much do you know about Turkey besides what I've just told you?"

"I know some . . . enough, probably more than most. I am an exile, remember?"

"I remember. And you think this makes you an expert. How were you exiled?"

"How?" asks Orhan.

"Yes, how? By boat, by plane, by submarine? How?" she asks.

"I left by plane," he answers.

"How very civilized."

"I would not call it that," he says, trying not to think about the dark cell.

"Did they mark your door?" she asks.

"What?"

"They marked our front door with the word *sevkiyat*," she says finally.

"Transport," whispers Orhan.

"At first, we treated it as just another example of the building tension. There was always tension, you see. It would come and go, like the tides of the river. And like the tides, it would subsist. We were used to it, our Muslim neighbors and us. We were part of a community, an extended family. Families fight, but they go on, don't they?"

"Yes," says Orhan, thinking of his father and aunt.

"At least that's what most of us believed. There were others who knew otherwise. People like my father. He lost two older brothers to the Red Sultan's army, so he knew what men could do to one another. And yet he was hopeful, some would say naive. He wanted to believe that things had changed. 'This isn't the Sultan's empire anymore,' he would say. They bewitched him with their constitution and their parliament." Licking her lips, she continues, "And so we were exiled. Herded like animals."

A long silence follows. Orhan feels its presence expanding between the two of them.

"That is terrible," he says finally, because it is. There are decaying buildings all over the Turkish countryside that testify to the presence of Armenians before the war. His favorite was the Sourp Nishan Monastery just outside of Sivas, where he played target practice as a boy, before it was converted to an army base. When the soil beneath your feet has seen a half-dozen civilizations and been consecrated by the priests of five different religions, you learn that everything must be repurposed. Pagan temples converted to churches converted to mosques and back again. Why not a twelfth-century monastery into a military barrack? This was not sacrilege, only practicality.

Orhan never thought much about those abandoned buildings until, during his stay in Germany, Armenians from the diaspora began protesting in front of Turkish consulates. In places like Los Angeles and Beirut, they insisted on using the word *genocide*. Turkey wasn't perfect. He, of all people, understood this, but innocent people die in wartime.

"Agh," she moans. Her breastbone rises up before sinking

down again, making her look like a deflated balloon. "I was only fifteen, a child myself. I had nothing left. We were hungry. Weak." The words are only a whisper now. Her voice cracks beneath the silence in the air. "Bedros, Aram, and I. Hiding in a grove of apricot trees." Seda pauses between each sentence, letting her voice rest. Then she begins again, each time with a little more strength. "I fell asleep. When I woke, Bedros was gone. I climbed up the hill, carrying Aram in my arms. I climbed out of the valley and up the next hill. And there he was, pegged beneath a farmer who was beating him senseless. I gasped. I couldn't help it. The farmer heard.

"I ran a long time, with the farmer's thumping feet behind me. My arms burned from carrying Aram. Panic and fear surged through me. And then, like a siren calling, I heard the gurgling river. I ran until my ankles were submerged in the cold water and I could no longer hear the farmer running after me. The minute I touched that water, everything slowed down.

"The river's sound drowned out everything else—my fear and my hope in equal parts. I looked down at Aram, listless, half alive. His sunken eyes could no longer produce tears. They glassed over as he stared past me. His cracked mouth finally went silent. I held his parched body in front of me and I suddenly understood that I could not save him. I remember lowering onto my knees into that shallow riverbank. The water's surface was like a membrane. On the other side was silence. Peace. No bayonets, no blood or starvation. Just peace.

"I remember thinking Aram would be my little Moses, floating toward safety. And so I slid him into the murky water. He slipped into death in that peaceful way he used to slip into sleep in Mairig's arms.

"My first feeling was one of relief. There was such lightness in my arms, in my whole being. I remember taking a breath in that lightness. It was a glorious breath. The last free breath I ever took. Because when I looked down at the empty space between my forearms where he once was, I suddenly realized what I'd done. I jumped in the water but I couldn't swim."

The tears pour down her face. They fall out of her eyelids but seem to be falling inward too, so that her whole face wells up and her nose starts leaking.

"I don't remember anything after that." She fixes her wild eyes on him.

Orhan crosses the few inches of distance between them and takes the old woman's papery hand in the cave of his palms. He wants to tell her it's okay, that we must all find a way to first forgive ourselves, then one another; but he can't bring himself to speak for a long time.

"There's nothing you could have done for him," he says finally.

"I don't know how long I ran or where I managed to hide," she tells him, "but when Fatma found me, I was unconscious, still holding Aram's swaddling cloth."

"Fatma?" asks Orhan.

Seda nods. "Your aunt saved my life. Gave me strength when I had none."

"My God," says Orhan. Suddenly, this strange woman's connection to his life is less tenuous. He understood all along that Seda was a part of his Dede's past but had not expected that his aunt had saved her life. Then again, there are hundreds of people and their descendants who can claim the same about his auntie Fatma. In another time or place, there might be monuments constructed in her likeness.

"She ran a small inn in Malatya. Helping an Armenian was punishable by death in those days, but she took me in."

"She is a good woman," he says simply. "I'm sorry, but I still don't understand how this all relates to my grandfather."

She withdraws her hand from his. "There is still so much to tell," she says. "And I am doing a bad job of telling it."

"No, you are doing great," says Orhan, hoping she does not retreat back into her silence.

She nods at this, saying, "I suppose I could begin the way all ancient Armenian tales begin: *Gar oo chegar* . . . There was and there was not. You see, like all of life, a story is and is not."

And this is how she begins her tale, with her and Dede playing as children underneath the mulberry tree, its dark berries raining down upon their unsuspecting heads.

AT FIRST, SEDA's words spew out of her mouth in fits and spurts, reminding Orhan of a clogged faucet that suddenly starts working. But before long, the sentences come pouring out in a steady never-ending flow until she is interrupted by an uncontrollable fit of coughing.

"I'll get you some more water," he says, grabbing the empty pitcher. Seda concedes by nodding her head midcough.

Pitcher in hand, Orhan finds his way to the nearest water fountain. When he's filled the container, he does not walk directly toward Seda's room, but meanders in the hallways, trying to process everything she's told him. Lost in thought, he almost passes an open doorway from which Mrs. Vartanian's head is poking out.

She startles him and Orhan blushes just a little, thinking how the bent old woman sometimes scares him.

"Psst . . . psst . . ." she hisses, her hand beckoning him.

He takes a few measured steps toward her.

"Please, effendi, Mr. Gendarme, sir," she addresses him in Turkish, her voice reverential, devoid of its usual spite. Her breath is sour and smells of medicine.

"I am no gendarme," he tells her. "My name is Orhan."

Her eyes are pinned to his face but have a far away look about them.

Mrs. Vartanian nods. "I am marching to Aleppo," she says, turning her slippered feet toward the corridor that leads to the garden.

"What are *you* still doing here?" Betty's voice comes from behind him.

Orhan turns to find her walking toward him.

"I don't know who you think you are, letting little old ladies fall. What you talking to Mrs. Vartanian about anyway?"

"She thinks she's on some sort of death march."

"I know what she thinks, Mr. Orren. Haven't you wreaked enough havoc?" She takes one more look at him and smiles. "I'm assuming you're on your way out. It's way too late for you to be up in here."

"Yes," Orhan lies. "But I'll be back tomorrow."

"Well, all right," she says, her eyes studying his face. "You get anything out of Ms. Seda?" she asks.

Orhan nods.

"Really? Well, I'll be damned! What she say?"

"Many things."

"Anything that niece of hers would wanna hear?"

"Yes, I think so," says Orhan.

Betty nods with approval. "I have to clock out," she says. "You see yourself out now, you hear?" She turns down the empty hallway.

When Orhan returns to Seda's room, she is sitting up in her bed.

"Feeling better?" he asks, placing the pitcher on the bedside table.

"*Evet,* yes," she says, but her eyes have retreated further into their sockets.

"That is good," says Orhan. He pauses, preparing himself to ask her about Dede's will.

"There is still much to tell," she says, grasping the bed rail to prop herself up.

"Where I come from, everything is more or less covered up or left unsaid," Orhan says, thinking of Auntie Fatma's doilies. "Have you told any of this to your niece?"

"What do you know about my niece?"

"Nothing. Only that she is very interested in the past."

"She is already drowning in the past. They all are," says Seda. "She has too much past in her veins and you have none. I'm just evening things out."

"So you're not going to tell her any of this?"

"What I do and don't tell her is my business."

"No one would judge you for what happened."

"You don't understand," says Seda. "It isn't just what happened with Aram. It's Kemal I don't want to explain."

"He turned all our lives upside down for you and you don't want to have to *explain* him? You are right, I do not understand. The situation back home is not good. My father has hired a lawyer to contest Dede's will. A very good lawyer."

"I don't know anything about a lawyer," she interrupts him. "He was a clever man, your grandfather. He knew exactly what he was doing. He wanted you here for a reason."

Orhan wishes he knew what that reason was.

"Kemal gave me a drawing once. We were separated during the deportations, but providence reunited us after the war. It happened at Fatma's in Malatya," Seda says, pressing her head into a pillow. "It was God's hand working a miracle. I was so shocked to see him I thought he was a ghost." She lets out another short laugh. "We had a few precious weeks, and then he had to go."

"Kemal's plan was to establish himself in Istanbul, then send for me," Seda continues. "He had been gone six months. Half a year. Seventeen moons dipping into my little window. Fatma was big by then, no longer able to hide her condition."

"Her condition?" asks Orhan.

"She was pregnant."

Orhan lets the information wash over him. He struggles to imagine Auntie Fatma as a young pregnant woman. As far as he knows, she was never married. Inside her stout body rests all the comfort and nurturing that three generations of Türkoğlu men could ever want. She is unlike any other woman Orhan has ever known. A woman who stands apart from all the rest not just because of her sharp mind and even sharper tongue but precisely because she is immune to the limitations of motherhood and matrimony.

"Was this at the inn?" he asks.

Seda nods, coughing into her fist. "She lived in fear of her bey returning to find her as big as a house. What would happen to us then?"

"Her bey?" he asks.

"Yes, Nabi Bey, the lieutenant governor of Malatya was an important man in her life back then. In his absence, things had gotten so much worse around the khan. The soldiers and lodgers were not as careful with her, the food supply not as consistent. Even the stable boy had taken to disappearing into the mountains for days at a time.

"I received no letters from Kemal," Seda continues. "Not a

single word arrived from Istanbul. I began to think he had forgotten me. And Fatma agreed.

"'Why so glum?' she would ask me. 'You didn't really think that boy was going to whisk you away, did you? Men are like dogs. They will lick a bone until someone hides it. They may dig a little here and there, but if they find another bone somewhere, they forget about the first.'"

"That sounds like something she would say," says Orhan.

"I was beside myself with sadness," Seda says, smoothing the crumpled skin of her brow with a hand. "A new kind of sadness that only occurs after you've managed to find some hope. A fresh wound after a prolonged recovery.

"That is when she convinced me."

"Convinced you to do what?" Orhan asks.

"To write and tell him I was pregnant."

"To tell my grandfather *you* were pregnant?"

"Yes."

"And were you pregnant?"

"No. It was risky and deceptive, but what choice did I have? I knew nothing about men and she knew so much. Her plan was that I would claim her child as my own and raise it with Kemal."

Orhan's chest constricts and his ribs tighten around a pocket of breath that travels up and gets trapped in his throat.

"'You owe me this much,' she said. And she was right. She had saved my life at great risk. At first, I could not fathom lying to Kemal, let alone raising a child of some . . ."

"Who? Raising the child of who?"

"Only Fatma can answer that."

Orhan feels his pockets for his cigarettes before remembering he can't smoke in the nursing home. There are no words he can manage, no words to speed this experience along so he can find out what happened to Auntie Fatma's child.

"As you probably know, Fatma can be very convincing," Seda continues. "She reminded me that I had taken an innocent child's life and could now save the life of another."

"You told him you were pregnant with his child," Orhan says in disbelief.

"Yes," she says. "I was so desperate to be out of that khan. To be given a new chance at life. So I wrote the letter. I don't know if he ever received it or had it read to him. I never got a chance to find out, because three weeks after sending it my uncle Nazareth showed up at the khan. He was ragged and disguised, but I knew him right away. Nothing can explain the joy I felt when I saw him. He had come for me. After combing every village on the deportation route from Sivas to Syria, he found me.

"He thought he knew where Bedros was and this only made my heart grow even more glad. Our plan was to go to Syria, where Uncle Nazareth believed Bedros was living in an orphanage, and then on to Lebanon, where my uncle had a contact.

"It was clear that Kemal had abandoned me. Fatma could barely sustain herself after the baby was born. And here was my uncle, alive and well, with a plan. I left all of it. Fatma, Kemal, Sivas, the deportations, my life, all of it."

"You kept the name Seda," Orhan says.

"Yes, it was the only thing I kept from that life. I could not go back to being Lucine. Lucine died with Aram. And I never allowed myself to look back. Never. Not even when I was reunited with my brother Bedros."

"So you did find him?" asks Orhan.

"Yes, in an orphanage in Beirut. My niece, Ani, is his daughter. But the Bedros I found was very different from the Bedros I'd known as a young girl. Instead of the boy, I found a man consumed by hate and revenge. My brother called himself a freedom fighter, but others would call him a fanatic. How could I tell him I had loved a Turk? How could I tell any of them? It was impossible. There was only one story. A story of hate. So I stayed quiet. Always quiet, even more so when I got your letter."

Orhan takes a deep breath. His head is reeling with the past. He tries to picture Dede walking into that khan after all those years of pining away for this woman, only so she could walk away from him like it was nothing.

"So my father . . ." he says.

"Mustafa is Fatma's child," says Seda.

The blood drains from Orhan's face and heads down to the bottom of his feet.

"All these years . . ." he begins, thinking about all the big and little ways Auntie Fatma spent her life loving all of them, the Türkoğlu men. And suddenly he is saddened beyond measure.

"And the father?" he says.

"Perhaps Nabi Bey. Perhaps another. I'm sorry," says Seda. "This must be very hard for you. You thought she was your aunt."

"I thought he was my grandfather," he manages before staggering to his feet. "I have to go," he says, and leaves the room.

CHAPTER 33

Decrepit Seed

ORHAN MAKES HIS way back to the sea of mauve and green that is the reception area. Sitting down, he sinks so deep into one of the couches that he swears he can suddenly feel the weight of a century's worth of deception and longing bearing down on his shoulders. Like the crumbling Byzantine structures all over Sivas, he is being pressed, layer upon layer, by the past.

If what the old woman says is true, then he and his father are not even related to Kemal. They have no right to his fortune. He thinks about the lawyer Celik, whose name literally translates to "steel," an element that describes the man's iron will. His ancestors were probably sheepherders, Orhan thinks, to make himself feel better. When Atatürk declared Turkey a republic, he forced everyone to pick a last name. Strong names like Celik, meaning "steel," and Demir, meaning "iron," were common.

Orhan's own last name translates to "son of a Turk." He hopes that Dede's lawyer, Yilmaz, lives up to the meaning of his surname: one who never gives up. Because if his father succeeds in taking over the company, there is no telling what will become of

Dede's life's work or the family fortune. Mustafa doesn't know the first thing about textiles or exporting, or money, for that matter. He may build a mosque or donate it all to some extreme nationalist faction full of illiterate angry men. For years, when Dede was alive and Orhan was running the business, Mustafa kissed the hand that he could not wring. Now all that could change.

The blood pumps through his body, boiling with anger. The images of Seda's story dance around in his head. A young and vibrant auntie Fatma. His *dede,* an insecure boy, in love with his employer's daughter. He feels the tears slide down his face.

Feeling suffocated, he gets back on his feet and makes his way to a pay phone tucked inside a hallway near the restrooms. Breathing deeply, he stares into the dark narrow cavity where the money should go. Though he's used a phone his whole life, he is stupefied. With enough money, he could speak to and hear anyone. Words travel from one person in the world to another—truth and lies and inconsequential syllables, laughter and tears too. All of human expression exchanged here for a small price. Yet no person or machine is equipped to interpret these words, give them a finite meaning. No one and nothing to explain it all.

It takes nine rings for Auntie Fatma to answer the telephone. When she does, she sounds breathless from the exertion.

"Ha? What news?" she pants.

The anger swells up in his throat, so he can't bring himself to speak.

"Hello? Are you there? Speak up, boy."

"Auntie," Orhan says finally. The word, a lie, sits heavily on the telephone line. It is a stone brick in a dividing wall that stretches from Sivas to California, from World War I to now. His entire world is made of one brick, one lie, one word placed carefully on top of another.

"Grandmother," Orhan says, whispering it in her ear.

Fatma is frozen and speechless on the other end of the telephone line.

"Would you have ever told me?" he asks.

"No," she says finally.

"Why not?" he asks.

There is another long silence followed by a heavy sigh. "Why criticize the decrepit seed of an otherwise fruitful tree? There's no point in it," she says.

"You can't build something on a lie, Auntie."

"Nonsense. It was the only seed I had. And I used it. And I'm not ashamed or regretful. I spent my days loving those who mattered to me. What else is there in life?"

Orhan cannot think of a thing.

"Not like her," continues Auntie Fatma. "She ran from his love and it broke him apart. Even when a nail comes out, it leaves a gaping hole. Your grandfather struggled in Istanbul. He made some contacts, started a small stall, but within months he had a disagreement with his partners. He left with nothing and returned to Karod, where what was left of the family textile operation was waiting for him."

"It was not his textile business to come back to," says Orhan.

"What are you talking about? Of course the business was his."

"Those cauldrons. That house. Everything we have, everything Tarik Inc. was built on, belonged to Seda once," Orhan says.

"That's ridiculous. Who told you that?" Auntie Fatma snaps.

"It's the truth. Seda's real name is Lucine Melkonian. Dede knew it."

"Lucine? Seda is Lucine?"

"Yes."

Auntie Fatma is silent for a long moment.

"All those times he said that name, he was talking about Seda," she says, more to herself than to him.

"Yes."

"What does it matter?" Auntie Fatma says suddenly. "The Hagia Sophia once belonged to the Greeks. You don't see us handing it back to them, do you?"

Orhan snorts at this. "She says you saved her life," he says.

"Your *dede* should have left the past alone," she says. After a minute, she asks, "What else does she say?"

"Many things."

"What many things?" Auntie Fatma raises her voice.

"I don't know. Stories about her and Dede when they were young. Stories of deportation and murder."

"I liked it better when she didn't speak," says Fatma. "She never spoke, you know. Back then."

"Well, she's speaking now," says Orhan.

"Forget her. Don't waste any more of your time with her."

"There's more," he says. "She's got a niece who's obsessed with the past. She keeps going on and on about genocide. Threatened to get a lawyer."

"You need to call Yilmaz right away," says Fatma. "He'll be dealing with that lawyer of your father's and he needs to know about this. Don't be timid, my boy. Remember, according to our inheritance laws, all this belongs to you, not Seda. I don't care who her father was. You know what happens when a thief steals from another thief?" she asks.

"I'm not in the mood for one of your proverbs," Orhan says.

"God laughs. That's what happens. God laughs."

"You're missing the point." Orhan rests his forehead on the edge of the pay phone. "None of it belonged to Dede to start with."

"It was abandoned and he knew how to run it," she snaps at him. "Besides, he did come back for Seda. She's the one who didn't wait for him. She's the one who chose to leave. Followed that half-starved uncle of hers and, of course, the ghosts of her people."

"You lied to Dede," he says.

"Your father was only a baby. Kemal saw him and went to him immediately. I let him believe what he wanted to believe. That the child was his, a parting gift from the woman who'd haunted him all those years."

"And you went along with him," Orhan says.

"*Evet,* yes. I offered to help him take care of what he thought was his child. I tried to get him to forget her. I did everything,

everything in my power. We started something new, he and I, our own kind of family. But then, as he got older, he regressed further and further into his past. He sat in front of that withered old mulberry tree day after day, sketching till his hand cramped. He took to calling me Lucine, a name I had never heard until a few months ago. It was unbearable, let me tell you.

"He took to dyeing his damn skin the way he used to dye wool. You don't know how many times I ran out there with a towel in my hands and a curse on my lips. And this business of putting Seda's name in the will. For what? I've never seen such idiocy."

"When you went back to Sivas with him, was there anyone there?" asks Orhan.

"Just a Greek boy named Demi. He knew all the formulas for the dyes. Why do you ask?"

"Don't you see," he says. "None of it belonged to Dede. And even if it did, if he wasn't my grandfather, then I can't inherit a thing."

"Nobody knows that," says Fatma.

"She knows it," says Orhan. "And her niece will know it soon enough."

"Nobody will believe them," she says. "This is no time to be weak. I don't care what you do. I'll be dead soon, and your father will figure himself out. But this is your future we're talking about here."

"Don't say that. I can't bear it right now," says Orhan.

"What?"

"The part about you dying."

"There, you see. It doesn't matter what you call me."

"I'll call you grandmother," says Orhan.

"It doesn't matter, I tell you," her voice rises with the reprimand. "Mother. Grandmother. Genocide. Deportations. Seda, Lucine. None of it matters. There is only what is, what happened. The words come much later, corrupting everything with meaning. Call me what you want, but love me, Orhan. Because that's the only thing that matters."

But love is a word, thinks Orhan before hanging up. Love is a goddamn word. And which ones we use does matter.

CHAPTER 34

The Photographer

ORHAN WALKS AROUND in a haze of melancholy, carrying his arsenal of images through the empty halls of the nursing home. When he peeks into her room, Seda is in a deep slumber, as if the outpour Orhan witnessed was her last on earth.

The Leica's strap lays flat across his chest like a loving arm, the familiar weight swinging at his middle, comforting him. It is late in the evening and there are few residents shuffling along. Vapors of chlorine and lemons emanate from the shiny linoleum. Orhan finds himself looking for Mrs. Vartanian, but there is no one to spit at his shoes.

The door to the dining room is shut, but the murmur of voices comes through anyway. Someone has placed a freestanding sign at the entrance: BEARING WITNESS: AN EXHIBIT ABOUT MEMORY AND IDENTITY. Orhan presses his face to the glass-paneled door. The room has been completely rearranged. The chairs and tables have disappeared, along with the stale air of decay. Large black-and-white photographs line the white walls. Each panel features the face and torso of an elderly person set against a black background.

Orhan is relieved to step inside this space awash in images. He approaches a photograph whose subject he recognizes. Mrs. Vartanian's face is displayed as a black-and-white landscape. The horizontal lines that drift across her forehead move from the dark side of the frame toward a light source. The bags under her eyes sag in deep U-shaped crescents, reaching past her drooping nose. A thin-veined hand covers her unseen mouth. Orhan notices that each knuckle is tattooed with a symbol of some sort.

"Haunting, aren't they?" someone says.

Orhan starts and steps back to find Ani staring at Mrs. Vartanian's image. Seda's niece is dressed in black again, her dark eyes and hair mimicking the backdrop of the photographs.

"Yes," he says.

"The exhibit won't be open until tomorrow, but you're welcome to look." She glances at the camera swinging from his neck. "Are you a photographer?" she asks.

"No, just a visitor," says Orhan turning back to the photograph.

"She's actually a resident here," says Ani, pointing at the image of Mrs. Vartanian.

"What are those symbols on her knuckles?" he asks.

"Tattoos. Many of the deportees were branded by the Arab and Bedouin tribes that abducted them," she explains. "I'm Ani Melkonian, by the way." She extends her hand.

"Nice to meet you," he says, shaking her hand. "Orren," he says, pronouncing it the way Betty the orderly had. It's a small deception, but it lodges itself in his throat like a fish gone bad. "Is this your project?" He gestures toward the wall.

"I'm not an artist, if that's what you mean." she says. "But I organized the show."

"It's very intense," he says.

"Yeah, nobody does sorrow like the Armenians. Besides, art is always intense when it's transformative. Only kind of art worth pursuing."

Orhan turns away from the photograph to look at her. Something in the way she's looking at the photograph reminds him of his youth. "Are you saying all art should be political?" asks Orhan.

"I'm saying art can change things."

"So there is no value in a still life," he says smiling.

"With the world as fucked up as it is, why would anyone choose the still life?"

Because it's a thing of beauty. "Because he feels like using the color red?" he ventures out loud.

"I guess I just prefer intense," she says. "Have you seen a film crew, by any chance?" she asks, finally turning to face him again. "The documentary guys are supposed to be here by now." She looks down at the clipboard in her arms. "Two guys. One old. One young, hopefully carrying a large camera?"

"No, sorry," says Orhan.

She sighs and looks up at him again. "I'm trying to pair each photograph with an oral history."

Why ruin the images with words? thinks Orhan.

"The idea is to document the voices of the surviving eye-witnesses."

"Eyewitnesses," Orhan repeats.

She looks at him as if he's stupid. "To the genocide," she says.

A young man with a headset pokes his head through the dining-room door. "Ani, we need those mikes," he says.

"Okay, I'm on it." She fishes through her purse and produces a ring of keys.

"And bring the blue binders if you can," he adds before disappearing behind the door again.

"I have to go to my car," she says to Orhan.

"Need help?" he asks.

"You don't mind?"

"You could tell me more about the exhibit," he says, walking alongside her.

"The photographs you saw were taken by Gerard Nova. There'll be some oil paintings by tomorrow, as well as oral histories. It's really about bringing our past out into the light."

"I prefer to keep my past in the dark," he says with a chuckle. "Under lock and key."

"You must have an interesting past."

He shrugs. "Not really," he says, thinking how if you paid enough attention to your past, it would grow and grow, obscure your present as well as your future.

"Well, you can deny your past all you want, but it's a part of you. Acknowledging it only gives you more power. Anyway, the idea is to record these stories for posterity."

"Not sure what good that will do," he says more to himself than to her.

"My mother nursed me with mother's milk but also with

sorrow. It flowed from her heart to her breast, into my insides where it probably still rests. She herself had ingested the same from her mother. They call it transgenerational grief now. We call it being Armenian. I had a Cuban friend claim she could spot the Armenian children at Glendale Middle School by the sorrow in their eyes. There is no cure to speak of. Of course, you could always 'convert.' Strange that we use that word even though it is not a religion but a nationality. But we have no nation, haven't had one in a long time, so I guess the word works."

"A disease of grief," says Orhan.

"Except there's really no cure for inherited grief. Some people look for the cure in the soil of the homeland. They call it reparations. Others seek the salve of an apology, recognition. I stopped trying to escape this sorrow long ago. I accept it the way I accept the color of my eyes and the width of my hips. It is part of who I am."

"Is that what the exhibit is about? Finding a cure for your grief?" Orhan asks.

"That or just more probing of the wound."

"You people know how to keep a wound fresh."

"We don't have a choice," Ani says.

"Sure you do. You could forget it. Everyone else has."

"Impossible. It would be a betrayal."

"What is a memory if not the reliving of an experience?" Orhan asks, thinking of his own past. "Why relive this over and over again?"

"Because it happened. Remembering it is all we have in the face of denial. Silence is the enemy of justice," she says in a mocking voice. "That was my father's motto, anyway. The *baykar,* or the cause, with a capital *C,* is a sacred thing to an Armenian." Ani fixes her dark eyes on him. "I'm oversharing, aren't I? I tend to do that," she says, smiling for the first time.

"No, I wanted to know," Orhan smiles back at her. He walks a dozen steps before formulating a proper question. "This cause you were talking about. What's the objective?"

She stops in front of a cream-colored sedan, its backseat crammed with boxes. "It's about getting Turkey to admit to the genocide. You can't get over a thing when the perpetrator denies it even happened. That's why eyewitness accounts are so important."

She reaches into the car and grabs a cardboard box. "Could you help me with this?" She hands him the box without waiting for an answer and dives back into the back seat of the car.

"War is a terrible thing," Orhan says to her backside. "Everyone suffers." It is the safest sentence in the world, but he knows he's said the wrong thing because his words paralyze her. She extricates herself from the backseat and turns to face him.

"What did you say your name was again?" she asks, knitting her brows.

"Orhan," he pronounces it clearly this time. He knows she is ingesting his name because she fixes her kohl-rimmed eyes on his face and takes a deep breath.

"There is a difference, Orhan, between wartime atrocities perpetrated by both sides and a state-sponsored campaign of genocide meant to exterminate an entire race."

"There's no real proof of that, is there?" Orhan asks, unable to silence himself.

"There are telegrams proving that the decision to annihilate the entire Armenian population came directly from the ruling members of the Young Turk Party," she says, looking him directly in the face.

Orhan doesn't respond to this. He is no historian.

The light vanishes from Ani's eyes. Her mouth falls open and a kind of dread falls upon her soft features. She places one hand on the car door to steady herself.

"Who did you say you were visiting?" she asks.

"I didn't," he says. The box in his arms suddenly feels like a boulder.

"You're the one who wrote the letter," she says, pressing her lips together to form a tight line. Before he can answer, she jumps in again. "I remember the name now from the front of the envelope. Türkoğlu, wasn't it?" She pronounces his name not like an American or even a city Turk, but like an Anatolian.

Orhan goes mute. His stomach tightens and curls in on itself. I've done nothing wrong, he reminds himself. "I . . ." he begins. "Yes," he says.

"I haven't read your letter Mr. Türkoğlu, but my aunt hasn't been the same since she got it," she says.

Orhan nods at this, admitting guilt.

"What do you want? Why are you here?"

The question is simple enough, but it sounds profound coming from her. Orhan is not sure how to answer it.

"Please, call me Orhan," he says, wishing they could rewind and go back to the nursing home, when Ani treated him like a kind stranger. "I'm here because my late grandfather put your aunt in his will," he says finally.

An uncomfortable silence hangs between them.

"So you thought you would just pump me for information?"

"I didn't pump you for anything," he says.

"How did they know each other?" Ani asks.

"I was hoping she would tell me that," he says.

Ani scans the floor, as if she's lost something. "What has he left her?" she asks.

"Some sketchbooks," Orhan lies, then thinking better of it, adds, "and a house."

"A house," she repeats.

"In Sivas," he adds.

"Sivas," she repeats.

"Do you know Sivas?" he asks, trying to lighten the mood.

She does not answer him right away. She slams the car door and locks it instead. "Not directly," she says as she starts walking back to the home. "My father described it as a paradise."

Orhan scoffs at this. "Maybe he was talking about a different place," he says to her back.

She does not slow her steps. She walks like she's fleeing from a demon.

"Memories are tricky things," he goes on. "Happy or sad, they are always accompanied by a sense of loss." He knows he's treading on thin ground, but he can't seem to stop talking. "The past does not define me and it shouldn't define you." He flings these words at her receding back. They come out louder and more forcefully than he'd intended. Ani stops her hurried steps and turns so suddenly that Orhan almost collides into her.

"What a Turkish thing to say." She says each word softly, individually, letting each one land in the tiny space left between their faces.

"Are you insulting me?" Orhan asks.

"You don't even know your own past," she says, resuming her gait.

"How would you know?" he says, thinking how infuriating it is to constantly be talking to her back. "You don't know me. I live with my past every day."

"Then we have something in common," she says. "Only I have to live with my father's past too, and my aunt's, and the past of every other surviving member of my race."

"What are you talking about?" asks Orhan, his frustration rising.

"Genocide." She raises her voice. "I'm talking about genocide."

"What does all that have to do with me?" Orhan yells back at her. "My grandfather fought in the First World War. He defended his country from Russians, the British, the French, and a bunch of Armenian insurgents who would have gladly handed him over to his enemies. How does that make him, me, guilty of anything?"

"What does it have to do with you?" she asks, raising her voice to meet his. "Everything," she shouts, her arms making a wide circle. "It has everything to do with you."

How ridiculous to be arguing with this stranger. "Listen," he says, regaining his composure, "if you want to debate some event from a hundred years ago, go ahead. I'm only here to get a signature, maybe even some closure."

"You want closure." She pronounces the words like a declaration, her voice tight and controlled.

"If I can get it. Yes," he says, placing her box at the dining-room door.

"I see," Ani says, nodding her head in what looks like sarcastic agreement. "Closure would be good," she says, "but you're not going to get it from my aunt."

We'll see about that, thinks Orhan.

"I'd like closure too, Mr. Türkoğlu. Perhaps I'll get a lawyer to help me get some closure."

"If you think that scares me, you're wrong," Orhan lies. "No Turkish court would give our house to a perfect stranger. I'm only here because I'm a decent person."

"And because you want closure," she says in a mocking voice. "Will you still be in town tomorrow?" she asks.

"Probably," he says.

"Good. You should come to the opening of the art exhibit," she says walking back into the dining room. "There'll be lots of closure then. Until then, stay far away from my aunt."

⋘ CHAPTER 35 ⋙

Semantics

"YOU KNOW THERE'S no difference between withholding and lying, right?" Ani is standing in her room.

"Good morning to you too," Seda says. The morning light glows horizontal in the slats of her blinds. She rubs her face in an attempt to shake off the sleepless night. Two sleeping aids and still no sleep. Ani's heels pound across the floor. She clicks the blinds open and whirls them all the way up, letting the sun flood the room.

"I can handle all your withholding. I'm used to it."

"Who's lying?" says Seda.

"You told me he was from the *Armenian Herald*."

"No, *you* said he was from the *Armenian Herald*. I just didn't correct you."

"Semantics," says Ani.

Seda sits up and motions for Ani to get her wheelchair.

"I'm ninety. You think you could wait to assault me until after breakfast?"

Ani places the chair, wheels locked, against Seda's bed. "No one's assaulting. We're talking," she says.

"Semantics," Seda says, lowering herself into the wheelchair.

"What's going on?"

"Nothing."

"A man leaves you a house and it's nothing?"

Seda can feel Ani's eyes boring into her. She doesn't dare look up.

"Why?" Ani's voice cracks. "Why is it so hard for you to talk to me? I don't deserve this." She turns to face the window, away from Seda. Seda can hear the tiny whimpers escaping from her throat. They sound exactly the same as they did when she was a child. And just like then, Ani has managed to make this about her.

"What do you want to know?" Seda says.

"Everything." Ani spins around. "Like who left you a house in Sivas?"

"Someone from my past."

"Who? Who from your past?"

"An old friend. A Turk."

"A friendly Turk just decided to leave his family home to you? Did this house belong to your family before the genocide?"

"We lived in it, yes."

"Let me get this straight. Turks take everything you have, kill every member of your family, and when you somehow survive, kick you out of their country. Then sixty years later, one goddamn guy finally has a crisis of conscience? Thinks it's probably a good idea to right things before he croaks and leaves you a house? Am I right?"

"Not exactly."

"When were you planning on telling me this? Do you realize what kind of legal repercussions this could have? It's an admission of guilt."

"I knew you would do this," says Seda.

"Do what?"

"Turn this into something it's not."

"What is it not?"

"I don't want to have anything to do with the house. Or with Sivas. I just want to live my last days in peace. Is that so hard for you to understand?"

"Peace comes at a price. You of all people should know that."

Seda spins her chair around and rolls toward the door. "You don't want my story. You've got your own story. The one you've plastered all over the walls."

"What other story is there?" Ani shouts back at her.

"I'm tired. I need my breakfast." Seda starts heading toward the dining room for her morning meal before remembering that it's Friday, the day of the exhibit. The dining room has been converted into a gallery of the past.

Kemal wasn't just any Turk. And he had nothing to do with what happened to my family. He was a good man. What could he do?

⊶⊰ CHAPTER 36 ⊱⊷

Witness

ORHAN ARRIVES EARLY on the day of the exhibit. He parks his car inside the gray fog of the empty lot and rests his groggy head on the steering wheel. Last night Seda's words appeared in his sleep. Gendarmes and refugees were being eaten by giant silkworms from a mulberry tree. Auntie Fatma and Dede both made an appearance. They were scrubbing a basin full of paper money and coins. When he asked them what they were doing, they told him that the money was tainted. There was also something about a train or was it a wagon?

Inside the Ararat Home, the bronze bust of the mustached writer is gone and there is a new receptionist at the front desk.

"I'm here for the exhibit," he says, hiding his satchel beneath the high counter. "Ticket?" she says, eyeing him suspiciously.

"I'm the lighting engineer," he lies. "Ani asked me to come by."

"All right, down the hall to your right," she says.

Orhan signs the now familiar clipboard. The Ararat Home is completely deserted in the way only an old folks' home or cemetery can be. With all the doors shut, the hallway is endless and barren. He drifts past one shut door after another, letting his fingers brush the walls that take up the empty spaces between doors. His body feels raw but transparent like a jellyfish's. When the pair of walls that make up the hallway lean in closer together, he turns toward the garden, thinking, I am not one thing or another.

If he is not a photographer or a businessman, then what is he? If he is not Kemal's grandson, then who is he? Mustafa's son. But then who is Mustafa? Fatma's son. And who is Fatma? Someone who loves. That is it. He is someone who was, is, loved.

And if he is Turkish, what does that mean? Is he the prodigal son of a democratic republic or a descendant of genocide perpetrators? Maybe he is all of those things and none of them.

He steps onto the garden path, with its carved explanation of history inscribed in stone. He follows the timeline from Byzantium to 1915 and on to the present. There is only one version of events, and there it is beneath his feet. If only someone could do the same for him. Carve who he is in words and numbers that quantify and make sense: a singular interpretation of Orhan Türkoğlu.

But he is not singular. No one is. Not him, not Dede, not Seda. And if they are not singular, how can history be? Orhan reaches into his satchel for the legal papers when he realizes he must have forgotten them in Seda's room the night before. He makes his way to her door but finds it locked. He knocks gently, then with more purpose, but no one answers.

Orhan heads toward the dining room, hoping to find Betty or

maybe even Seda, but when he swings the door open, he's confronted with the somber reality of the art exhibit. The room is dark, except for the light projected on the black-and-white photographs that pop against the white walls. Men and women stand with their backs to the massive images. From the backs of their heads, Orhan can tell that they've all made an extra effort. The men have removed their newsboy caps and combed their sparse hair to one side. The women have had their short bobs teased so that rows of fluffy helmets line the room.

Orhan steps inside and presses himself against the back wall, still close enough to the door to make a stealth exit. The bronze bust from the reception area has been moved to the front of the room and placed next to a podium where a gray-haired man is talking into a microphone.

"And so I humbly call on President Bush to honor the proud history of the United States as a champion of human rights throughout the world by recognizing the memory of the 1.5 million who perished in the Armenian genocide," he says.

"The governor," someone whispers. He turns to see Ani holding her clipboard.

"You came," she says. "I wasn't sure you would."

Orhan nods and is about to respond when a microphoned voice interrupts.

"Thank you, Governor," says a woman with a heavy accent. "Our first speaker is Mrs. Varti Vartanian, originally from Kharpert. As you all know, this testimony is being recorded for posterity and will be collected into an oral history, so please keep your questions and comments for the very end."

Mrs. Vartanian's bent back miraculously straightens when she stands before the microphone. Even then, her white froth of hair clears the podium by only a foot. She begins her story in Armenian, her arthritic hands gesticulating left and right. Orhan can't understand a single word of her tale, but the tragedy enters the room, fully formed. Palpable.

That is when he hears it. A single understandable word floats among the undecipherable syllables. It is uttered in Turkish. *"Oğlum."* My son. Then, *"Çocuk."* The child. These are her memories, her burden to carry. But somehow he feels a degree of ownership for this story, and all the other stories that will and will not be shared in this room.

Mrs. Vartanian ends her story, dabbing at her eyes with a small handkerchief. Her back gradually curves again; her head hangs like a lantern from her neck. An orderly shows up at her side and leads her by the elbow away from the podium. The speaker with the accent announces the name of the next witness, but Orhan keeps his attention on Mrs. Vartanian. She looks spent and exhausted from telling her story. Leaning on the orderly, she makes her way down toward the back of the room.

She stops a few steps shy of the exit. Her doll is propped in a chair only inches from where Orhan is standing. She turns her neck and her eyes rest upon the doll next to Orhan. Her gaze climbs up slowly to his face.

"He doesn't belong to you," she whispers, her voice filled with anger.

"I know," says Orhan, handing her the doll. Mrs. Vartanian lays her cheek on top of the plastic face and inhales.

Without thinking, Orhan lifts his camera and takes a photo of her cradling the child. The act of pressing his eye to the hole and seeing the world framed, a neat little border around its perimeters, gives him an immeasurable sense of comfort.

His next shot is of Ani, who stands only a foot away. She looks his camera in the eye, an expression of defiance on her face.

He clicks the shutter, letting the aperture swallow her image up. He lowers his lens and stares back at her.

"You were right," he says.

"About?" she asks.

"These stories. They define me just as much as they define you."

She exhales.

"Thank you," she says.

"For what?"

"For looking at these photos, listening to these stories. Sometimes it feels like we're just talking to ourselves when who we really want to talk to is you."

"Me?"

"You and the rest of the world."

Orhan nods. "About my grandfather's will," he begins.

"That's between you and my aunt," Ani says, lifting a palm to stop his words.

Orhan fidgets with the camera in his hands.

"I thought you said you weren't a photographer," she says.

"I thought I had to be one thing or another," he says. "Not everything is black-and-white."

He brings the camera back up to his eye, clicking the shutter every time that life, in all its lovely and miserable guises, shows up in the frame. He takes picture after picture of the residents as they share their stories. Though he cannot understand their words, Orhan is able to capture the emotion in their faces, the vibrations of their sorrow, and their need for solace. All of life, Orhan realizes, is a story within a story; how we choose to listen and which words we choose to speak makes all the difference.

He zooms in for a close-up of an old man covering his face, when someone grabs his forearm. He looks down to see Seda in her wheelchair, with Betty gripping the handles behind her.

"You're here," he says. "I thought you said you wanted no part of this."

Seda looks at the camera, then back at him and smiles. She lifts a bundle of papers up toward him and presses them to his chest. They are his legal papers, signed and dated.

"You keep the house," Seda whispers.

Orhan's chin drops with the weight of her words. This is why he came. What he wanted, but instead of relief he feels shame. "What about you?" he asks.

"I'll keep my story," she says.

"I don't know what to say," he says. "Except I'm very sorry."

"We are all sorry for something. It's what makes us human," says Seda. "But sometimes empathy is not enough. Sometimes empathy needs to be followed by action."

She turns away from him then and with some assistance by Betty, approaches the podium, where she begins to tell her tale all over again.

She begins with, "My story is very different from all of yours."

CHAPTER 37

Fatma Forgiven

CELIK'S OFFICE IS exactly how Orhan imagined it. His father's lawyer has chosen the corner suite in one of the tallest buildings in Istanbul. The place is all black lacquer and gold. Orhan guesses that the color scheme is designed to communicate modernity and wealth. And if those two things fail to intimidate, splashes of red in the abstract art remind one that, if necessary, Celik could draw blood.

Orhan and Fatma are alone in the empty conference room. Seated at a glossy black table as vast and vapid as the room itself, they wait in silence for Mustafa and his lawyer, the man named after steel. Orhan's own lawyer is notably absent. The only one he wanted was Fatma, and she is here, sitting to his left. At least he hopes it is her. She arrived this morning, sporting a dramatic black burka that covered everything from her head to her feet. Today's costume, unlike the head scarf she sported at the funeral weeks ago, is more of a shroud. Even her eyes are hidden behind a small square of black mesh embedded in the headpiece. Getting her out of the car and into the elevator had been an almost-fatal experience. Orhan hasn't asked her why she is dressed like a Saudi housewife, but everyone is entitled to their prebattle rituals.

"You look ridiculous," he whispers to her, thinking her black burka and head full of gold teeth actually match Celik's decor.

"Nothing scares these Kemalists more than a devout Muslim," she says. "I'd whip out my prayer rug in the middle of this meeting if I were you."

Orhan snorts. "You know I don't own one, Buyukanne."

It is their little game now. He calls her grandmother whenever they are alone, which is often, since his father refuses to speak to him. It never fails to make her smile.

"Where is that bastard Celik? I'm boiling under this black curtain," she says.

At that moment, Mustafa appears at the door, a cloud of cigarette smoke floating above him. There was a time Orhan would stand out of respect for his father, but today he remains seated. Mustafa limps into the room with the help of his cane. Ignoring Fatma, he goes straight to Orhan's chair.

"What the hell is she doing here?" he says.

Fatma plays dead under her burka.

"This affects her as much as it does us," Orhan says.

"What's this?" he asks, turning to Fatma and fingering the black cloth. "Finally found God?"

"Something like that," says Fatma.

Mustafa makes his way to the other side of the massive conference table. He sits in the chair as he would in a throne.

Celik glides into the room a few seconds after Mustafa, a

musky cologne trailing behind him. "Hakan Celik," he says, shaking Orhan's hand. When his eyes fall upon the black ghost that is Fatma, Celik stops suddenly. He takes in the dark slopes of her shrouded body as if they were the apocalyptic remains of a ravaged society. He stares at her with disgust, as if she has annihilated every modernist tendency he and his like have fought hard for. He clears his throat before assuming his place next to Mustafa.

"Where's Yilmaz?" he asks, without looking up. He slaps a manila folder on the table.

"He couldn't make it," Orhan lies. The truth is Orhan had to beg Yilmaz not to come. The fewer people in the room, the better.

"Good. It's a simple case anyway. Very cut-and-dry. No need to complicate it." Celik says it all in one breath. "This will is bogus. You know that. Under Turkish law, the amount of the inheritance depends upon the closeness of the surviving heirs to the deceased. As Kemal's only son, your father is entitled to the majority of his wealth. The good news is your father wishes for you to stay on as acting president of Tarik Incorporated for now, until he decides otherwise. And if all goes well, the whole estate will eventually be passed on to you at the time of his death. So you see? No harm, no foul. A case of semantics and timing. That's all it is."

"And the house?" asks Orhan.

"Naturally, it belongs to your father now."

"I'm sorry. I can't accept that."

Celik fixes his eyes on Orhan. He uses his thumb to twirl the gold ring on his pinkie. "Your grandfather's will is a sham," he says. "Yilmaz should have advised him about our inheritance laws."

"I'm certain Mr. Yilmaz understands the law perfectly well," says Orhan.

"I don't really have time for this," Celik says, closing the file and standing up. "I've got a whole roster of cases to get to. We'll have to resolve this in court."

Orhan waits to see if the man in bluffing, but Celik storms out faster than he came in.

"I can't understand you," Mustafa shouts. "Why must you shit in every pot we own?"

"I'm keeping the company and the house," says Orhan.

"What?" Mustafa's face matches the red inkblots in the art-work. "You're either a madman or an idiot."

"I will take care of you and Fatma. You don't have to worry about that. You can stay near me, in one of the apartments in the city," says Orhan, "but I have other plans for the house."

"Are you dense? You heard the man. I am his son, his first heir. You have no right. Not until I am dead!"

"What if I told you that you are not who you think you are?" Orhan pronounces the words slowly, enunciating each one separately.

"What are you talking about?"

"You are not Kemal's son, and I am not his grandson," Orhan says.

"What the hell is he talking about?" Mustafa asks Fatma. Fatma inhales, sucking in a pouch of black cloth around her mouth.

"We are not legally entitled to any of it," Orhan continues. "We come from her," he says, nodding at Fatma.

Mustafa looks from Fatma to Orhan and back again. He leans across the table, grabs Fatma's headpiece and pulls it off.

Fatma fixes her eyes on him. "It's true. I'm sorry, Mustafa," she says. She lowers her eyes and points to her groin area. "You came through here."

Orhan blushes at her words.

For a moment, Mustafa is frozen in stunned silence.

"I gave birth to you," says Fatma, "and I mothered you. All these years, that's what I've been doing."

"You . . ." Mustafa begins but does not continue.

Orhan waits a moment to let his father digest the news. "There's more," he says. "Will you tell him, Buyukanne?"

Mustafa looks perplexed by Orhan's use of the word *grandmother*.

"Kemal is not your father," says Fatma. "He and I. We never—"

"I don't believe you," Mustafa interrupts.

"It's true. I'm not sure who your father was exactly," says Fatma.

"What are you talking about?"

"Fatma did what she had to do to survive," says Orhan.

Mustafa sits back in his chair. Mouth agape, his eyes dart from Fatma to Orhan and back again.

"You could go ahead with the lawsuit," Orhan continues, "but I'm sure you understand that I would be compelled to share this new information. It would be most embarrassing, to you and to our whole family."

"You would admit to being a whore?" Mustafa squints at Fatma.

"God forgives all sins," says Fatma.

Mustafa stands, giving his chair a dramatic push, but his body is visibly shaken.

Orhan stands too, afraid his father may lose his balance. He reaches for his father's arm, but Mustafa pushes him away.

"Get away from me," he says before limping out of the room.

CHAPTER 38

Transformation

THE CAULDRONS SURROUNDING the house have been cleaned and restored, their smooth copper surfaces gleaming in the sun. The house itself has been renovated to its former splendor, its mustard-colored stucco bright against white wood-trimmed windows. Everything is brighter in the spring air. Orhan stands some thirty feet away, across the street, taking long drags from his cigarette. He doesn't dare go inside, where his father and Fatma have been engaged in daily battle.

Mustafa's legal fortitude did not melt upon hearing the news of his questionable parentage. The sting of illegitimacy only served to confirm to him that the whole world was out to betray him. Orhan checks his watch: 5:42 a.m. A speaker mounted on the highest minaret of the mosque crackles. The voice of the *muezzin* cuts against the gray sky, calling believers like his father to their morning prayers. At the sound of footsteps and the clicking of his father's cane, Orhan turns his back and steps into a nearby alleyway. Only a coward hides from his own aging father. But he isn't entirely cowardly, he reminds himself. The legal battle for his ancestral home ensues, and in that, he has been downright heroic.

Orhan waits for Mustafa to disappear entirely before extinguishing his cigarette and walking toward the house, where Fatma stands by the open door.

"Good morning, Buyukanne," he says kissing her cheek.

"I get many more kisses since you've started calling me grandmother," she says.

"Where's your burka?" he says, stepping inside.

"Don't be an idiot," she says, smiling.

"How long do we have?"

"An hour."

"The exterior of the house looks good," he says.

"Like a butterfly landing on a donkey's dick," she says, making him laugh with one of her favorite Turkish phrases.

Inside, the house looks emptied and gutted. The home, once cluttered and covered almost entirely with doilies and kilims, is now a blank space. The bare floor looks naked without its ancient carpets. His *dede*'s green lounge chair sits like a modern art installation in the middle of the room.

"What happened here?" he asks.

"Home improvement."

"It looks like an empty museum," he says.

Fatma shrugs. Two metal folding chairs lean against a blank wall where the television and shelves used to be.

"Where's the television?" Orhan can't imagine his father sitting in the room without it.

"Out for repairs," she says winking at him.

Orhan gives her a doubting look.

"What are you trying to do here?" Orhan asks. "Smoke him out?"

"No," she says, shaking her head. "I thought more about what you said about basing my whole life, our lives, on a lie. It was wrong. Necessary back then but wrong. I can correct it now."

"By stripping the house of furniture?"

"By starting fresh. Every word from my mouth, every object in this house, will be based on the truth. No more decrepit seeds."

Orhan nods. "That may take longer than we thought," he says.

"I'm not going anywhere," she says, grabbing a folding chair and placing it near Dede's chair. "Besides, a good general doesn't leave a front until it's conquered."

"We are fighting over a dilapidated house," he says, knowing full well that there is so much more at stake here—things he cannot define to anyone but her. Reclaiming the house is the first step toward reclaiming his family's and his country's past.

"I wasn't talking about the house," she says, folding her crumpled hands in her lap like a schoolgirl. "I was talking about your father's heart."

She looks so vulnerable and frail. Orhan wants to reach over and embrace her shrinking body, and he almost does, but she stands up, breaking the moment in half.

"Besides," she says, her voice cheerful now. "The house isn't dilapidated anymore. Did you see the stucco outside? And the cauldrons? Good as new."

"We can paint, and scrub, and remove things, but the past is always here," he says.

"Everything is built on something else," Fatma says.

"Yes, but we've built an entire fortune on her loss, an entire country on their bones," says Orhan.

"An unlucky Bedouin will get fucked by a polar bear in the desert," she responds. "What can be done about it?"

"Acknowledge it, I suppose," says Orhan. "Isn't that what Dede was trying to do with his will?"

He turns away from her and Dede's chair and walks out of the house. He doesn't stop until he is engulfed in the abundant foliage of the mulberry tree. Lush leaves, so large they can be worn as masks, hang low and wrap around him like a bright green cloak. Adorned with the deep reds and purples of the fleshy fruit, they sway in the wind, brushing Orhan's head and shoulders. He hears the sound of Fatma's footsteps amid the whispered chatter of the wind and leaves.

"A miracle of nature," she says. "The thing just came back to life."

"It's beautiful," says Orhan. It is in this place of reincarnations, under the leaves of the mulberry tree, that Dede's bones lie. Here with the umbilical cord of the woman he loved, where worms feast and emerge as moths, it's as if the earth itself is telling a story of its betrayals and resurrections.

"We will win this battle. I will see to it. One way or another," Fatma says.

"Yes, but what then?" he asks, thinking of Seda's words about empathy and action.

"That's for you to decide. I'll be gone soon enough."

Orhan closes his eyes against the thought. "We can turn it into a museum," he says suddenly, partly to chase the thought of her dying away from his mind.

"A museum?" laughs Fatma. "Who would come to a museum in the middle of nowhere? And a museum of what? Sorrows?"

"No, of exiles," says Orhan.

"Exiles?" asks Fatma.

"Sürgün Gallery," he says, half jokingly, gesturing in the wind.

Fatma lets out a bellowing laugh.

"A place for the voiceless," he continues. The idea germinates in the very syllables coming out of his mouth. It comes out fully formed, as bountiful and fertile as the tree he is standing under. Orhan pictures the walls of the house displaying the works of artists whose identities have rendered them voiceless in Turkey. The second floor could house some of the photographs from the exhibit at the Ararat Home, alongside his own.

"The basement could be dedicated entirely to the past owners of the house," he says out loud, picturing his great-grandmother's wooden loom displaying the green kilim, rumored to have been woven for the sultan himself. A picture of Dede, clad in a three-piece suit and standing before the first offices of Tarik Inc., would grace the wall, along with a plaque describing his life. A glass case would house all of his sketchbooks and Auntie Fatma's hand-crafted doilies. And of course, the house's original Armenian owners would be there too. A photographic timeline of the Melkonian family displayed along the length of the back wall. He would use the word *genocide*. He'd make sure the story was there in all its horrific detail, under the heading DEPORTATIONS AND MASSACRES.

"That's a ridiculous idea," says Fatma, interrupting his thoughts. "Anyway, the house isn't even ours yet. It may never be."

"Maybe," says Orhan. "And maybe not. How does that proverb go?"

"You're quoting proverbs now?" she asks, amused.

"You know, the one that goes 'Do good and throw it into the sea,'" he says.

"If the fish don't know it, God will," she says, finishing for him.

"Iyilik yap denize at, balık bilmezse Halik bilir," he repeats in Turkish.

On a leaf beneath his left elbow, a silkworm, thick as a finger, wraps itself in a blanket of silk. Soon the larva will disappear into the protective confines of its cocoon, where the possibility of transformation awaits.

Acknowledgments

THE FIRST-TIME NOVELIST is a dreamer and a fool. I'd like to thank the following people for indulging these two qualities in me. My mom was the first to encourage reckless dreaming. Thanks, Mom, for letting me choose freely. Garin Armenian read every word twice and indulged me when I wanted to have long talks about imaginary people and places. This book wouldn't be the same without the candid feedback of Holly Gaglio and Marrie Stone. Barbara DeMarco Barrett and the Writer's Block Party provided a community and encouragement when I needed it most. Deniz and Aytek showed me all the beauty in Turkey. Khatchig Mouradian was an early reader and champion of my work. My editor, Kathy Pories, for her unwavering support and her discerning eye. Eleanor Jackson, for being the best agent/fairy godmother I could wish for.

I am deeply indebted to writers before me who've shared the story of this tragedy: Micheline Marcom's *Three Apples Fell from Heaven,* Carol Edgarian's *Rise the Euphrates,* Nancy Kricorian's

Zabelle, Peter Balakian's *Black Dog of Fate,* Margaret Ahnert's *The Knock at the Door,* and Mark Mustain's *The Gendarme,* to name a few. The historians, scholars, and journalists who champion the truth prove daily that the pen is indeed mightier than the sword. Thanks to Raymond Kevorkian, Ara Sarafian, Roger Smith, Hrant Dink, Ronald Grigor Suny, Fatma Gocek, Taner Akcam, and Richard Hovannisian.

My gratitude and deepest respect to the survivors, including my great-grandmother, Elizabeth Aslanian, who taught me that though we are products of our past, we need not be prisoners of it. My sons, Alec and Vaughn, who will inherit this transgenerational grief, provided the need for such a book. Boys, may your minds stay hungry and your hearts full. Last, but by no means least, I want to thank my husband, Vram, without whom this book would only be a dream. There are not enough words for what you mean to me.

Ohanesian, Aline.
Orhan's inheritance